my

D0122078

TONE DEAF

TONE DEAF

OLIVIA RIVERS

Sky Pony Press

NEW YORK

Sky Pony Press books may be purchased in bulk at special discounts for sales promotion, corporate gifts, fund-raising, or educational purposes. Special editions can also be created to specifications. For details, contact the Special Sales Department, Sky Pony Press, 307 West 36th Street, 11th Floor, New York, NY 10018 or info@skyhorsepublishing.com.

Sky Pony˚ is a registered trademark of Skyhorse Publishing, Inc.˚, a Delaware corporation.

Visit our website at www.skyponypress.com.

10 9 8 7 6 5 4 3 2 1

Library of Congress Cataloging-in-Publication Data is available on file.

Print ISBN: 978-1-63450-707-3
Ebook ISBN: 978-1-63450-708-0

Cover design by Sarah Brody
Jacket photo credit: iStockphoto

Printed in the United States of America

To Mom,
for your endless love and unwavering support.

AUTHOR'S NOTE

Due to the limits of written English, italics are used in this book to signify the use of American Sign Language (ASL). However, please note that ASL has its own vocabulary and grammar system that separates it almost entirely from English. If you'd like to learn more about the unique beauty of ASL and Deaf culture, check out the nonfiction resources listed in the back.

1

ALI

ROCK CONCERTS AREN'T meant to be watched like silent movies. Period. End of story. No exceptions.

So what the hell am I doing here?

I turn toward Avery with my arms crossed, ready to ask her this exact question for like the fiftieth time. She doesn't notice me, not that I can really blame her. Surrounding us is a sea of girls wearing blue and green, all of them screaming, jumping up and down, waving their hands to a beat I can't hear. The vibrations of the noise strike me from all sides, like some sort of tidal wave. We're close to the stage, and even though there's not a single person sitting, at least the rows of seats keep a bit of space between me and the strangers packed around us.

It's still not enough.

Avery finally glances over at me, her eyes wide with excitement and a goofy grin plastered on her face. Typical. If I even mention the words "Tone Deaf," my best friend turns into a babbling, fangirly mess. Usually, her enthusiasm is contagious—I might not get Avery's love for the pop-punk band, but I'm no stranger to feeling passionate about music.

Tonight is different. All my enthusiasm for this concert fled about three hours ago, when we jostled through the crowded gates of the stadium and plunged into the unruly mass of Tone Deaf fans. Between the ruthless Los Angeles heat and the anxious pounding of my heart, I'm now covered in sweat, and my nerves are screaming at me to get the hell out of here.

Avery pulls me into a quick, giddy hug, and I wince as her fingernails accidentally dig into my shoulder. Her nails are painted in alternating shades of blue and green, the same colors on Tone Deaf's album covers and the posters plastered all over Avery's bedroom. Honestly, her boy band obsession is more endearing than annoying, but of all the musicians in the world, did she *have* to pick Jace Beckett to fall in love with? Jace is the sort of lead singer who gives the entire music industry a bad rep—he completely ignores the fans who praise him, and he goes out of his way to bad-mouth anyone who criticizes his band. Flip through any entertainment magazine, and there's bound to be some story about Tone Deaf's lead singer publicly mocking a music reviewer or giving a journalist the finger. My former piano instructor had a name for famous musicians like Jace: "popular disgraces." Personally, I prefer the more accurate term "total jerk."

I've tried to point Avery toward some very cute up-and-coming prodigies from the classical scene, but nope, she wants nothing to do with the sweet nerds I grew up performing alongside. Her heart belongs solely to Jace Beckett and his pop-punk band.

He *is* a good performer—I have to give him that. Tone Deaf's lead singer jumps around onstage, singing into his microphone, expertly strumming his electric guitar. Every step he takes is in sync with the pulsing beat, and even though his movements are quick and energetic, he seems perfectly in control of both the music and the audience. His eyes are half-lidded, and it's obvious that his focus is on the song, not the crowd. Even after hours of performing, a small smile lifts his lips.

Avery grabs my shoulder excitedly as she bounces up and down in Converse that have "I Love Tone Deaf!" scribbled across them. Her blue and green shirt reads "Jace's #1 Fangirl," and her pigtails bounce around with her, showing off the green streaks she's dyed into her dirty-blond hair.

My best friend doesn't take the title of "fan" lightly.

She screams something, but she's twisted toward the stage so I can only see half of her lips. I shove her hand off my shoulder, which gets her attention. She turns toward me and blurts out something. I raise my eyebrows, trying not to look too impatient, and she repeats her words in both speech and sign language: *"They're announcing it!"*

She clasps her hands together and opens her mouth in an excited squeal. As I look around, I see other girls doing the same thing, everyone's eyes wide with anticipation as they focus on the stage and the huge LCD screen right above it. I'm close enough to the front that I have to crane my neck to see the screen—we're fifth row, middle. Avery has been saving up for these tickets for an entire thirteen months, insisting I come along since "even deaf girls need to experience their first *real* concert." I'm not exactly sure why performances at Carnegie don't count as real, but I know better than to argue with her when it comes to anything related to Tone Deaf.

Jace has finished his performance for the night, and he gives a short bow. As he looks down on the mass of fans in front of him—all squealing and jumping and ready to kiss his feet—his smile turns into a cocky grin. It looks completely fake, like the expression painted on a Ken doll, but none of his audience seems to notice.

The image on the screen changes to a close-up of Jace's face as he addresses the crowd. "Ladies and gentlemen!" he calls out, and a second later, little subtitles dance across the bottom of the screen with his words. I squint as I struggle to read them. Stadiums have to provide subtitles to comply with disability laws, but apparently there aren't any laws against making the letters ridiculously tiny.

The vibrations of the crowd die down a little, and Jace re-peats, "Ladies and gentlemen! Thank you for coming tonight and helping to kick off Tone Deaf's summer tour."

More cheers. More crazy jumping and blown kisses.

"Tonight a special fan will receive a special prize," Jace says. "Tone Deaf is giving away a backstage tour, so one of you can come meet us right after the concert." The subtitles are quickly replaced with a tiny legal disclaimer, and even though the text is too small to bother reading it all, I get the gist of it—crazy fans can win a half-hour meet-and-greet with the band, but the tour is of the stage and not anything in Jace's pants. Then Jace announces, "Everyone in the audience has received a wristband with a raffle code on it," as if every girl wasn't already aware of this.

I stare down at my own band: *A632D9*. I wanted to rip it off as soon as the ticket guy at the entrance put it on, but Avery had started freaking out, signing frantically that the code was defunct if I took off the wristband. I kept it on, just to please her, but not before arguing back a little.

"In ten seconds, the winning code will appear on the main screen," says Jace. He points upwards, and all eyes turn to the huge LCD screen I'm already staring at. A large "10" appears on the screen, quickly followed by a "9," then an "8."

A chant goes up in the crowd, and whatever else Jace wanted to say is drowned out as the concertgoers count down. At the "1," a roar of sound hits me, even more powerful than before. I clutch my arms to my chest and turn to the side, trying to ward off the sensations.

Something slams into my shoulder, and I yelp, glaring at Avery. She excitedly clings to my arm as she jumps up and down, and a huge, shocked grin spreads across her face.

Which can only mean one thing.

"You won?" I scream, hoping I'm loud enough to be heard over the crowd.

"Ali!" she shrieks. "Ali! It *happened*! Oh my god, I *told* you it'd happen!"

A bubble of excitement rises in my chest as I watch her smile grow even wider. Avery babbles a long string of words, but no amount of lip-reading skill could help me interpret what she's saying. Then she points eagerly toward the screen, and I turn, grinning as I read the code. I have Avery's code memorized; she'd been chanting it like a good luck charm before the concert started, drawing out all the O's like she was practicing for a kiss.

My grin falls from my face. I blink, hoping I'm seeing things wrong. But every time I blink, the screen just grows clearer.

It's not Avery's code. Not even close. Instead, the bright screen proudly displays: *A632D9.*

Well, shit. I just won myself a date with a rock star.

2

ALI

BODIES BRUSH AGAINST me as I struggle through the crowd, and I try not to shudder. My face must be pale, because Avery reaches down and takes my hand. If it were anyone else, I'd jerk away, but she gives my palm a comforting little squeeze, and I gratefully squeeze back. Avery doesn't skip a beat as she continues babbling about the raffle prize.

"—can't believe—Jace is just so—still can't believe—make sure he signs *all* of them?"

I glance up at her lips every once in a while and catch snippets of her words, but I don't bother with a response aside from a couple nods. What I want right now is to escape this crowd, not to hyperventilate over Jace Beckett. Although Avery has made it very clear that I'm not to leave the tour without getting as many autographs as possible. I have four of her CD albums and a rolled up poster in my purse, along with the metallic blue pen Avery brought for this very purpose. Earlier, I'd been teasing her for actually believing we'd get a chance for autographs, but I guess her optimism paid off.

I glance down at my raffle wristband, wishing Avery were wearing it instead of me. But I'd checked the tiny print on the back of my ticket, and it made the rules clear—in order to accept the prize, the code on my wristband has to match the code on my ticket, and the name on my ticket has to match the name on my ID. So passing off the prize to Avery isn't an option, but at least I can get all the autographs she wants and take some cool pictures for her.

Although, I guess I should try to be at least a little excited about meeting a rock star. Aren't I supposed to have some whole monologue planned out about how I love Jace and adore Tone Deaf and think their music is the best and want to marry him? I'm pretty sure that's the kind of stuff fans are supposed to say.

We near a small ticket stand at the back of the arena, which is apparently where I'm supposed to redeem my raffle code. There's a ticket-box in the side of the building, along with a line of girls all sporting wristbands and determined expressions. The worker behind the counter looks beyond exasperated. One girl marches up and displays her wristband, only to have the worker shoo her away. Huh. Who would have thought girls would try to fake their way into a raffle prize? But, then again, Tone Deaf fans are about as fanatic as they come.

Avery marches me right past the line of girls and straight toward the counter, staying by my side like some sort of personal wristband guardian. The other girls glare at me, and I glare right back. It's not really them I'm mad at, but they provide a good excuse for the scowl. Truth is, I really don't want a date with singer-boy. Tabloids might be sketchy sources at best, but when every single one of them prints stories about Jace Beckett mistreating his fans, it makes me suspect they're on to something.

Avery steps up to the counter, tugging me along. The worker gives a sharp flick of her manicured nails, gesturing for us to move to the back of the line. "Wait your turn," she snaps.

Avery says something, but her back is to me, so I can't see her words. The worker just scoffs and says, "Your friend's the winner? Just like all the other girls behind you?"

Avery puffs up, straightening her shoulders and standing on her toes. For someone who's only five foot four, she looks pretty intimidating. I shuffle my feet and try to disappear in her shadow. I don't want to get into any argument, and even if I could puff up like that, I'd probably just look ridiculous.

No, I'd *definitely* look ridiculous. I've always been the "cute" one: I'm barely over five feet and have way too many freckles, and glow-in-the-dark pale skin. The fine art of makeup is one I learned early on, so at least I no longer have the issue of people mistaking me for being super young. But no matter how old I look, it's kind of hard to come across as intimidating when I always need to look up to meet people's eyes.

Avery, on the other hand, is quite adept at transforming into teenage-mutant-ninja-girl. She's waving her arms around in what looks like kickass karate moves but is really just her version of exasperated flailing. The worker finally rolls her eyes and waves me forward, and I offer her an apologetic smile that she totally ignores.

Okay, time for tactic number two: I shove my wrist up on the counter, displaying the code on my band, and then lay out my ticket and ID next to it. The worker lets out a sigh—probably of relief—and waves her hand in a shooing motion at the girls behind me. "Okay, everyone, leave. *Now*. The winner is here, and she isn't you."

The girls waiting in line glare at me hard, but slowly disperse, hands on their hips. I'm sure Jace would much rather spend time with the tall blond who is shooting me daggers, or the redhead flipping me off. But, nope, I'm the winner. Little ol' deaf me, who hasn't ever heard a second of his music.

Whoop-dee-doo, hooray, and all that jazz.

The worker gives me a bored look and says, "Hang on. I'm going to phone backstage and get someone to pick you up for the tour."

I glance back at the retreating girls and take in their expressions: anger, sadness, jealousy. Lots and lots of jealousy. For one impossible second, I actually smile. Someone in this world—more than one someone—is actually jealous of me.

Then Avery tackles me in a hug, and something crazy happens: I start laughing. It all hits me then; I got the winning code. I get to spend the rest of the night backstage on a tour. I get to meet a freakin' celebrity.

Me. Not any of those other girls, but *me*.

I probably look like a maniac standing there in a near-abandoned area of the arena, laughing my head off. But then Avery also starts giggling, and I couldn't rein in my happiness if I tried.

We only calm down when we see a middle-aged guy heading toward us, his mouth pursed in concentration as he attempts to type on his smartphone while he walks. The wire of a microphone earpiece is tangled on the frame of his glasses, and he's wearing a polo shirt that states, in bold letters, MANAGER. He only tears his attention away from the phone when he reaches the ticket booth. The worker points to me and gives a thumbs up, and the guy shoves the phone back in his pocket as he reaches out his other hand for a shake.

"So you're the lucky winner," he says, offering me a smile that looks forced and haggard. He introduces himself with a name I don't quite catch, but then I see the smaller, embroidered letters on his polo: TONY ACCARDO, LEAD ARTIST MANAGER.

I accept the handshake and try not to pull back too quickly. Being surrounded by a crowd all evening has left my nerves ground down and raw, and physical contact is the last thing I want right now.

"I'm Ali Collins," I tell him, and then point to Avery. "This is my friend Avery Summers."

"Nice to meet you, Ali," Tony says. As if he's reading my mind, he shoots Avery an apologetic smile and says, "Sorry, but we can only bring the one winner on the tour."

"That's fine," Avery says, and she gives me a stern glance as she adds, "Isn't it?"

"Totally fine," I agree with a sigh, realizing she's not going to give me a chance to back out of this.

Tony nods a couple times and says to me, "Are you one of Jace's UK fans? You sound like it. We've been seeing more tourists come to his concerts since Tone Deaf hit the charts over there."

"No, I'm American," I say, and then my entire face flushes red. Really, really red. I know because Avery winces a little, and

Tony has to hide an amused smirk. I quickly explain, "I don't really have an accent, I just kind of talk strange." Seven years of not being able to hear your own voice does funny things to it. But Tony just cocks his head, clearly not understanding, so I add, "I'm deaf."

Tony's expression falls for a moment, then he quickly plasters on a smile. But he's not quick enough for me to miss his reaction. I bet he's thinking the same thing I am: Why should a deaf girl be the one to meet a music idol?

Tony slowly inclines his head toward the stage. "Well, come on. I'll show you to Jace. He's waiting backstage." He tries to smile again, like this is exciting, but the expression comes off as almost nervous.

What, does he think I'm some crazed fan who's going to go bonkers when I meet Jace? Maybe I should tell him the truth: that I've been mentored by some of the greatest pianists alive, and I know to act normal around celebrities. But I don't say a word, because that was the past.

"I'll wait for you in the parking lot," Avery chirps, breaking into my thoughts. She tugs on my sundress, straightening it a little, and quickly signs, *"You're gorgeous and he'll love you!"* Then she waves and walks away, my good-bye trailing after her.

I officially have the best friend in the world. What other person could lose their chance at their life's dream without a spark of jealousy? She's amazing, and I vow to tell her that later.

But, for now, I have a rock star to hang out with.

Tony taps my shoulder to get my attention, and I quickly step away from his touch. I shoot him an apologetic smile, but he hardly seems to notice. He's frowning now, although I'm not exactly sure what I've done to upset him.

Tony leads me toward the stage, and this time it's much easier to make it through the crowd. He's obviously an expert at navigating packed stadiums, and I follow carefully behind him as he nudges people out of the way and sidesteps the more intoxicated concertgoers. Tony gets us to the stage fast, and then he leads me up the stairs at its side and into the back. His shoulders grow tense as we pass people carrying lighting equipment and microphones.

I let my eyes roll. What is it about me that has Tony all anxious? I weigh a grand total of one hundred pounds. Even if I were some rabid fan, it's not like I could ever do any damage to a musician who's six foot two.

We turn a corner, moving down a small staircase and into the hallway behind the stage, and there he is. Jace Beckett, lead singer extraordinaire. Suddenly, my chest feels all tight and my stomach feels . . . fluttery. What the hell? Sure, the guy is hot, but that's no excuse for my stomach to turn traitor.

Jace is leaning against a wooden panel, his electric guitar clutched in his hands. His body language is casual and cocky, but he holds the guitar carefully, like it's some sort of Stradivarius. Well, at least he respects the instrument that made him famous.

He's talking with a blond dude, who I recognize as his backup singer and guitarist, Arrow. Arrow is tall—just a tiny bit shorter than Jace—and his hair is shaggy and styled into a messy look. I filter through all of Avery's past babbling, trying to remember something about the guy. All that pops into my head is: he's the oldest member of the band at twenty-one, and he's Jace's cousin. I mentally curse myself for not being able to remember more; maybe I should have paid closer attention to all of Avery's ramblings about Tone Deaf. If I'm going to avoid coming off as completely clueless, it'd help to know more than just his age.

My mouth starts drying out as I approach the two. I stumble, and then bite my lip to keep a curse from escaping. What's wrong with me? I used to be in these guys' shoes; I was the musical prodigy, the one performing in front of huge crowds. I have no excuse for being so anxious.

Jace and Arrow both lean over the guitar, and Jace gestures excitedly to a tiny box clipped to the instrument's fret board— probably some sort of fancy gadget to enhance the guitar's sound. Tony must call out a greeting, because Arrow looks up at us, but Jace keeps his attention steadily focused on his instrument.

I walk toward them, emerging from behind Tony and keeping my hands at my sides. I want them to know that I'm not going to go all fangirly on them, trying to tackle-hug them or dropping down on one knee to propose. Arrow shoots me an approving look tainted with surprise, like he was expecting me to do both those things. Jace glances up from his guitar just long enough to give me a small wave.

I urge my hand to work. *Move, move, move!* But I'm frozen. I'm only two yards away from Jace, so close to the music icon and . . . I can't move.

Suddenly, I get it. Like, really, *really* get it. In that frozen moment, it makes total sense that Jace has so many thousands of fans. He's stunning—tall frame, lean muscle, sharp facial features. Piercing eyes so blue that I wonder if he's wearing colored contacts. Black hair styled into a fauxhawk, with the tips dyed cyan.

But it's not just his looks. Actually, it's the way he handles his guitar that really grabs my attention. Standing there with the instrument in his hands, he looks ready to burst with confidence. Not cockiness, but confidence, like he knows the music, and he's sure the music knows him.

"Hey," he says. And just like that, he sets down the guitar, and his expression changes. Now it's that pained, fake smile he was wearing when he announced the raffle. "I guess you're the lucky girl."

I nod and do my best to smile. "Um, yeah. I guess I am."

He laughs. "You guess you are? You're not *sure* you're lucky?"

I blush and then quickly look at my feet, knowing my freckles are about to pop out like polka dots. Even makeup can't hide my Irish blood when I get flustered. But I force away my embarrassment and look back up at him, carefully watching his lips.

"I know I'm lucky," I amend, and I let my smile grow.

Arrow chuckles and elbows Jace in the side. "Looks like you've got a live one here, Jace."

I raise my eyebrows. "Live one?"

Jace rolls his eyes at Arrow and then turns back to me. "Yeah, a live one. You know, a girl who isn't trapped in la-la-Jace-land, where they're married to me and we make passionate love twenty-four-seven."

"Oh," I say lamely.

Jace cocks his head. "Are you English? You sound like it."

Tony speaks up. "No. Jace, she's . . . deaf." He cringes as he says it and shoots me an apologetic look.

I'm about to tell him he has nothing to be sorry for, but then I see Jace's expression change. His smile disappears. His chiseled jaw snaps shut. His eyes narrow into an accusing glare. And he's staring. *Right. At. Me.*

"Oh," he says, echoing my previous response in cold mockery. He whips his gaze to Tony, and without even trying to hide the words his lips form, he says, "Today of all days you want me to deal with some deaf chick? Seriously?"

"Take it easy, Jace," Arrow says. "It was a random raffle, it's not like anyone knew."

I edge back a few steps. I'm used to all types of frustrating reactions to my deafness—pity, concern, ignorance. But hostility? This is a new one.

I cross my arms over my chest and straighten my shoulders. Just because I can't pull off an intimidating look doesn't mean I'm going to cower. I scan Jace over, mentally cursing as I take in his all-too-familiar body language—clenched fist, tight jaw, wide stance. He's officially pissed, and I officially need to get the hell out of here.

"She's the winner, Jace," Tony says firmly. "Just give her the tour and be done with it, okay?"

Jace doesn't reply; he just keeps glaring at me, like he thinks that if he glares hard enough, I'll explode into bits of pitiful, useless dust. My eyes keep shifting to his clenched fist, watching for even the slightest twitch. My instincts scream at me to bolt, but fear claws at my brain, setting off all sorts of sirens and turning my legs shaky.

"Do you sign?" Jace demands.

Arrow groans and elbows his bandmate in the side, sharper this time. Jace cusses and shoots him a dirty look. Then his attention is back to me, giving me an even dirtier look.

"Dude, let's go," Arrow says. "If you're not going to give her the tour, just leave the girl alone."

Jace ignores Arrow, his eyes laser-focused on me. "I asked you a question. Do you sign?"

I nod, unsure how else to respond. "Yeah. I sign."

His lips curve into a tight smile that looks more like a snarl. "Then read this." Jace holds up both his middle fingers, points them at me, and then turns away. He strides off without another word, his fists still clenched and his shoulders stiff with tension. Arrow pauses just long enough to give me a pitying look, then hurries after Jace.

I stare after them in shock. For a second, warm relief floods me as Jace disappears around the corner. Then the warmth rises into heat, and my face burns with a mixture of embarrassment and anger. Tony places a comforting hand on my shoulder, and I shrug him away.

He shakes his head, a mortified expression widening his eyes. "I'm so, so sorry about that."

"What the hell is his problem?"

How *dare* Jace treat me like that? I don't even know him, and he's just going to act like I'm a freak? That's not right. Not right *at all*.

"He can be, um . . ." Tony nervously shuffles his feet and clears his throat. "Touchy."

"He's a total asshole," I snap. I point to Tony. "I want out of here, okay? Forget the tour. Take me to the closest exit."

I grit my teeth and take a deep breath through my nose, trying to keep from exploding. But, seriously, what just happened? Jace puts up with dreamy girls who are completely obsessed with him, yet he refuses to offer even a shred of respect to me. A normal, non-obsessive girl who just happens to be deaf.

"Here," Tony says, and he nods toward the stairs we'd used before. "Let's go." He walks toward the steps and then falters. I almost bump into him, and a curse erupts from between my gritted teeth. Tony bites at his lip. "Maybe . . . maybe one of the other band members could give you a tour? Arrow is a nice guy, and I'm sure he'd love to do it."

I shake my head. "No. Thanks, but definitely not."

Tony opens his mouth in a sigh and guides me away from the stage. Away from the humiliation, the hurtful words, the obscene gestures.

But the anger stays.

3

JACE

I BLAST THE latest Fall Out Boy album through my headphones, letting the pounding bass beat down the dark memories clawing at my mind. I force a couple of deep breaths and try to focus on my laptop, clicking through Twitter and reading the messages left by fans:

Rocking out downtown at the @ToneDeaf concert! Still can't believe I scored tickets!! #biggestfan #truelove

i've got the new @ToneDeaf album on repeat. #love i'm sooooo jealous of every1 at the LA concert!

Maybe if I tweet @ToneDeaf, Jace will reply . . . ;) #hopeful #futurehusband #love

I scoff at the last one and mute the girl's profile. It's strange how often I hear that word thrown at me—"love." Fans love my music, love my lyrics, love my looks, love everything about me. Everything except the *actual* me. They don't know me, and that's how I like it.

Of course, that doesn't let me off the hook when it comes to Tony's strictly enforced marketing efforts. Successful bands require fans, and fans require attention. It's a simple equation that forces me to spend at least a couple hours every week answering messages on social media.

I still haven't figured out if Tony is a genius at marketing or torture, but whatever you call it, Tone Deaf owes its fame to his skill. If it weren't for that, I'd ignore his advice and stay away from social media like the plague that it is. I got into this industry for the music, not for the vapid comments about my hair and fashion choices.

The RV door slams open, and Killer comes prancing inside. He looks like he always does after performing a concert—all smiles and light footsteps and happy-rainbow attitude.

I yank off my headphones and pin him with a glare. "Killer, what the hell? Have you ever heard of knocking?"

He walks over to the couch across the room from my desk and collapses in it. "Yeah. I think that's the word in the dictionary between oh-my-god-dude and get-over-it."

I turn back to my laptop screen and roll my eyes. On first inspection, Killer looks pretty harmless: super thin and kind of tall (but he still totally sucked at phys ed), nerd glasses that he's convinced are cool (he's blind without them), and skin he says is "a shade between cocoa and burnt umber." But, in reality, he's not harmless. Far from it, actually. He's a gigantic thorn in my side.

"You on Facebook?" Killer asks.

"No, Twitter."

"Then tweet Arrow. Tell him to get his pretty ass over here."

"I am *not* publicly calling my cousin's ass pretty. Use your own phone and text him." I shoot him a look as I stretch my arms above my head, trying to ease the pain in my ribcage. Jumping around onstage is expected of rock stars, much to my bones' despair.

Killer lets out a loud, put-out harrumph. With his high voice, it sounds more like a sneeze. There is a very, very good reason Killer is our keyboardist and not the lead singer. Sure, he has an awesome London accent, and he would have taken the spot, but the world has endured enough chipmunk imitations with that Bieber kid.

Killer pulls out his phone, although he's probably still going to tweet Arrow instead of sending a private text. I shake my head. When we first came into the media spotlight, Arrow had wanted to keep his bisexuality quiet. That lasted about three days, until Killer kissed Arrow onstage.

Killer is about as subtle as a bullhorn.

I hear a deep grunt and the click of nails against tile, and a second later, Cuddles comes trotting in the from the kitchen. My pit bull wags her tail madly as she shoves her head into Killer's lap, demanding an ear scratch. She has a strange love for Killer, even though he was the one who dubbed her with her ridiculous name. Cuddles weighs nearly as much as I do and has jaws that could intimidate a lion. But Killer clearly doesn't care as he pushes his face up against her nose and coos a hello, making my dog's tail wag even harder.

"What are you doing in here, anyway?" I mutter at Killer. "This is my RV, you know. You can't just barge in whenever you want."

"Arrow told me about your run-in with the deaf girl," Killer says, patting Cuddles on the head. "We thought you might want some company after what happened."

I raise an eyebrow at him, but he just grins his dorky smile at me, like he thinks my glare is the ultimate portrayal of undying love.

"Sooo," he says, drawing out the word in the annoying way he always does. "You want to tell me what happened?"

"Nothing happened," I mutter, but I can't stop my eyes from drifting to the little calendar in the corner of my laptop screen. June fifth. Why the hell did I have to run into that girl today of all days?

"Arrow says you gave her the finger. That's something."

"Do you two always gossip behind my back?"

"Jace, Arrow is my boyfriend."

I scoff. "Yeah, believe it or not, I've noticed. So what?"

"Webster defines boyfriend as 'a man who becomes deader than meat upon withholding gossip from his true love.'"

"Make that reason number twenty-one thousand eight hundred and ninety-three I'll never enter a serious relationship," I mutter.

"You still haven't answered my question," he says. Cuddles lays at his feet with a heavy thump, and Killer turns his attention back to his phone. He types a little and then repeats, "What happened with the deaf girl?"

"I was just in a bad mood."

"Don't try to fool me, Jace. You're always in a bad mood when it comes to deaf people, but not *that* bad."

"It's June fifth."

He stares at me blankly. "Huh?"

I rake a hand through my hair and hold in a frustrated groan. "How the *hell* can you have the first thousand digits of pi memorized, but still forget what today is?"

Killer squints at me and blinks a couple times. Then his eyes go real wide. "Oh. Shit. June fifth." Then, as if he thinks I'm the one who needs reminding, he adds, "Your mom died on June fifth."

"Correct," I say, offering him a slow, sarcastic clap.

There's a long minute of silence after that, the only sound coming from the humming RV generator and the soft whirring of my laptop. Then the door bangs open again.

"Hey, guys," Arrow says as he walks up the last step and into the RV.

Killer disgustedly throws his phone across the couch, where it lands safely on a cushion. "Seriously? I tweet you three times, and that's all I get? 'Hey, guys?' Not, 'Hello, my darling love,' or 'I missed you bunches, sweetie'?"

Arrow grimaces. "Since when do I call you sweetie or darling?"

"Well, you could always start."

I groan. "Guys, seriously, take it up with a marriage counselor. Preferably not in my RV."

Arrow hesitates as his gaze settles on me, and I know he's debating whether or not to bring up the anniversary of my mom's death. It's been six years, but that still doesn't make it an easy topic. Arrow never knew my mom very well—my dad shunned anything and anyone non-Deaf, and since Arrow doesn't know sign language, he just never got a chance to communicate much with her. But I know he hasn't forgotten about his aunt's death, and I give him a little shake of my head, sending a silent message: *Let's not talk about it now. Please.*

Arrow nods and collapses on the couch next to his boyfriend. He tosses an arm over Killer's shoulders and kisses his cheek, and just like that, Killer forgets that he's supposed to be grumpy. He throws both arms around Arrow's neck, closes his eyes, and nuzzles his face into Arrow's T-shirt.

"Good god," I mutter. "You two are sickening."

Killer sticks his tongue out at me without opening his eyes. "We make you horny, and you know it."

I turn back to my laptop screen, absently refreshing the page. "Killer, how many girls do I have to be with to convince you I'm not gay?"

He yawns and says, "At least one."

"Aren't you supposed to be the genius around here?" I ask, raising an eyebrow at Killer. "I thought an IQ of 140 would be enough to help you figure out I'm not a virgin."

Arrow barks a laugh. I shoot him a sharp look, but he just says, "Dude, no one needs a high IQ to know you're not a virgin. Anyone smart enough to read a tabloid can figure it out."

"Then go buy Killer a tabloid," I snap. "Get him off my back about being gay."

Killer wags his finger at me. "Sleeping with girls isn't the same as *being* with them."

I scoff. "Don't get all romantic on me, Killer."

"He has a point," Arrow says. "You've never had an *actual* relationship with a girl."

"Yes, I have."

"One-night stands don't count as relationships, Jace," Killer says. Then he scrunches his face and looks around the RV. "By the way, where's your company for the evening?"

"I didn't bring a girl back tonight."

Killer slaps the sides of his face, like he's stricken with shock, and makes a show of peering out the window.

I just roll my eyes, but Arrow takes the bait. "What are you looking for, babe?"

"Meteors," Killer replies.

"What?"

"Jace didn't bring home a girl after a concert. That means either the world is ending, or he wasn't in the mood."

"And the world ending is more probable?" I mutter.

"Naturally."

I shake my head and refresh my laptop, bringing up a new batch of @ToneDeaf tweets. I see #MarryMe in two of them and disgustedly close the browser. Can't they at least *try* to be original?

"I've been with girls for longer than one night," I mutter, although I'm way too late replying, and it sounds downright pathetic.

"Two nights doesn't count as a relationship, either," Killer says.

I have no response for that one, so I open up a MS Word document and start absently typing. "Free writing" is what Tony calls it; he says it's good to let the imagination go and just write whatever comes into my head. But after a minute, all that's on the page is: *"Once upon a time, there was an annoying dude named Killer. He died. The end."*

It's definitely not going to win me any short story awards, but maybe I can work it into a song . . .

The RV door bangs open, and I cringe as it crashes against the wall. "Jon, for the love of god! How hard is it to open a door without denting my RV?"

Jon saunters into the RV and makes a big show of closing the door softly. It's actually mildly impressive, considering the muscle the dude packs. Freshman year, our high school's coach tried to make Jon the star of the junior varsity football team. That lasted about one week, until the coach discovered that Jon couldn't bash into anyone without spewing a bunch of nervous apologies. But our music teacher figured out he's much better at bashing drums, and he's been at it ever since.

Jon raises his eyebrows at me as the door clicks quietly into place. "Better?"

I give a grunt of approval. Jon smirks as he walks over to the other couch right next to my desk, collapsing onto it. Cuddles ditches her spot at Killer's feet to lie down next to Jon, and he scratches her under the chin.

"So what'd I miss?" he asks. "I heard arguing."

Killer nudges Arrow in the side, and says, "We're trying to get Jace to come out."

Jon groans and covers his face with both hands. "I knew it. I'm the only straight one in the band."

I roll my eyes. "Jon—"

He points a finger at me and cuts me off. "No, Jace, I'm not dating you, so don't even ask."

I grit my teeth, keeping in a yell of frustration, and grind out, "I was going to ask you to kindly shut your obnoxious trap. Got it?"

All the mischief melts from Jon's expression. "You're in a worse mood than usual," he says.

"I'm fine," I snap.

Arrow makes a disbelieving sound in the back of his throat. "Jace, you just flipped off a completely innocent fan. I really don't think that counts as 'fine.'"

Jon's eyes narrow at me. "You flipped off a fan?"

"It wasn't that big of a deal," I mutter, but the lie sounds weak even to me.

"It's going to be a big deal when Tony murders you. Seriously, what the hell were you thinking?"

"I am having an extremely shitty day," I growl. "It just happened."

"Yeah, and you'll be having an even worse day tomorrow. You know how Tony gets when you pull stunts like this. He's going to take it out on all of us."

Killer clears his throat pointedly and says to Jon, "Dude, go easy on him. It's June fifth."

Jon's eyes suddenly go really wide. Then he says, "Oh. Right. June fifth," in a tone that might be either a question or an apology.

"How about instead of going easy on me, you all just go?" I wave a hand at the door of the RV. "Seriously, get out of here. I don't want to talk."

Arrow shakes his head. "Jace, look—"

"You're talking," I snap, cutting him off. "Exactly what I just said I don't want to do."

Arrow hesitates, but then he throws his hands up in defeat and walks out the door before things can get any more awkward. Jon is quick to follow, but Killer lingers for a moment longer. Just as I'm about to tell him to leave, he crosses his arms and says, "What's that saying you're so obsessed about? Your personal motto, or whatever?"

"*Serva me, servabo te.* What's that got to do with anything?"

Killer shakes his head. "Do you even know what that saying *means*, Jace?"

"Of course," I say. "'Save me, and I will save you.' It's like karma. When someone bothers to give a shit about me, I give a shit about them. Everyone else isn't worth my time."

"Exactly, it's like karma," Killer says. "It's supposed to be a two-way street."

"What's that supposed to mean?"

"It means you're always so mad at the world for not saving your miserable ass, but you never bother trying to save anyone but yourself."

"I don't need the world to save me, and I sure as hell don't expect it to." I make a sharp gesture to my guitar propped in the corner of the room. "*That* saved me. That gave me a career and a ticket out of hell, and I pay my respects by treating my music like an actual craft. You and Arrow and Jon helped save me, and I pay you back by treating you like brothers. Tony helped make us famous, and I pay him hundreds of thousands for it. But no one else has ever helped, and I have no reason to bother with them."

Killer shakes his head. "Jace, our band had a little bit of talent and a shit-ton of luck. And, someday, we're going to run out of luck. All bands do."

"If you're trying to make me feel better, you're failing miserably," I growl.

"I'm not trying to make you feel better, I'm trying to make you *do something* better. You built our band to escape your past, but it won't last forever. So maybe you should start caring more about the world, because you're not always going to have the band to cower behind."

I open my mouth to argue, but he shoves out his palm, stopping me. "You can yell at me for being an asshole later," he says as he heads for the door. "For now, just shut up for once and think about what I said." He doesn't give me any chance to respond before slipping out the door and leaving me alone with nothing but silence for company.

4

ALI

I CREEP INSIDE my dad's house and quietly close the front door. Even after living here for almost seven years, I still can't kick the habit of thinking of it like that: "my dad's house." Not *my* house. My home is far, far away in a NYC apartment that's tiny and cramped and absolute heaven. Because it's where my mom is, and where the air is always filled with the sound of my piano and the smell of oatmeal cookies.

Or at least that's how it used to be. Last I saw my home, it was covered with white sheets and silence. The air had smelled like a hospital, and even though it was totally morbid, I wanted to stay there forever. My mom may have been far underground in a coffin, but all my memories of her were stuck in that apartment.

Of course, I didn't get my wish. In a matter of days, I was shipped off to my dad's house in hot, dusty Los Angeles, California. I'd always wondered why my mom never let me see my dad, why she divorced him before I was even born.

Now I know all too well.

As I turn around, I face my dad. Speak of the devil. He's Chief Patterson to most people, but he insists I call him "Dad." He likes to desperately cling to the illusion that we're some sort of normal family, even if we both know it's a complete lie.

Seeing him in front of me makes my stomach drop. Usually, he avoids me, and I avoid him, and the careful distance we set between each other keeps things quiet. Until he drinks. Then the alcohol rips away his desire for distance and replaces it with a drive for violence, and all that quietness is shattered.

I force an innocent smile. It hurts my cheek, where the bruise from last week is still healing. "Hey, Dad."

The slap comes so fast, I barely see it. But I *feel* it. There's no way in hell I *couldn't* feel it. My dad has perfected his slaps over the years: hard enough to bruise, soft enough not to break the skin. My jaw snaps back, and I hold in a yelp. That'd only make things worse.

"Where were you, Alison?" he demands, his slurred words hard to read. His face is twisted with the anger that overtakes him every time he gets drunk. I have no idea what sort of horrific flashbacks he tries to hide from when he gets that haunted look in his eyes and pulls out a bottle, but I'm not sure I want to find out. He's never dared to speak about the monstrous memories that ruined his mind, and I've never dared to ask.

I've heard my dad's police buddies joke that he's a "master of disguise," because underneath all his gruffness is a "heart of gold." He's their retired chief, and the entire Los Angeles police department holds him up on a pedestal. Everyone sees him as a hero for creating protocols that reduced gang violence in at least half a dozen neighborhoods. And I guess he technically *did* do something heroic, but he's not the Superman everyone thinks he is. People have no idea how quickly a few shots of liquor can make his gold heart turn black.

Pain blossoms through my cheek and down my neck, and panic twists my gut. I feel like I'm about to lose my dinner. Maybe I'll hit his shoes if I vomit. Go down with a fight.

Yeah. Right.

My dad glowers down at me, and I do my best to read his lips while avoiding his gaze. It's an art I've mastered over the years: when his eyes get watery and red, look at anything but them. His receding hairline, his knobby chin, his graying hair, his strong jaw. *Anything* but his eyes.

"How many times have I told you? Curfew is at eleven."

It was actually at twelve last time I checked, but I know better than to even attempt to correct him when he gets like this. Silence is almost always the safest answer. I resist the urge to rub at the stinging skin on my cheek, knowing it's best not to draw attention to the fresh bruise.

Damn it, I really should have accepted Avery's offer to sleep over tonight. But she was so worked up about what happened with Jace, and I didn't want to hear any more on the subject. I just wanted some peace. I'd figured I'd be able to spend the evening quietly holed up in my room; my dad had been in a surprisingly good mood earlier today, and I had expected it to last at least though the evening. Apparently, I was wrong.

I could cry about it, but I've lost enough tears over him. Now I need to focus on the good: in four months, I'll be eighteen. Then I can run away and no one can stop me.

"Well?" my dad says.

"I'm sorry."

"Sorry isn't good enough," he snaps. "You're always sorry, but you never listen to me."

I bite my lip just in time to stop myself from saying, *"Maybe I'd listen if you bothered to make sense."* It's true, though. The demands he makes of me are often downright stupid. He wants me to get straight A's so he can "be proud of me." I want to get D's, so that my teachers will realize I really *do* still need the help of an ASL interpreter, despite my lip-reading allowing me to squeak by with passing grades. He wants me to attend Los Angeles State and "follow in his footsteps." I want to go to Gallaudet University, where I'll be part of a community that embraces my deafness instead of pitying it. He wants me to get a job in law enforcement. I want to vomit at the thought.

"Really, Dad," I say quietly. "I'm sorry. It won't happen again. I promise." My cheek is already starting to swell, and it aches as I speak. But I force an appeasing smile to stay on my lips.

He grunts and turns away from me, walking unsteadily toward the kitchen. I let out a long breath. But apparently I'm too loud, because he whirls around. "*What* did you say?"

"Nothing," I squeak. "I didn't say anything."

He glares at me for a long moment, and then shakes his head and strides back to the kitchen, leaving me there alone. I let out another relieved breath, but make sure to keep it quiet. Then I sprint up the staircase to my room in the attic.

Old movies make attic rooms out to be scary—making your kid stay in one is always some sort of punishment. In reality, it's the exact opposite. Mine is cozy and big and far away from my dad.

I collapse on my bed and stare up at the ceiling. Avery's room still has the glow-in-the-dark stars we put up there in second grade, and her bedroom is also home to about five dozen pictures of her family, friends, and animals. Her walls are covered in good memories.

Mine are bare. I keep all my favorite pictures carefully bundled in my desk drawer, ready to be scooped up and packed the first chance I get to move out of here. This isn't home, and it never will be.

I reach up and touch my sore cheek, wincing as my fingers graze the flesh. Tomorrow, Avery will lend me an ice bag, and I can hang out at her house for the day. It's the one place I always feel welcome.

Over the years, Avery's parents have tried reporting my dad to Child Protective Services at least twice, but it did nothing to help. My dad simply has too many connections for the reports to be taken seriously. CPS has assured Avery's parents that my home is safe, and that I'm just a "troubled kid." I don't think either of them quite buy it, but they're both people who are wary of the authorities and too scared to directly argue. I can't blame them for their fear. They make up for it by letting me spend as much time as I want over at their house.

But I can't go over there until the morning, so I pull out my phone and open up Google Chrome, figuring I'll distract myself by reading some forum posts. I've been following the DeafClan forum for almost four years now—they have an entire sub-forum dedicated to bands, and it was how I first discovered that being deaf didn't have to mean ditching music. A lot of classical music has lost its magic—the vibrations are more subtle, and the memories are too painful. But the DeafClan forum introduced me to the idea that feeling the vibrations of rock songs is almost as good as hearing them. Since then, I blast music whenever I get the chance, and it never fails to bring back good memories of dancing around the kitchen with my mom, listening to her sing along to her favorites by the Beatles.

I scroll through the newest forum posts, pausing to read a long message chain about the newly restored Elvis Presley album coming out in a few weeks. The excitement in the messages is contagious, and part of me is dying to join in on the online conversation. Even though I've gleaned hundreds of song recommendations off this forum, I've never actually posted anything. I tried making an account once, but I deleted it before I even finished registering.

Everyone else on the forum is Deaf—part of the non-hearing community and proud of it. Me? I've never even had a Deaf friend, let alone been part of their community. All through middle school, I worked with my school district's ASL interpreters and speech therapists. Through hundreds of hours of tutoring, they made me fluent in ASL and a champion lip-reader. But I've only ever used those skills to make communicating with hearing people easier. I've never really had the chance to converse with Deaf individuals.

Sure, I've read practically every single forum thread on DeafClan, and spent way too much time daydreaming about attending Gallaudet University, where I could dive headfirst into Deaf culture. But those are just daydreams.

At least for now. As soon as I turn eighteen, I can hightail it out of this house and do whatever the hell I want with my education and my life. I glance at the clock at the top of my screen; it's 12:37 a.m.

Only four months, two days, and five hours before my birthday.

5

ALI

AVERY RIPS OFF the last Tone Deaf poster from her wall and throws it in the corner of her room. There's a pile of posters there, all ripped to pieces, with Jace's face scribbled out on each one of them.

I sit at her desk, below a patch of glow-in-the-dark stars. It's ten o'clock in the morning, and the stars have faded back to white plastic, but it's still comforting to see them. The day we put them up there, Avery's mom had invited me over and made us butter cookies, and we'd eaten them up in Avery's room. I was still getting used to being deaf, and Avery was still getting used to having a deaf neighbor. We'd struggled to keep up a conversation made up of poor sign language and even poorer lip-reading, and giggled at all our mistranslations.

I had tried to tell her about my mom's oatmeal cookies, how they were the best in the world, and how I missed them. But that made me burst out sobbing, a language we both understood. Avery had held my hand while I cried, and promised she'd tell her mom to make me oatmeal cookies next time I was over.

"I still cannot believe he did that," Avery signs frantically, breaking me from my thoughts. She strides to the corner and kicks the pile of paper scraps. Then she stomps on one of the posters of Jace's head. *"What an asshole."*

I absently doodle on a piece of binder paper and try to ignore her outburst. I should have known better than to tell her what happened last night. As soon as I knocked on her door this morning, she'd burst into a fit of anger toward Tone Deaf. Then she noticed my face and burst into another fit. Thirty minutes later, she still can't decide who she hates more: my dad or Jace Beckett. She seems to be leaning toward Jace at the moment.

I'm trying to draw a puppy—something cute and cuddly and comforting—but I keep focusing too much on the eyes. They turn piercing and light-colored. I crumple up the paper and throw it in the corner with the other scraps of uselessness.

"Let it go, Avery," I say. "He's not worth the time."

She throws her hands up in the air. *"You're right, he's not worth the time,"* she signs. Her signing is slower than mine, but after four years of taking ASL classes, she's close to fluent. She never got the specialized tutoring in ASL that I received, but she did decide to take ASL as her second-language course in high school. *"I can't believe I've spent two years swooning over that guy! He's just—"* She makes a disgusted face and shakes her head, abruptly turning away from me.

I pull out another piece of paper and start doodling a kitten. What I really want to work on is the lion I've been meticulously drawing for the past week. It's actually turning out pretty well, even though half my room is now covered in charcoal-pencil dust, and I'm itching to finish it. But I left the drawing and all my art supplies back at my house, so binder paper and a mechanical pencil will have to do.

My sketched kitty is sleepy, with very closed, very non-Jace eyes. I don't tell Avery what I'm thinking: that I can't believe she wasted all that time, either. How many times did I tell her to lose the Tone Deaf obsession? Like ten thousand. But she wouldn't listen. If she'd just listened, then I never would have gone to that concert, and Jace never would have . . .

No. I can't blame Avery. It's not her fault.

Avery sighs and, as if she's reading my mind, signs, *"This is all my fault. I'm so sorry, Ali. I never should have dragged you to their concert."*

I quickly sign back, *"It's not your fault. Not at all. You're not responsible for that asshole's actions."*

She turns away and scrubs at her face with her hands. It's obvious she's holding back tears, but I don't have it in me to comfort her. If I tried, I'd just burst out crying myself.

"Look, Avery," I sign. *"Just forget about it, okay? It happened, and now it's over."* I point to the pile of crumpled posters as proof.

She shakes her head and signs, *"We should go to the media. He can't just get away with treating you like that. He can't!"*

I roll my eyes and scribble out the cat. It looks all lopsided and pitiful, and I don't have the patience to fix it. *"If you heard Jace treated someone like that, would you have believed it two days ago?"*

"Yes. Of course."

I give her a pointed look. She lets her head fall back and reluctantly signs, *"No. I guess not. Two days ago, I would have thought he was too good to do anything like that."*

"And that's exactly what all the Tone Deaf fans out there would think. They wouldn't believe me. Besides, it's not like I have proof of what he said to me."

Avery flops onto her bed and crosses her arms over her chest, her lips pursed in a pout. I can tell she still wants to try reporting Jace, and a small part of me wants to smile at her loyalty.

"He needs to pay for this," Avery grumbles, although I don't know if she means for me to see the words.

I shrug. "His attitude will catch up to him eventually."

Even as I say it, I know it's a lie. He's a freaking rock star, a celebrity, a modern god with hordes of followers. He can do anything, and nobody will care. Well, as long as he does his shit to someone like me—someone who doesn't matter.

"Eventually isn't soon enough," Avery says.

I don't respond, and we fall into silence. I start sketching a sleepy puppy, and Avery sulks on the bed, glaring at the ceiling. Then I feel a buzzing in my pocket, startling me and making me draw a thick, dark line through my cute puppy.

Crumpling up the paper, I toss it in the corner with the others and tear my phone out of my pocket. A new text waits for me on the home screen.

Sorry.

I bite my lip, hiding a frown as I wonder which of my meager group of friends has heard about my run-in with Jace. I don't recognize the number, which is weird. When you use your cell phone as much as I do, everyone gets programmed into contacts. Texting is one of the easiest ways to communicate with hearing people, so I use it all the time. Not that it's made my small group of friends grow much; getting close to people is near impossible when I'm constantly hiding everything about my home life. But at least it helps.

I toss the phone onto Avery's desk, not bothering with a reply. No matter who it is, I don't want to take part in a pity party.

It buzzes again, and I reluctantly look at the screen: *I was a jerk. Sorry.*

What the . . . no. It can't be Jace. He doesn't know my number, and even if he did, I don't think an asshole like him would ever bother with an apology.

Avery taps on my shoulder. I turn to find her standing beside me, hands on her hips, lips still in a pout. "We need to do something, Ali. We . . ." She trails off as she sees the text on my screen. "Who is that?"

I shrug. "Don't know."

"Wrong number?" she asks, although her frown is just as suspicious as mine.

"Probably."

The phone buzzes again. *Alison. Come on.*

My heart picks up its pace. So it's not a wrong number. And, as far as I know, there's no one else who should be apologizing to me.

No one other than Jace.

41

I reach for the phone, but Avery grabs the arms of the desk chair and spins it so I'm facing her. "No," she says. "You are *so not* going to waste your time giving that douchebag a response."

I nod in agreement, but I can't form any words. How in the hell did he get my number? My heart keeps pounding, and I close my eyes, just wanting the whole situation to go away.

Avery grabs the phone and starts typing, but I snatch it away before she sends some insulting message. I hug the phone close to me and wag my finger at her. "We're not going to get in a pissing war with him." I say it out loud, so she can't pretend to misunderstand me. "Like you said, he's not worth our time."

She throws her hands up and glares at me. I'm used to exasperating Avery, but I've rarely seen her like this; she looks genuinely upset with me. "Let me talk to him."

"No." This is something I need to deal with myself. He insulted *me*, he flipped *me* off, and so it should be *me* who deals with him.

Before Avery can protest, I jog into the hallway, clutching the phone close to me. I turn into the bathroom right outside her room and lock the door. Taking a deep breath, I sit on the edge of the bathtub.

Vibrations run through the tile, and I know Avery is outside banging on the door, trying to get me to come out. I pull out the phone and erase the part of the message Avery already typed. Once the last swear is cleared from the screen, I start my own message.

How did you get my number?

The response comes almost instantly. ***Ticket sale records.***

I groan. Avery was the one who saved up for the tickets, but she'd had me make the actual purchase, since I'm better at scrounging up online deals. I'd been certain the info I gave the ticket site was private, but Jace probably isn't the type to care about confidentiality. He's got the money to get past any kind of barrier. Lucky bastard.

Another text pops up on my screen: *I'm really sorry.*

No you're not.

But my manager thinks I should be.

I squeeze my eyes closed just as my phone vibrates again. I clench it tight, resisting the urge to chuck it across the room. After a long minute, I stare back down at the screen. I'm not about to drop the conversation now and let Jace think he got the better of me.

You need money?

I'm slightly surprised at how articulate his texts are. Most guys use as many abbreviations as possible when they text, which drives me nuts. But not Jace. Well, that's *one* thing about this conversation that's not infuriating.

How is that any of your business? I text back.

I'll give you 3k if you let me make up for being a jerk.

I rub my temples. This is so *not* how this conversation was supposed to go. I was supposed to tell him off, say he was an asshole and that he can't just go around treating people the way he does. Money was never supposed to be a factor in this.

How does he even know how broke I am? How desperately I need cash? For every second Avery has spent daydreaming about Tone Deaf, I've spent a minute dreaming about escape. To get away from this city, away from the air that's strangely hot and dusty. To run back to NYC, where beautiful chaos rules and no one notices you unless you want them to.

To escape to a place where my dad could never find me.

"Damn you," I mutter, clenching the phone tighter in my hand. I hesitantly type back, *What do you want from me?*

Just finish the tour. Take a couple pictures with me. I promise I won't even talk to you.

I laugh as I read his reply. Jackass. Like ignoring me is some type of gift? Seriously, what's his issue? Sure, he's made his living off music, but that's no reason to hate anyone who can't hear his work. I think of all the people I've seen posting on the DeafClan forums about his music, and suddenly wish I had my own account, just so I could warn them that Jace doesn't deserve his fans.

And why is he even offering this to me? Probably to keep me from going to the media, like Avery suggested. After all, Jace doesn't know for sure that I don't have any evidence of what he did. I'm sure some girls would have tried to discreetly film their encounter with a celebrity, which is probably what he's worried about. But if Jace gets a couple of pictures with me, both of us smiling, then no one can claim he's done anything wrong.

My breath catches in my throat as I realize these texts would probably give me enough evidence to convince a news outlet of what an ass he was to me. But . . . damn it. The number he's using has a local area code, probably from a phone he borrowed. There's nothing to prove it's actually him. Which leads me back to the impossible issue of getting the media to believe me over a celebrity.

No, I type back before I can stop myself. *I don't need your pity.*

This isn't pity. This is my manager keeping you quiet.

Well, at least he's honest. But still a jackass.

I grit my teeth and flick to his first text, getting ready to delete every word he's sent. A message screen pops up, asking, *Send conversation thread to trash*? Just as I'm about to press *OK*, another text appears.

8k. Final offer.

My throat goes dry. With eight thousand dollars, I could easily get a plane ticket to New York City and pay for a few months' rent. And combined with the money I've saved up over the years, I'd have enough for a semester at a community college, which would give me a chance to improve my grades and get accepted into a nice university . . .

No. I'm not really considering this. Am I? Even though he's the one offering the money, it's still pretty much blackmail. And I'm above that . . . right?

More vibrations run through the tile floor from Avery outside the door. I wipe a sweaty palm on my jean shorts, darkening a small splotch of the denim.

I take a deep breath and text back, **When do you want to meet?**

Tonight. 8:00. Meet at the stadium stage.

I quickly select each of the messages and delete them. But there's no satisfaction now. Instead, my stomach rolls, like I'd just swallowed a cocktail of antifreeze and boiling tar. I reach over and unlock the door, and Avery comes rushing in. "What did you say to him?" she demands, her agitation causing her to sign and speak at the same time.

"I told him to f-off and never text me again," I say. I know if I told her the truth, Avery would insist on coming with me tonight, and I don't want that. It's going to be hard enough to stop myself from strangling Jace, without also having to hold back my overprotective best friend.

Her lips purse in a suspicious frown. "I heard your phone go off a few times."

I force a smirk onto my lips. "He doesn't take rejection well."

That makes a smile spring onto her lips, and she nods decidedly. "Awesome. You gave him what he deserved."

"Yup."

She holds out her hand and wiggles her fingers. "I've got to see this conversation."

I shrug my shoulders hopelessly. "Sorry. I already deleted it. Didn't want any trace of him on my phone."

For a moment, Avery's frown reappears, but she quickly replaces it with a triumphant smile. Then she runs over and envelops me in a hug. My bruised cheek presses against her shoulder, and I try not to cringe.

I hug her back, driving away whatever remaining suspicions she has. I try to push away my guilt over the lies I've just told. *Jace Beckett, you'd better come through on your end of the bargain.*

6

JACE

"I SHOULDN'T HAVE to do this."

I'm not sure who I'm talking to; Tony isn't listening to me, and I'm sick of hearing my own voice.

"You were an absolute asshole to her, Jace," says Tony. So apparently he *is* listening. You never know with that guy; he always has his ear to a phone or his nose pressed against a screen, so it's hard to tell if he's paying attention or not.

He's on the couch with his phone in his hand, clicking through emails. Probably all of them are about me or some event I'm about to participate in. As my manager/royal-pain-in-my-ass, it's Tony's job to keep my career in order.

Tony quickly types out a message before glancing back up at me. He looks nothing like a band manager should: short dirt-brown hair, pale complexion, wire glasses that sit on the end of his nose. He hardly looks professional, let alone stylish, like most people in the music industry try to be. But what Tony lacks in appearance, he makes up for in marketing genius. There's no way Tone Deaf ever would have gotten off the ground without his skill.

"Jace? Are you listening to me?"

I ignore him and focus on the notebook in front of me. In my sloppy handwriting, the front reads, THE PERFECT SONG. Although, I'm beginning to wonder if that will ever be true; I've been working on this song for years, and it's far from perfect.

Strong hands clasp on my shoulders, making me flinch. I still half expect those hands to cause pain, even though I know Tony would never hurt me. But the fear is ingrained in me, and it makes my words sharp as I growl, "Get *off* me, Tony."

He keeps his hands right where they are, and even gives my shoulder a little squeeze. Bastard. He knows how much I hate it when he does emotional crap like this.

"Jace, listen to me," Tony says, his voice surprisingly even. "You were terrible to that girl. She doesn't deserve what you did, and you know it."

I grunt in response and turn back to my notebook, reading over my revised first lines: *When clarity's gone and logic is done and love flees out the doorway,*

When kisses hurt and your heart is cursed and so carelessly cast away . . .

. . . And then nothing. I'm stuck on the next line, and even though I have three dozen previous drafts of this verse, nothing seems to fit.

Tony sighs and lets go of me. I slowly release a breath and unconsciously flex my shoulders, checking for damage.

"I've told you before," he says, "stunts like this could ruin you. We've all seen it happen before. One bad media story can flush a music career down the toilet."

"I don't care," I mutter, knowing I sound like a three-year-old.

"And what about the rest of the band? Are you willing to ruin *their* careers, just because you're too petty to make things up to this girl?"

Damn it, I hate it when he does this. He's pulled the think-of-your-bandmates card plenty of times before to convince me to act like a nice little rock star. He knows our band is a family, and that I could never hurt any of them. Never.

I raise my hands in exasperated defeat. "I'll give her the tour. Just don't expect me to suck up to her or anything."

Tony rolls his eyes. "I'd never expect you to suck up to any-one."

"Good."

A knock comes at the RV door. Before I can even respond, the door whips open and Killer pokes in his head. "The deaf girl is here!"

I rub my eyes with my palms and bite my lip to hold back a yell of frustration. "Thank you for announcing that to the entire neighborhood, Killer."

"Dude, she's deaf. You really think it matters how loudly I say it?"

I sigh and stand from my chair, stretching to work out the kinks in my neck. This is the part of the job I hate: the people. I got into this business because of the music. Not for the fans, not for the attention, and definitely not for the socialization. Unfortunately, all those things are necessary if I want to keep the band alive.

Tony gives me a pat on the back, which I shoot him a glare for. How hard is it for him to keep his hands to himself?

"Thirty minutes," he says. "That's it. Give this girl thirty minutes of your time, take a couple of smiling pictures with her, and then you can forget about her forever."

I walk out of the RV, silently chanting his words: *thirty minutes, thirty minutes, thirty minutes.*

And then forget about her.

Forever.

7

ALI

I CROSS MY arms over my chest and gaze around, taking in the empty stadium. One of Tone Deaf's tech crew members greeted me at the entrance gates and led me here to the base of the stage. Then he ran off to fetch Jace, leaving me to wait.

It's been hardly one day since the concert, but everything looks different. The giant screen is off, and the only lights on the stage are the dim backup ones. There's no audience, no sound vibrations or packed bodies. Just plain old silence.

I take a deep breath to calm my nerves and tap out a beat with my foot, driving my frustration into a steady rhythm. I guess I should just be happy I'm getting eight grand out of this. But I'm not happy; no amount of money is worth the sort of humiliation Jace flung in my face. A soft breeze ruffles my hair, but it does nothing to cool my flaming temper.

I look over the seats in the stadium, toward the lot in the distance where I parked. My dad let me borrow his old Pontiac tonight, like he sometimes does. My feet itch to run back to the car and drive away. This was a mistake coming here. I shouldn't be here, shouldn't be giving in to Jace's bribe. It's not right.

Before I can convince myself to leave, I see Jace coming toward me. He emerges from one of the hallways right beside the main stage, moving like he has a lead ball chained to his leg.

As Jace approaches, his expression isn't predatory, but instead wary, like he's afraid of what he'll see. He comes to a halt right in front of me. "Thanks for coming, Alison."

"I go by Ali," I say in what I hope is a growl. "Not Alison." Only my dad calls me Alison.

I stare at his feet, not wanting to even see whatever scathing response he comes up with. I'm surprised to find he's wearing a beat-up pair of Vans instead of some designer brand. Huh. I guess he's not into the whole "famous and fashionable" thing.

Jace strides back toward the hallway he just came out of, motioning for me to follow. I stay at his side and try to keep my expression neutral. I can't let Jace see that he's getting to me. He's not even apologizing for what happened last night. No, he's just acting like nothing is wrong, like I'm just another obsessed fan who actually wants this tour.

I force in a deep breath. It'll be over soon. I just need to get through it.

The guy from the tech crew who greeted me earlier meets us in the hallway. He's scrawny and wears thick glasses, and I'd bet he's hardly any older than Jace. But as he follows along with us, he gapes at Jace like he's witnessing a god, and he keeps snapping pictures of us with his phone. Great. I guess those images will be the evidence Jace needs to keep away a media scandal.

We reach the sound room, hidden away just a couple dozen yards from the main stage, and Jace vaguely gestures around. "This is where all the sound controls are."

I take in the equipment in front of me. Most of it I'm familiar with, but some of it's different. I walk around the room, running my fingers over the analog mixer, the power amp, the signal processor. I still remember my piano teacher making me learn all the stage technology when I was little. I'd thrown a fit; I wanted to play music, not learn about boring sound systems. But he'd insisted, saying that part of respecting music was respecting the devices that help create it.

I trace the ridges on one of the processor's knobs. The technology hasn't changed much since I last performed, but now that I can never be a part of it, the equipment feels cold and foreign under my fingertips.

"You're missing a monitoring system. How do you play without one?"

The question slips out of my mouth before I can stop it. I don't really want to know, right? Right. I shouldn't have a casual conversation with Jace, not after what he did.

Jace raises his eyebrows and walks over to me, his arms crossed firmly over his muscular chest. He pauses to pat a small analog mixer, like it's a dog needing attention, and then says, "Most of this equipment belongs to the stadium, but we like to use our own tech for the important stuff. Like the monitoring system. It's already been packed up for our next show."

I take a step back. "So then you're leaving soon."

"Tomorrow afternoon, thankfully."

I try not to wince. The way he looks at me with disdain as he says "thankfully" makes me think I'm the one he's happy to be leaving behind, and not this city.

"When do I get my money?" I demand.

Jace looks toward the tech crew guy, who's standing in the doorway. He's busy taking another picture of us and pretending he isn't hearing a word we're saying.

"I'll give you the check when we're done with the tour," Jace says.

"Forget the tour. You give me that money, and I promise to not go to the media."

He laughs in my face. "I don't trust promises, sweetheart."

I feel like I'm going to explode. Sweetheart? Does he really think he can call me condescending pet names, after how he treated me? But I guess he doesn't think that. He *knows* it. After all, he's the one with the money and the leverage. I'm tempted to call this whole thing off just to spite him.

Instead, I take in a deep breath and ask, "Why do you use an analog mixer instead of a digital? Wouldn't a digital mixer be better for punk music? Especially with all your guitars?" If I have to endure Jace's presence, I might as well talk about something I'm interested in.

Jace blinks at me, and his sneer slowly melts into a frown. "You know about PAs?" he asks slowly. I can tell by the way he hesitates at the word "PA" that he's trying to test my vocabulary.

I roll my eyes. "Of course I know sound systems."

"How?"

"I've performed before."

Jace lets out another scoff. "What venue would allow *you* to perform?"

"Carnegie."

His eyes grow wide. "Carnegie Hall?"

I nod. There's no way I can form any words right now. I haven't talked about my past for a long, long time, and there's a familiar stabbing pain in my gut as I mention Carnegie. I remember that night so well—I'd been terrified but exhilarated as I performed with a group of highly advanced piano students. It felt like every single eye in the audience was glued to me as my little hands flew over the keys. Everyone was waiting for me to screw up and prove that kids don't belong in the most prestigious music hall in NYC.

I performed perfectly. And that was the real start of my music career.

Jace's eyes narrow with suspicion. "Tell me where the 'h' note is on a keyboard."

"There is no 'h' note."

"Then tell me what an analog mixer does, as long as you're so interested in mine."

I rattle off an explanation that leaves him looking mildly impressed. "Great. So you've read a Wikipedia article about them."

"I'm not making it up! I used to play."

"Then prove it," he demands.

I shake my head. "I'm deaf now. I don't play anymore." I don't say what else I'm thinking: that I haven't touched an instrument since the surgery permanently stole my hearing. That I don't think I could if I tried. That the pain of it would kill me.

Jace smirks. "That's what I thought. You can't play now, and never have been able to."

"That's *not* true."

"It's what I'll believe until you prove me wrong."

Jace and I glare at each other for a good five seconds, and then he abruptly turns toward the door. "I'll show you the equipment trailer next," he says and begins walking away, not waiting for me to respond.

Eight grand, I remind myself. *This is worth it for eight grand.*

No, it's not, a small voice in my head whispers. *Nothing is worth digging up those memories.*

But I ignore the voice and follow him out the door.

8

JACE

I TEAR OFF my damp T-shirt and throw it in the corner of my room. The heat outside combined with my angry, anxious nerves have left me covered in sweat and feeling downright gross. I wish I could swap out the painful memories that have been crowding my mind for days, but for now, a fresh shirt is the best I can do.

I search through my closet for a T-shirt, knowing I need to hurry up. I'm procrastinating bringing Ali her check, but I really don't want to go back out there and have to talk with her again. Twenty-seven minutes I spent with her on the tour. Twenty-seven minutes too long. She spent every moment scowling at me, and I spent every moment knowing I deserved her anger, and probably worse.

But apologizing for flipping her off would have inevitably led to her demanding an explanation. And I'm not even sure I have one of those to give, at least not after getting to know her a little on the tour. Yesterday, her deafness had seemed like a giant, painful reminder of the past I've worked so hard to escape. Today, her deafness had hardly even mattered. Her disgust for me was far more distracting. Guilt usually isn't an emotion I let myself feel, but it kept clawing at my mind every time she'd shoot me one of those angry, frustrated glances.

I left her by the equipment trailer, promising I'd return in just a few minutes with her check. I've already written it out and have it waiting by the door, but I'm suddenly tempted to rewrite one for a higher amount. The money obviously means a lot to her. Every time I mentioned it, she got this desperate glint in her eye that made my guilt even stronger.

A knock comes at my door right as I shrug into a long-sleeved shirt. It's way too hot to be wearing anything with sleeves—between the heat and the cramped, dusty landscape, Los Angeles has got to be one of the most miserable cities ever. But the long-sleeved shirt is a comforting reminder of one of the few good things from my past—growing up in Denver, with its thick snow and chilly air.

"Come in," I call, and Jon pushes open the door to my room. He leans against the doorway and crosses his arms, his lips pursed in a tight scowl. After the lecture Tony gave us this morning, I don't think Jon is going to forgive me anytime soon for giving a fan the finger.

"Did you get the pictures?" he asks.

"Yeah." I take my phone out of my pocket and toss it to him. "I already forwarded them to Tony."

Jon nods and starts flicking through the images on my screen. I wait for him to show approval, but his scowl just deepens. "What happened to her face?"

"Huh?"

"Her face. It's all swollen on one side." He walks over and tilts the phone so I can see the picture on the screen. It'd been taken right outside the sound room, and Ali and me are both wearing smiles that look painfully fake.

Surprise jolts through me as I realize Jon's right. I haven't looked closely at Ali all evening; her glares have kept me from meeting her eyes. But the swelling is obvious now that I examine the picture. I reach over and flick to the next image, and I wince as I see the swelling in that one, too.

I snatch the phone out of Jon's hand and scroll to the last photo in the series. The sweltering heat had left all of us sweating by the end of the tour, and some of Ali's makeup had worn off. Without the thick plaster of foundation on her cheek, I can see the greenish shadow of a fresh bruise.

"Shit," Jon says, peering over my shoulder at the picture. "Did she have that yesterday?"

"I don't know," I admit. But it doesn't matter if the bruise was there yesterday, because it shouldn't be there at all. I flip back a few pictures until I find one that shows her arms. Cold nausea slams into my gut as I see what I was both expecting and dreading—a band of bruises curling around her forearm, like a hand grabbed her there. The bruises on her arm are faint, but the fact that they're old just makes me feel worse. Whatever happened to her face wasn't a one-time deal.

Jon gives his throat an uncomfortable clear. "Do you think . . . ?"

"Yeah," I say, not bothering to finish the sentence for him. I know we're both thinking the exact same thing. Jon comes from a decent family, but he's spent plenty of time fetching ice packs for me and helping me wrap sprains.

"Shit," Jon repeats.

He sounds sad and concerned, but it's nothing compared to the emotions roiling inside me and lighting my nerves on fire. I don't need this right now. Hell, this is the *last* thing I need. June fifth is always a horrible day, but it's only supposed to last twenty-four hours. Then I can spend 364 days shoving away the memories from my past and pretending none of it mattered.

Except it does matter, because now it's re-entered my life in the form of a girl who is clearly in trouble. I think of how careful she was to keep space between us during the tour, and of the desperate look in her eyes when I mentioned the money. Could this be why?

"Um, do you want to sit down?" Jon asks, his voice strained and uncertain. "You look like you're about to pass out."

I let out a shuddering breath I hadn't realized I'd been holding. My heart thunders in my chest as I take a couple shaky steps toward the bed and sit on its edge. I have the sudden urge to grab the sheets and pull them over my head, to just hide from this situation like I used to hide from my nightmares when I was a kid. Not that it ever helped much back then. It was impossible to escape bad dreams when I was living with a monster.

Jon bites his lip. "You stay here, okay?" He hooks his thumb over his shoulder, gesturing toward the door of the RV. "I'll go give the girl her money."

"No," I say.

"No? Jace, you promised it to her. You can't back out."

"I mean, no, you're not going to give it to her." I stand up and stride toward the door, walking fast so Jon can't see how shaky my legs are. "I am."

Jon sidesteps in front of me, blocking my way out of the room. "You're not going to ask her about the bruises, are you? We're trying to keep this girl *away* from the media. Stirring up drama isn't going to help things."

"Drama?" I repeat, my voice a growl. "Someone hurt that girl. That's not drama, that's a crime."

Jon holds up his hands, as if to ward off my glare. "Okay, sorry, that was a bad word choice. But my point stands. There's no way you're going to help things by getting involved in this."

I press my palm against my forehead, wishing I could just shove away the thoughts rattling around my mind.

She's being hurt.

She's in danger.

She needs help.

"I have to try," I say to Jon.

He heaves a frustrated sigh. "Look, Jace, you don't even know for sure if she's being abused. Maybe she just—"

"—fell down the stairs?" I say, my tone dripping with sarcasm. "Slipped on a wet floor? Got accidentally hit with an opening door?" I shake my head. "I'm sure she'll have some sort of excuse. And I'm sure I'll recognize it, because it'll probably be one I've used before."

Jon gives a frustrated sigh. "Look, Jace, I know you're going through a rough time right now. I get it. And, yeah, those bruises are really suspicious, so I understand why you're worried about this girl. But her safety is absolutely not your con-cern."

"If you really think that, then you don't understand at all," I say. Then I shove past him, stopping only to grab the check before I rush back to Ali.

9

ALI

I GLARE AT the pavement, my teeth gritted so hard that it makes my bruised jaw hurt even more. What's wrong with me? I never let people like Jace get to me. He's a worthless jerk, and what he says doesn't matter.

Except it does. He didn't just attack me with words; he attacked me with my past. I've tried so hard to forget about my musical career, and he tossed all that work out the window. The pain is back, just as raw as it was that day I woke up from surgery and couldn't hear. Damn it. Damn *him*.

I take in a shuddering breath. At least this tour is almost officially over. He went to get my check, and as soon as he hands it over, I'm out of here. If he ever comes back, that is. It's been a solid ten minutes since he left, and I'm starting to wonder if he's going to cheat me out of the money.

I lean against the side of the equipment trailer, letting the sun-soaked metal warm my back. I take a deep breath and close my eyes, just for a moment, just long enough to regain my composure. When I open them, I'll be calm. I'll forget about Jace's insults and the memories he stirred up. I'll take the check and run far, far away.

Something lightly touches my shoulder, making me yelp in surprise. I snap my eyes open and find Jace in front of me. He has his hands nervously stuffed in the pockets of his jeans, and he's wearing a long-sleeved shirt now. Why did he change into that, of all things? It's still like eighty degrees outside, and his forehead is already covered in sweat. Maybe the dude is some sort of masochist; he hurts everything and everyone, including himself.

His throat bobs as he clears it, and he shuffles around for a couple seconds, his eyes glued to his feet. I stay exactly where I am, doing my best to look intimidating as I stare up at him. I think of how my mom used to laugh when I was learning a new song; she said I looked ferocious when I concentrated that hard. I try to channel that expression and glare straight at Jace.

Jace stares down at his hands, holding them far in front of him, like they have some sort of terrible disease he's afraid to catch. Then he pushes up his sleeves, even though they're already scrunched up around his muscular biceps. He takes a deep breath, and I step to the side, wondering what in the hell is going on. He's not even talking. He's just standing there, occasionally shooting me little glances that almost look . . . scared.

He keeps staring at his hands for a bit longer, and then he takes a shuddering breath. "Hey."

"I want my check," I say, trying to keep my voice calm.

"I'll give it to you in a second," he mutters.

"No, *now*."

Jace shakes his head and takes a step toward me. He keeps coming closer, until he's only a foot away. He peers closely at me, his eyes squinting as he examines my face. I unconsciously reach up and cover my cheek with my hand, hiding the bruised area from sight.

"It looks like someone hit you," Jace says, gesturing to my cheek.

"No," I quickly say, shaking my head.

He points to my arm. "You're bruised there, too."

"It was just an accident," I insist. "And it's definitely not your business."

Jace takes another half-step toward me, bringing us impossibly closer. Finally, he looks into my eyes, and I'm able to see his full expression. It's not right. Jace is supposed to be angry and condemning and pitiless. But his eyes are . . . sad.

He raises his hands, gives them one more disgusted glance, and then signs, *"Let me help you."*

I stare in shock at his hands. What? *What?* I hesitantly raise my hands and sign back, *"I'm totally fine. No one's hurt me, I swear. I just fell."*

I half expect him to burst out laughing and mock me for my signing, for him to tell me that he doesn't actually know ASL, and he's just messing with me. But, instead, he gives me a small, sad smile.

"You're lying," he signs.

I ignore his accusation and ask, *"How do you know ASL?"* Sometimes I'll run into people who know a sign or two, but Jace's skills are obviously beyond that. His hands move with an ease that makes me think he's fluent.

"It doesn't matter," Jace signs. *"We're talking about you, not me."*

I shake my head. *"No, we're not."*

He laughs a little. Although, by the way his chest moves, I guess it's more of a hesitant chuckle than that scathing laugh from before.

"You're too stubborn for your own good."

"I'll be the judge of what's good for me and what's not."

He gestures to my bruised face again. *"That doesn't seem to be working out too well for you."*

Tears press at my eyes, threatening to break free, to spill down my cheeks and wash away the makeup, to give everything away. I squeeze my eyes shut and take a shuddering breath, trying to keep them at bay. *Think of something happy,* I tell myself. *Puppies, or kittens, or ponies.*

But when I think of those things, all I can picture are those ASPCA commercials that make Avery tear up every time they come on. I rub my hand over my eyes and feel moisture. Great. Just *great.*

Suddenly, there's a strange warmth on my swollen cheek, but it's not rough or angry. I open my eyes to find Jace standing close, his lips pursed in concern. He brushes away another tear with his thumb.

That's all it takes for me to start crying. Not the uncontrollable sobbing I was expecting, but something even worse. The tears are silent and hot as they stream down my face, and my chest doesn't heave, even though I can feel my heart pounding away. It's the type of crying that gives everything away: the kind that whispers I'm used to pain, to keeping it in, to never letting it out.

Jace pulls me into his arms, shocking me so much that I forget to resist. He wraps his arms around me awkwardly. For a moment, I'm ready to jerk away from him, but then I feel something drip onto my forehead. I look up and find him determinedly avoiding my gaze, his eyes strangely red and puffy as they stare at something in the distance.

We just stay there, me trapped in his arms, but not *really* trapped. It dawns on me that this is the first time in years that I've come in contact with a guy without feeling at all threatened. His arms are strong—but it's the kind of strength that keeps things standing, instead of tearing them down.

After what feels like a long time, Jace gently pulls away. But he keeps his hands on my arms as I shift away.

"How can I help you?" he asks.

"You're already helping," I mumble. Then I take a step back, breaking his grasp as I realize I still have no idea what's triggering this sudden kindness. I swallow hard and revert back to sign language. I'm still half expecting him to not know ASL, like maybe what just happened was a dream or hallucination. *"I'm going to use that check to get out of here. I'm going to buy a car and escape."*

He frowns and signs, *"Who's coming with you?"*

So he really *does* know ASL. Weird. No, bizarre is more like it. *"No one's coming with me,"* I reply slowly. *"I don't need anybody."*

"Well, where are you going? Do you have family to take you in?"

"No. But I'm going to New York City."

67

His frown grows into a grimace. *"What? Why the hell would you go there?"*

I flinch at his words, and he seems to realize he's being too harsh. He smiles thinly as he signs, *"It's not safe to be wandering around New York alone."*

"I'll be fine."

He scoffs. *"Just like your face is fine?"*

His mocking words are like another punch, and I stumble back, hitting the side of the trailer. Why did I ever think his concern was sincere? I almost laugh at my stupidity.

I turn on my heel and walk away. I'm getting out of here, with or without the money. I need to get away from Jace, from this bizarre conversation, from this city, from my dad.

Then a strong hand grips my elbow. Strong, but still not rough. In fact, Jace is surprisingly gentle as he stops me and turns me to face him. His hand is warm against my skin, maybe even a little comforting.

He lets go of me and signs, *"Wait. I want to help."*

I swallow hard, trying to steel myself for the truth. *"No, you don't."*

He rubs his face and lets out a long breath. "Look, Alison—"

"A-l-i," I correct, finger-spelling it for him.

He signs back, *"Fine, A-l-i. You need to know that I'm really terrible with words. Actually, unless it's lyrics, I'm just plain shitty at using language."*

I keep my expression stony and uncaring. I'm done listening to him. Done with him, period.

He holds up his hands, as if in surrender. He keeps them there for a long moment before dropping them to sign, *"I'm sorry. I'm really, really sorry for what I said. For everything."*

The way he locks eyes with me as he signs this makes me suspect he's being sincere. Is that even *possible*? I don't think jerks like him are capable of saying anything outside of the bullshit spectrum.

But my bullshit-o-meter isn't going off. And, for someone who gets by with constant lies, I'm great at detecting when people aren't telling the truth.

"I'm sorry. For everything." As if he's not just apologizing for his actions, but for everyone's.

I sniff back more tears and hesitantly sign, *"It's okay."*

"No, it's not okay. It's never okay for someone to beat you up. You don't deserve that. Do you hear me? It's not okay."

His signing grows more and more frantic. When he finally stops, his hands are shaking, and he's breathing hard.

I stare at my feet.

Jace holds out his hand for me to take. "Let me help. Please. I want to do more than just give you money."

I cross my arms and look away from the temptation of his outstretched hand. "What, are you afraid to part with eight grand?"

"I'll give you any amount you need, if that's really what you want from me."

I scoff. "And what if I ask for your entire bank account?"

"You won't."

I hesitantly meet his eyes. They're still sincere, surprising me almost as much as the look on his face: concern. And not the fleeting type of concern most people have shown when they ask about my bruises. This is real, genuine concern that feels like it could last forever.

Or at least until the problem is solved.

Jace's smile slowly wilts into a frown, and it takes me a moment to realize that I've just been staring at him for like a minute. I shake my head, trying to get a handle on my confusing thoughts, and sign, *"I don't have a single reason to trust you."*

He reaches his hand toward mine, until our fingertips almost touch. *"Then let me give you one."* He swallows hard, and then starts speaking so fast, I can barely read his lips. "Our tour ends in New York City. Come with me. The band, I mean. It'll make traveling a lot safer, if you're with us. And I can help find you someplace safe to stay, once we get there."

I shake my head. *"You don't get it. My dad's a retired police chief, and I'm a minor. As soon as I start running, he's going to hunt me down, and he'll have an entire police force to help."*

Jace frowns. *"You're what, seventeen?"*

"Yeah."

"They won't chase too hard after a seventeen-year-old. You're too close to being an adult."

I look up at the sky, wondering how much to tell him. *"My dad . . . he's relentless."*

Jace simply shrugs. *"So am I."*

"You don't get it. He'll—"

"He'll have my best lawyers after his ass if he even tries to come after you," Jace interrupts. His expression turns fierce, the harsh angles of his face reminding me of a hawk. *"I'll keep you safe. I promise."*

"I thought you said promises didn't mean anything to you," I mutter before I can stop myself.

He frowns, as if he isn't used to being challenged like this. Tough luck; I'm not going along with anything until I know his motives. "Well, this is different," he says.

"How?"

"Because *I'm* the one making the promise. And I always tell the truth."

I scoff. "The truth? You're a celebrity. People like you live off of lies."

His expression darkens. "I'm a musician, not a celebrity, and anyone who says differently can go to hell."

I stumble back a step. I don't like these mood swings the dude keeps having. It's like he has two people stuck in him— angry Jace and nice Jace. And I'm not sure which one I'm scared of more— the side trying to shove me away, or the one begging me to do something utterly stupid.

"Come with me," Jace says again, interrupting my thoughts. "Please. I can help."

"But . . . my dad is going to try to find me. The police will be after me. And you're nineteen. You could be accused of kidnapping."

"Are you hearing me, Ali? I don't give a shit. We'll hide you, keep you out of sight. No one will ever know you're with the band." He signs, *"When's your birthday?"*

"In four months."

"Perfect. Our tour lasts four months. By the time we make it to New York, you'll be eighteen, and you won't have to worry about anything."

His words strike me one by one. I won't have to worry about *anything*. I'll be free, away from my dad, out of his hold.

Jace offers me a small smile. It's the sincere sort of expression he showed me when he was up onstage, and it makes me want to believe that he'll really help, that everything will be okay.

"You'll really do this for me?" I ask.

"*Anything to get you safe, A-l-i,*" he signs, and then reaches out his hand again for me to take.

A thousand doubts run through my head as I stare at his outstretched hand. My heart pounds frantically, and I swear I can hear it begging me to accept his offer.

"*No,*" I say, signing it and saying it out loud. Then I shake my head to make sure he gets the point. "I can't go."

I don't know him and don't trust him. I'd be an idiot to run away with him. And I may be helpless, but I sure as hell am not an idiot.

Jace's expression falls faster than I thought possible. He blinks a couple times, and his mouth opens and closes. He's clearly not used to hearing "no" from anyone.

"I'm sorry," I whisper.

He shakes his head and takes a step away from me. "Here," he says, pulling a check out of his pocket. "Your money. At least take this." He shoves it into my hand, and then he's gone, striding back toward his RV before I have a chance to say anything more.

10

ALI

I FLOP DOWN on my bed with a groan, and even though my room is too warm, I can't stop shivering. What the *hell* did I just do? Running away with Jace might have been my only chance at escape. For years, I've been telling myself that as soon as I turn eighteen, I'll be free. But I know it likely won't work out that easily. Getting away is going to take more than a few hundred dollars and determination. I need resources—the sort of resources Jace has to offer. The sort I just turned down.

I press my palm against my forehead, trying to push away the confused thoughts rattling around in my skull. I swear I can feel the check for eight grand burning against my skin, even though it's tucked safely in my jean pocket.

I did the right thing. Period. I have to believe that. Even if Jace made me the exact same offer again, I still wouldn't accept.

Although I have a feeling it will be awhile before another rock star asks me to run away with him.

Maybe this is a good thing. Maybe I just avoided disaster. But, then again, maybe . . . *maybe* I was right about what I saw in Jace's eyes. Real, genuine concern. I've never had anyone look at me like that, not even Avery. I know my best friend cares, but whenever she sees my bruises, there's always a bit of confusion mixed with her horror. It's like the violence is so terrible, she can't even comprehend it.

There was no confusion in Jace's expression. Just a gut-wrenching seriousness that makes me suspect his concern for me was real.

I jump off my bed and head for the small desk in the corner of my room. My ancient computer sits there, patiently waiting to be used, and I switch it on. Pressing my palm against the console, I focus on the small shudders that run through the computer, letting the familiar vibrations soothe my anxiety.

I adore this computer. Sure, it's old and finicky, but it has all my website coding programs on it. Coding is just like music—math and art twining together to make something new and beautiful. It's been my hobby ever since I took a computer science course my freshman year, and I've actually gotten good at it. Or at least good enough to share my designs with others. A lot of up-and-coming bands need websites to showcase their music, but most can't afford the expensive fees for a professional site design. That's where I step in. Whenever I see an especially promising band mentioned on the DeafClan forum, I'll reach out and offer to design a website for them.

It's not like I have any professional training, so my designs are far from top quality, but they're good enough to help beginning artists get more exposure for their work. And, someday, I'll learn how to make those sleek, gorgeous designs that professional bands use for their sites. Someday soon, hopefully. If I can just get into a good college, I might be able to learn enough to make coding into a career.

As soon as my desktop screen pops up, I click open Google Chrome and search *Tone Deaf band criminal activity*. It's a bit on the nose, but I want proof that I was right to distrust Jace. He's bound to have some sort of criminal record, right? It seems like all famous musicians do.

A bunch of search results pop up—everything from parents saying Jace should be sued for his provocative lyrics, to someone claiming Killer is an illegal immigrant. But there's no reliable source that proves Jace—or anyone in the band—is actually a criminal.

One link reads *"Criminal Lyrics,"* and I recall Avery mentioning a debate in the Tone Deaf fandom about what the lyrics of this song mean. "Criminal" was one of Tone Deaf's first hits, but even after the song topped charts for weeks on end, Jace never bothered to give his fans an explanation for it. I click on the link, cringing as it brings up a Tone Deaf fandom website that's a mash of bright green graphics, blue fonts, and a misspelled header. The entire thing is an insult to web designers everywhere, but I ignore my urge to exit straight out of the site.

The blog post contains the lyrics for "Criminal," but they're written in neon-green font that's nearly impossible to read. I squint and tilt my screen a little, and the lyrics become legible:

Am I better off living through death,
Or dying an invisible ghost?
Am I better off speaking in silence,
Or screaming so loud no one will hear?

I fake a smile,
But it's killed by you,
I fake a soul,
But that dies, too.
So I fake my life,
What else can I do?

Take me in, spit me out,
And I scream and scream and scream and shout,
But you can't hear my pain,
My blood's nothing but a worthless stain.

I fake a smile,
But it's killed by you,
I fake a soul,
But that dies, too.
So I fake my life,
What else can I do?

And if one day I wake up gone,
Maybe people will see through,
But until then the lies will rule.
And sometimes I think I'm better off dead,
But then I realize I already am.

I'm trembling again by the time I finish reading, my eyes lingering on the last lines. I swallow hard. This shouldn't be getting to me, right? Lyricists are just fiction writers.

Or maybe they're not. I think back to the pain in Jace's expression as he frantically pleaded for me to come with him. He knows. He knows more than the facts, more than the situation. He knows *me*.

A vibration runs through the wood of my desk, making me jump. I glance down and find my cell phone sitting next to the keyboard. The cracked screen reads: *7 New Messages*.

I groan, knowing they're from Avery. I probably should have checked my messages sooner, but I was in such a daze when I left the stadium, I didn't even notice my phone go off.

I take a steadying breath and scroll through her messages.

hey, you wanna see a movie 2nite?

???

don't see ur light on. u home?

where r u?

ali???

r u ok???

I groan and hide my face in my hands. Why didn't I tell her where I was going this evening? I never should have lied and made her worry. In the morning, I'll apologize and tell her everything, and she can reassure me that I was right to reject Jace's offer.

I realize there's still one new message that's unopened. I click back to my inbox, and my breath catches as I recognize Jace's number.

Come with me. Please. You can still change your mind.

I feel the vibration of footsteps run through the floor, and I quickly shut down my phone. If my dad found out I'd been texting Jace, if he knew I'd even considered running away . . . that would be bad. Really, really freaking bad.

I want to hide the phone somewhere, but it would look too suspicious, so I calmly place it on my desk and turn toward my doorway. My dad stands there with his eyes narrowed and his lips lifted in a sneer. He takes one, two, three footsteps, and he's right in front of me.

I swallow hard, watching his fists uncertainly. One is clenched, like he's ready to hit me, and the other holds a thick white envelope. My dad slams the envelope down on my keyboard. I stay quiet, knowing better than to protest.

"What the hell is this?" He's talking fast, his sneer making it hard to read his lips. But he's using a type of universal sign language that makes him easy enough to understand: his gritted jaw says he's pissed; his narrowed eyes scream his anger; and his clumsy stance tells me he's far too drunk to rein in his emotions.

I hesitantly glance away from him and look to the envelope. My heart leaps into my throat as I recognize the emblem in the corner: the word "Gallaudet" under a slim, double arch. I've stared at that emblem so many thousands of times as I surfed the Internet and daydreamed about college.

The letter is from Gallaudet University.

For a moment, I'm confused. Why would they be sending me a letter? I'm not on any of their mailing lists, and—

My application. Holy shit, it must be a response from the admissions office. I applied last year and got rejected, which was crushing, but no big surprise. My grades are barely average, and since it's so hard to communicate with my teachers, the recommendation letters I got were lukewarm at best. But then a couple months ago, I decided to reapply for the spring semester. It was a long shot, but I'd poured my heart into the application essay and had crossed my fingers that it would be enough.

I didn't expect to ever get a letter from them, because according to their website, only admitted students would receive notice by mail.

Which means I got in.

I stare in shock down at the envelope. It takes me a moment to realize I'm grinning like an idiot, but then I don't care enough to stop. Gallaudet has been my dream ever since I was twelve and first stumbled across the university's website. It has brilliant professors, one-of-a-kind courses tailored for people with hearing impairments, and a student body that is mostly deaf.

And now I get to go there.

It takes a hard slap to pull me back to reality. I yelp and press a hand to my stinging cheek. My head spins a little, and as I blink a couple of times to clear it, I look up at my dad. His angry expression hasn't changed, although instead of staring at me, he's now locked his glare on the envelope.

I realize the envelope is already open, its top ragged where my dad pulled out the letter. That means he's read it and knows I was admitted. So he should be happy, right? He's always complaining about how I do nothing useful, and now I have the chance to attend a top-notch school.

"Why?" he asks.

I hesitate, unsure what sort of reply he wants. When I don't give an immediate response, my dad slams his fist down on my desk, narrowly missing my beloved keyboard. I have one second to feel relief, but then the fear comes rushing back.

But instead of avoiding his furious gaze, like I usually do, I stare back. This is my college, my life, my decision. I don't know what he's so upset about, but he has no right to stop me from attending the school of my dreams.

"Why did you apply?" he demands.

"I thought I might have a chance." I gesture to the envelope. "And I did! Dad, I got in, and—"

"And you won't be attending."

My heart stutters and comes to a grinding halt. Then it starts beating overtime as anger sears through me. "What?"

"You heard me."

"No," I snap. "No, I *didn't* hear you. Don't you get it? I'm *deaf*. As much as you hate it, I can't hear a single word you say. So why not let me go? Gallaudet is in Washington, DC. I'll be far away from you, you won't have to bother with me, and—"

"Enough!" His fists clench again, and I have the common sense to shut up. "You're not going to argue with me on this, Alison. Gallaudet is the type of school that will ruin you. They teach you to embrace your weakness when you should be fighting it."

"How could I fight it?" I demand. "We both know nothing can make my hearing come back."

"That's no excuse to wallow in self-pity for four whole years of college."

"It's not self-pity! Gallaudet is like its own culture. All the people there would understand me."

"*You're* the one who needs to start understanding things, not anyone else," he snaps. "It's about time you buck up and face real life. This world has no room for the weak, and I'm not sending you to a school that will make you even weaker."

This is the point where I should shut my trap and go along with what he's saying. But I can't. The anger pulsing through me just won't let me drop the argument, even if it's for the best, even if it's going to get me hurt. I shove away from my desk and stand to face him directly.

"I'm not weak! Don't you get that? I'm *different*. That's all. And the only bad thing about being different is that it scares people obsessed with being normal. People like *you*."

His eyes narrow. "You're saying I'm scared?"

"I'm saying you're terrified. Ever since I've moved in, you've treated me like I'll never amount to anything. If I go to Gallaudet, I'll prove that I can do anything I want with my life. I'll prove that everything—*everything*—you've ever told me about being deaf isn't true. You know it, and that scares you out of your mind."

He uses a punch as his answer. It lands on my cheek, which is already stinging from his slap. But that slap is nothing compared to the force behind this blow.

Stars dance in front of my eyes, and I gasp in shallow breaths, trying to stay conscious as pain floods through my face. I blink again and again, urging the stars to go away. They finally do, but I almost wish they hadn't. Now I have to watch as my dad picks up the envelope and rips it in half.

"You're not going," he says. "End of conversation." Then he drops the tattered remains of the envelope on the floor and storms out of my room.

For a long moment, I just stare down at the ripped letter. Then I glance back at my computer screen, reading the last lines of Jace's song: *And sometimes I think I'm better off dead, But then I realize I already am.*

I'm not going to let that become me. I'm not going to let my dad destroy my future. But I know I can't fix everything by myself, and there's pretty much only one person who can help me at this point.

Jace.

With a shuddering breath, I pick up my phone and reply to his text. ***I'll come. When do you want to meet?***

I'm going to leave with him. Maybe it's stupid, or even insane, but damn it, I don't care. I need to get away. Sure, I have eight grand in my pocket, and I can escape temporarily with that. But there's no way I'd last long on my own, not when I'm still a minor and my dad has every legal right to drag me back here.

Plus, as a former police chief, my dad has enough power and contacts to make escaping on my own nearly impossible. Getting past airport security would be way too risky, and even if I could board a plane without being stopped, buying a ticket would make it obvious where I was headed. I'd just be caught the second I landed in New York. Driving would make it harder to immediately track me, but a young girl traveling on her own isn't safe. A single flat tire on an isolated road could land me in serious danger.

If I'm going to make a clean escape, I need outside help. And if Jace wants to give me the resources I need to stay under the radar, I can't pass that up.

For a moment, I think of asking Avery to come with me to New York. I know she'd agree. She's always wanted to go there, and she'd be a good travel buddy, and . . .

No. I'm not dragging her into this. She starts her summer job in just a few days, and after that, she's heading straight to UCLA for college. Her future is right here in Los Angeles, with her supportive friends and loving family. And I can't tear her away from it so carelessly.

I jump in surprise as a text pops up. But it's from Jace, not Avery.

Meet me at the stadium's RV lot tomorrow at 10 a.m. Come in the back way over the fence. I'll be waiting.

With shaking hands, I send a quick reply: *OK.* Then I open up a new message to Avery: *I have a chance to get away and I'm taking it. I can't tell you where I'm going, since my dad will ask you. It's safest for us both if you just don't know. I'm sorry. I'm leaving my phone so he can't track me, but I'll message you as soon as it's safe. Please don't worry about me. I'll be okay.*

I set my phone down on the desk and turn my back to it. I'm sure Avery is going to send a panicked reply, but I can't let her convince me to stay. Grabbing a duffle bag from my closet, I start packing. I move quickly but quietly, careful not to make too much noise as I stuff clothes into my bag. Sweatshirts and T-shirts and some tanks, along with shorts and jeans. If we're going to cross the country, we'll be in all types of weather. I think. I haven't traveled for years, and I don't remember much about it. Hell, I don't even know where we're going exactly. All I know is that I'll end up in New York City.

Hopefully.

The chills are back, and a sour taste itches the back of my throat. I keep swallowing, trying to stop from puking. This is a terrible idea, but . . . I *have* to go. I have to do something to protect myself. I have to give myself a chance.

I glance at my clock. It's 10:38 p.m., which leaves me almost twelve hours to pack before I meet Jace. My dad will be away at his skeet-shooting club by 7:30 tomorrow morning, and then I'll be able to sneak out of the house. Maybe if I pack quickly, I'll have time to sleep before I leave . . .

Yeah, right. I won't be getting any sleep. Not until I'm safe in New York, away from my dad, away from this hell.

And back home.

11

JACE

"SHE'S *WHAT?*"

From across the RV's small living room, Arrow stares at me with his eyes squinted in disbelief. His mouth quirks into a half smile, like he's hoping what I said is a joke, but worried it's not.

"She's coming with us," I repeat. I turn in my desk chair and pretend to be busy clicking through some music downloads, trying to look as casual as possible. Maybe if I approach this like it's a completely normal subject, then Arrow will believe it *is* normal. And maybe I'll start believing it, too.

Yeah, right. It's pretty obvious Ali somehow broke my brain, and it's going to take more than a little pretending to fix it.

I stare out the window above my desk, watching the sunrise. Maybe this wasn't the best time to tell Arrow. It's barely eight o'clock, and no one in the band is ever happy after waking up early. But Ali will be here in just a couple hours, and that means telling the others about her can't wait.

Arrow sighs and runs a hand through his hair. Twice. It's a good thing he wears that I-just-rolled-out-of-bed style, or else his hair would be a mess, and Killer's fashion radar would go off and wake him up. Killer's asleep on the couch, his head in Arrow's lap and his mouth lolled open. He really should be awake for this conversation, but I know better than to try rousing Killer when he's napping off a hangover.

"You're serious?" Arrow asks me a little too loudly. Killer stirs, his glasses slipping off his nose and clattering to the floor. He mumbles something in his sleep and nuzzles closer to his boyfriend. Arrow doesn't notice any of this; he's gawking at me like I just announced I'm pregnant.

"Oh, come on, dude," I mutter. "It's not that shocking."

Arrow shakes his head and laces his fingers behind his head, like he's trying to keep it from exploding. "But . . . she's *deaf.*"

"I know."

"You publicly gave her the finger. No, *two* fingers."

"I know."

"And now she's suddenly tagging along? All the way to New York?"

"I already told you. Yes, she's coming. And, no, you're not going to change my mind."

Arrow pinches the bridge of his nose, as if he thinks he can physically hold back a headache. "This is a bad idea, Jace. No, a *terrible* one. Inviting an underage girl to travel along with us? Hell, are you *trying* to get arrested?"

"It's not like anything is going to happen between us. This is about helping her and nothing else. She's in trouble."

Arrow groans. "What, did you knock her up or something?"

"Of course not," I snap.

Arrow gives me a disbelieving look and crosses his arms over his chest. Great. Every second I stay silent, his suspicions are just going to get bigger. I shake my head and quietly say, "She's being abused. Honestly, I don't know much about it, but she's got bruises all over. That's why I offered to help her get away."

"How old is she exactly?" Arrow demands, although he speaks slower, like he's finally starting to consider what I'm saying.

"Seventeen."

"Then she shouldn't have any trouble getting away on her own."

"She says her dad's a police chief. According to her, he won't just let her escape."

Arrow throws his hands up in the air. "Are you hearing yourself? 'She says.' 'According to her.' How do you know this girl isn't just some rabid fan who's lying to you?"

I cross my own arms over my chest, mimicking Arrow's defensive position. "Well, for one, she's deaf."

"We have deaf fans."

"Seriously? Rabid deaf fans?"

Arrow looks away and mutters something, but doesn't bother with a real argument. An awkward silence passes, filled only with both of our heavy breaths and Killer's quiet snores. Then I hesitantly say, "It's just a couple months, Arrow."

Arrow scoffs. "Jace, thousands of girls attend our concerts every year, and I'm sure lots of them have abusive boyfriends or families. What makes this one girl so special?"

"Because she . . ."

I trail off, not wanting to say what's on the tip of my tongue: *Because she looks like me.* That look in her eyes, of fear and anger and self-loathing, is the same one I see every time I glance in the mirror. Well, the same one I *used* to see. All that's there now is the blank stare I've mastered over the years. But Ali hasn't mastered that expression, because she hasn't escaped yet.

Because I haven't helped yet.

Arrow raises an eyebrow at me. "What? Because she what?"

"Because I know she's in trouble," I snap. "I know that look. You know that look."

He flinches. I do, too. We avoid each other's eyes for a long moment, as if we're both afraid we'll see the past reflected there.

"Fine," Arrow finally says, his words emerging slowly. "The deaf girl can come."

"Her name is Ali," I correct. I don't like how all my band-mates have taken to calling her "the deaf girl," especially since I think they picked up the habit from me. But I was wrong to ever call her that. She's more than just a girl, more than a deaf person. She's a person with a name, someone who lives and breathes and . . . *feels.*

"Whatever. Ali can come." Arrow points an accusing finger at me. "But if she messes things up, I'm blaming you. We'll *all* blame you."

"I'll take full responsibility," I say.

"Good." Then Arrow frowns. "We're leaving in just a couple hours. When's she going to join us?"

"She's meeting me at ten. But as far as anyone else knows, she's not going to be here at all. This is between you and me and the band. No one else can know."

Arrow stares at me blankly for a long moment. Then he shakes his head and says, "She's in deep shit, isn't she? I mean, it's not like we've never broken the law before, but this is . . . different."

"Yeah, I know. But she needs help, and I'm not just going to ditch her."

Arrow nods slowly and chews at his lip, considering this. Then he asks, "Does Tony know about this?"

"Tony would never let her come. He'd be too worried it would cause a publicity scandal."

"So then he doesn't know."

"No."

Arrow stands up and gently clasps his hand on my shoulder. I flinch at the unwelcome warmth of his hand, but for once, I don't pull back.

"You realize Tony would be right, don't you?" Arrow says. "If someone figures out you're hiding away an underage girl in your RV, it'll cause a scandal for sure. The media isn't going to care that you're barely a year older than her. They'll label you as an adult and her as a little girl, and your reputation will be ruined."

"I know."

"And you're still sure you want her to come?"

"Totally and completely sure."

He nods and lets his hand fall away. "Then just tell me how I can help."

12

ALI

I'M PRETTY SURE my legs are going to fall off before I make it to Jace. Between the scalding hot sidewalk and the rub of my poorly fitted sneakers, my feet feel like they've been through a meat grinder. Three miles hadn't sounded so bad the night before, when I made my final escape plans: take dad's old car, drive it to a café downtown, and then walk a couple miles to the stadium. Easy peasy.

Plus, the café is right next to a bus stop, so when my dad eventually finds his missing car, he'll hopefully be convinced I hopped a bus. I'm crossing my fingers he won't search too hard for me, but I know it's useless to be so optimistic. During his law enforcement career, he frequently helped find kids who ran from their homes. If he doesn't launch a full-out search for me, it would look suspicious, and risk ruining his carefully maintained reputation.

Under the heat of the sun, walking those three miles felt like a marathon. Somehow, I made it to the stadium without my legs completely cramping up, and as best I can tell, no one followed me. But now all I want to do is curl up in a ball and never move again. I'm dizzy from walking, my stomach is still sore from throwing up my breakfast earlier, and I'm sure my face is all puffy from lack of sleep.

I'm a total mess. Jace is probably going to take back his offer when he sees me.

I take a shuddering breath, trying to quell the thought, and push on. I've already jumped the back gate leading into the stadium, like Jace instructed me to do last night. Did he have to be so vague? ***Come in the back way over the fence. I'll be waiting.*** He didn't even mention that the gate is like eight feet tall. Thank god for Avery and all those tree-climbing lessons she gave me when we were little.

I heave my duffle bag into a more comfortable position. My muscles ache in protest, and I glance down at my bag. Even though I can feel it tugging at my arms, I'm still terrified I'm going to lose it. It's all I have; I didn't want to bring more than one bag in case someone got suspicious and stopped me on my walk over here.

What I'd been able to fit in the duffle isn't nearly enough to last me four months, but it will have to do. Besides, I have the money I've been saving for the past few years: eight hundred and twenty-eight dollars, and thirty-seven cents. Not much, but at least it's something. Plus, I have Jace's check stuffed in the bottom of the bag. I haven't cashed it yet—he's already doing enough for me at the moment. But it's my backup plan in case Jace loses interest in helping me.

Just a few hundred yards to go. I can see a mass of RVs and trailers parked in the distance, heat shimmering around their tires, people scurrying around as they load up equipment. A drop of sweat falls into my eyes, and I adjust my grip on the bag so I can scrub it away.

Something nudges my shoulder. I yelp and whirl around, my heart pounding overtime, my fist clenching into a tight ball. Just as I'm about to start sprinting toward the RVs, my vision clears, and I see Jace.

He looks exhausted, like he got as much sleep as I did. But he's standing beside me, a hesitant smile on his lips, and holding out a hand. For a moment, I think he wants me to take it, but then I realize he's offering to carry the duffle bag. I shake my head and grip it tighter. I don't need to be any more in his debt.

He rolls his eyes and tugs it out of my grip before tossing it onto his shoulder. Then he points to the RVs in the distance and signs, *"Come on. We're leaving earlier than I thought. We need to get back."*

I shuffle my feet a little and narrow my eyes. He didn't have to just grab the duffle like that. *"How am I going to get in your RV without anyone seeing?"*

"Easy," he replies. *"My RV is on the edge of the group. The entrance is facing the back. No one will see you."*

"And the driver?" I ask.

"Arrow and I trade off," he signs. *"We're the only ones who drive. I don't like other people in my home. So only Arrow will see you."*

My eyes grow wide, and I swallow hard, trying to gulp back my panic. He told Arrow about me?

Jace smiles apologetically. *"All of the band knows about you. We don't keep secrets. But it's just the four of us who know. No one else will ever find out."*

I nod, but my stomach feels all tight again. I take a step away from Jace, hoping I don't puke on his shoes.

He gestures to the RVs again. *"Let's go."*

I trail after him, trying not to scowl at the pavement beneath my feet. I've learned to hate walking on the stuff. It soaks up vibrations and leaves me clueless to approaching footsteps, which is exactly what I don't want right now. Most of Tone Deaf's crew is a safe distance away, hopping in and out of trailers and giving thumbs-ups as they do last-minute checks on vehicles. But these people are still strangers, and still a potential threat to my escape attempt, and my heart pounds frantically.

Surprisingly, getting into the RV is just as easy as Jace said it'd be. Jace holds open the door for me and I slip right in, no one the wiser. The RV is dark, with all the shades pulled down, and my stomach twists wildly as I step inside. Maybe this isn't a good idea. Maybe I'm just getting myself into even more trouble. Maybe—

A movement in the corner of my eye cuts into my panicked thoughts. I whirl toward the couch, where I spot the moving object. A dog. A huge mutt that looks like a cross between a pit bull and the grim reaper. I stumble back.

Jace lets the door close, cutting off the light for a long moment. Then he flicks a switch, and the overhead lights illuminate the RV. I blink against the sudden brightness and take another step away from the dog.

The massive pit bull yawns, displaying two rows of glistening white teeth. Then it lazily stretches and jumps down from the couch, landing with a thump that shakes the floor. It trots over to Jace.

"This is Cuddles," he says, nodding toward the dog.

I take a few more steps back and frown at his words, sure that I'd read his lips wrong. "What?"

He quickly finger spells the name for me. *C-u-d-d-l-e-s.* Then he sighs at my confused expression and says, "Killer named her. He likes to think he's funny."

Jace reaches down and scratches the dog's head. As tall as he is, he doesn't even have to bend over to reach her, and Cuddles wags her stump of a tail and opens her mouth. I cringe, but all she does is gently lick his hand.

Jace gives her one more pat and then glances over to me. I try to smile and pretend I'm not scared, but my lips are frozen, and my face feels cold and clammy, despite the heat outside.

"You don't like dogs?" Jace signs.

"Not big ones."

"I'll go put her away for a while," he says, grabbing her collar. "You guys can get acquainted later, I guess."

Jace walks away with Cuddles, the giant mutt trailing along obediently after him. Her pawsteps send vibrations through the thin flooring of the RV, and I shudder, backing away.

Jace heads down the RV's small hallway, into a room that I assume is his bedroom. I stand there anxiously tapping my foot and taking in my surroundings. I've never been in an RV before—we always traveled by plane when I was younger—but I imagine this RV is about as luxurious as they come. It's way larger on the inside than I expected—from here, I can see a bathroom, a small living area with an office space tacked next to it, and an entrance to the kitchen. A short hall leads toward the back of the RV, where Jace has just disappeared to.

The furniture looks like it was all plucked straight from a magazine—sharp and modern designs, and fabrics in dramatic shades of blue. I think it should look stylish, but knowing that a nineteen-year-old guy lives here, it just gives the RV a hotel vibe, like it's a home that's never really been lived in.

The only personalized touches are the posters of bands on the pastel-blue walls. I read the titles one by one: *Fall Out Boy, AWOLNATION, Forever the Sickest Kids.* There are at least five more littering the walls, and I try not to look too surprised as I trail a finger over the glossy paper of the nearest one. Who would have guessed rock stars could get all fanatic about other bands?

I follow the posters into the living area, which has two couches facing each other and a giant flat-screen TV mounted on the wall. There's a small mound of pillows and blankets on one of the couches, and I can practically hear it calling to me. I glance down the hall where Jace disappeared. I don't want to look like I'm getting comfortable too quickly, but my feet are seriously about to drop off. I shake my head, deciding I don't care what he thinks, and fall back into the pile of blankets.

There's a thrashing movement from under me, and I shriek, the sound scraping my throat as it escapes. Jumping off the couch, I whirl around. What the heck is hiding under the blankets? Another dog? Dammit, I hope I didn't just squish anything.

The blankets flop back, and staring up at me with blood-shot eyes is a young guy who I instantly recognize as a member of Tone Deaf. His name is Killer, I think. He was the one playing the keyboard at their concert the other night.

Avery's always babbling about how adorable Killer is, but he doesn't look like that right now. He's squinting at me with an expression that screams of pain. I stumble back, gasping for breath and trying to assess the damage.

Killer takes one look at me and then groans and lets his head drop back into the pillows. He glares through half-closed eyes and doesn't say anything, which just makes the whole thing more awkward. But he doesn't seem to be in distress. So that's good, right?

"Darling," he finally says, his lips moving in a soft way that tells me he has a British accent, "it's generally considered impolite to sit on someone with a hangover. Screaming is also rather rude."

I stutter out a couple of incomprehensible words, unsure how to reply. Then I feel a hand tap my shoulder. It's warm and gentle, and I immediately recognize the touch as Jace's. I mumble an apology as I turn toward him.

Jace pulls away his hand and signs, *It's going to be hard to hide you if you scream every time you see one of the band.*

"Sorry," I sign lamely. *"I'm a little on edge."*

"Yeah. I can tell."

He glances over to the guy on the couch, who has taken the last few moments to fling the blanket back over his head. "That's Killer," Jace says to me, and then he finger spells the strange name to make sure I get it.

I nod and hesitantly say out loud, "Hi."

Killer fishes a hand out of the blankets and gives me a limp wave.

Jace rolls his eyes. "Killer had a little too much to drink last night. You'll have to excuse him. He's a bit of a lightweight."

Killer's hand thrashes around, like he's trying to find some-one to smack. But Jace expertly backs away, and Killer withdraws back under the blankets. I smile a little, not bothering to hide it.

Jace gestures to the other couch. *"You can sit over there."*

I nod and obey, sitting on the cushion right across from Killer. I force in a shuddering breath and do my best to actu-ally relax. But I can't get my muscles to loosen, and my hands are shaking a little. I fist them into balls to try to hide their shaking, and then quickly unclench them, realizing that it's just making me look even more like a nervous wreck.

Jace stands between the couches, a safe distance between both me and Killer. I wait for him to take a seat on one of them, but he just stays there, his arms crossed over his chest. He's wearing a thin black T-shirt, which does a nice job of showing off his defined muscles, and a ripped pair of dark skinny jeans. Usually, I don't like it when guys wear skinny jeans, but Jace pulls them off. Hell, he could wear a kilt and pull it off.

He shuffles his feet, and his throat bobs as he clears it. "So . . . do you want a drink, or something?"

I flinch at his words. Me? Drink? After all the times I've been punched by a drunk? "I don't drink."

Jace grimaces a little. "I'm not talking about alcohol. I would *not* offer you alcohol."

Then he looks at me expectantly, raising one eyebrow. It always annoys me when people do that. I mean, if you're going to raise an eyebrow, why not go all-in and raise them both? People always look awkward when they only raise one.

Except for Jace. He doesn't look at all awkward. This seems to be a recurring theme with him; he can get away with anything—dirty Vans, quirked eyebrows, overactive middle fingers—and still look hot.

My god. I'm starting to sound like Avery.

"Well?" he signs. *"What do you want?"*

I blush deeper and deeper until I'm pretty sure my face looks like a lobster's. That's right; he's been waiting for me to tell him what I want to drink. Damn, I really need some sleep. When I wake up, maybe I'll actually be able to carry a non-awkward conversation.

"Water," I reply. "Um, please."

He walks into the adjoining kitchen without saying anything else, and my heart starts pounding again, making my head ache from the racing pulse. Was that the right thing to do? Should I have insisted on getting my own water, instead of having Jace get it? I mean, he's a celebrity. I don't think he usually spends his time fetching water for girls. Especially not for sweaty, shaking, sunburned girls.

Killer flops the blankets off of his face and squints at me. "Darling, if you're gonna tag along, you need to learn the Jace Rules."

I frown. "The Jace Rules?"

He holds up a hand and starts counting them off: "One— don't lie while you're near him. Two—don't touch him. Three—don't bring anything with carbs or refined sugar into his RV. Four—don't ask about his feelings. And five—don't even mention drugs or alcohol."

I'm pretty sure rock stars are supposed to *want* all those things. Well, maybe not the carbs, but still. It seems like Jace missed the memo that famous musicians are supposed to live on the edge. Not that I'm complaining—if his rules mean that

I don't have to put up with anyone drunk, I'll gladly follow along.

I nod uncertainly to Killer. "But aren't you kind of . . . ?"

"Completely hungover," Killer supplies, rubbing his temples with a wince. "Yeah. About that. Jace will make exceptions to his rules for the band, because we're stubborn and he trusts us not to screw him over. But you'd do best to just follow them. If someone outside of the band annoys Jace, he has no problem shoving them out of his life." Killer rolls his eyes. "He's finicky."

Even though Killer doesn't directly say it, I get the message: if I piss off Jace too badly, he'll just tell me to leave, and my chance at freedom will disappear. My stomach starts churning again at the thought.

I glance over to the small kitchen. Jace stands at the counter, gripping the edge of the granite like his life depends on it, but he's not moving and seems to just be staring out the window. I don't stick around to find out what he's looking at. Instead, I head back toward the entrance of the RV, looking for the bathroom I spotted earlier. I want a few moments alone to splash some water on my face and clear my thoughts.

As I pass by the RV's entrance, I spot my duffle where Jace dropped it by the door. I pick it up and stare at the door uncertainly. If I leave now, I could probably get back to my house before my dad realizes I ever left. I could go back home, to where things are miserable, but at least predictable. As soon as he figures out I've run away, I really don't know what my dad will do. He'll try to get me back, that's for sure. He has so little control left in his life, and he's not going to give up the power he has over me without a fight. But I have no idea what lengths he'll take to get me back, and I'm scared to find out.

I take a deep breath and then head into the bathroom. No. I'm not going to give up this opportunity Jace is offering. Although, judging by how awkward and uncertain he's acting this morning, I'm afraid his pity for me isn't going to last very long. Musical background or not, I don't fit in here. Jace's whole life revolves around playing music and being in the spotlight, whereas my only goal is to stay quiet and hidden.

I open my bag, touching the cash and the check at the bottom just to reassure myself they're there. All I need is to get away from this city, to a place where I can't be recognized, and then I can safely branch off from Jace. That way I won't have to keep depending on his pity, and I can make sure he won't be harmed by anything my dad does.

I'll wait just a few days. That's all the time I need to spend with Jace. Then I can travel the rest of the way to New York on my own.

13

JACE

I STARE OUT the tiny kitchen window and watch as the last trailer is bolted shut, ready for travel. Earlier, I pulled the shades down on all the windows so no one could peer in and spot Ali. But I left the shades open on this window, since it's taller than the others and impossible to snoop through. If all the trailers are packed, we should be leaving any minute. Although driving is the last thing I want to do. Anxiety and uncertainty keep stabbing at my mind, and I want to play some music, drown out my thoughts in chords and notes and riffs.

"Dude," Killer calls from the living room. "How hard is it to fetch a glass of water? You've been in there for five minutes."

Right. Water. That's what I'd gone in the kitchen for.

I quickly grab a glass and fill it, then head back to the couches. My stomach drops when I see that Ali's gone. She didn't leave, did she? She's been pale and jittery, but I didn't think she was freaked out enough to ditch her plans of escape.

Killer squints at my worried expression, yawning as he runs a hand through his hair. "She didn't leave," he says. "She's just in the bathroom."

The RV door slams open, and Arrow comes striding inside a moment later.

"Hey," I say to him. I set the water down on the small end table and sit on the couch across from Killer, moving so Arrow has room on the other end.

"Hey, Jace," Arrow says. He sits on the couch, careful to leave a few feet between us, reminding me why I like him so much. Then he turns toward Killer and says in a way-too-bright voice, "And, hello, my darling sweetie. Are you having a lovely morning?"

Killer grunts and mumbles something before burying his face back into his cocoon of blankets. Arrow turns to me, a wry smile on his lips. "Someone wouldn't listen when I said he couldn't handle another shot last night."

"Someone is going to hit you if you keep rubbing this in," Killer mutters.

Arrow chuckles, but I can't bring myself to laugh. I don't like that the rest of the band drinks. I don't like it *at all*. Sure, they don't do drugs, but only because they know I'd leave the band if they did. But they insist on drinking, and even though they rarely do it in front of me, it freaks me out every time I see one of them nursing a hangover.

Arrow ignores my frown and stands from the couch, moving to the other one. "Scooch," he says to Killer. Killer curls up into a tighter ball, and Arrow sits beside him. He drags Killer halfway onto his lap and gently smooths his hair. "You want some Tylenol or something, babe?"

"Can Jace get it?" Killer mumbles.

"Nope," I say. "I'm not your servant."

Killer ignores me and says to Arrow, "Just stay here, 'kay?"

Arrow rolls his eyes at me, but I catch the small smile on his lips. It's a happy little expression, the kind he always wears around Killer. When those two are together, they're always acting like the world is made of rainbows and butterflies, as if everything is perfect and nothing could ever go wrong.

But I can't resent Arrow for it. Like practically every member of my family, the dude had a shitty childhood. His dad OD'd by the time he was eight, and his mom was sent to prison pretty soon after for dealing. Arrow drifted through the foster system like a ghost for a long time after that, too skinny, too scared, too traumatized to have much of a life.

Killer changed that. The dude might be annoying as hell, but I can't help but like him. Without Killer, my cousin would probably still be in that ghost state.

Arrow strokes Killer's cheek with the back of his hand. "Promise not to drink so much next time?" he murmurs.

"Promise. Swear. Cross my heart, hope to die," Killer groans. "Never, *never* drinking that much again."

I scoff, and Arrow shoots me a glare. "What?" I demand. "You do realize how many times he's said that, don't you?"

"Don't talk so loud," Killer grumbles.

"I'll talk however loud I want. This is my RV. What are you doing in here, anyway?"

Killer shrugs his shoulders and winces. "Tony and Arrow were talking in ours. Really, really loudly."

I raise an eyebrow at Arrow, and he gives me a thin smile. "I was distracting Tony while you got Ali into the RV." He nibbles uncertainly at his lip. "You're sure you want to keep all this from him?"

"Positive," I say. "He's too good at his job. If he thinks Ali is any type of threat to my reputation, he'll report her."

Arrow shrugs, but doesn't disagree. I turn my attention back to Killer. "So you decided to crash in my RV? Without permission?"

"Yup. Besides, your pillows are comfier," he says, like this is some sort of excuse.

Arrow smirks at me, and I throw him a half-hearted glare. Killer is a nuisance and an ass, but he's also loyal and devoted. Mostly to Arrow, but also to Tone Deaf. We never would have gotten the band off the ground without his tech skills.

"Next time, ask," I say.

"Yeah. Sure."

Our conversation is interrupted by coughing coming from the bathroom. A second later, I hear a faint splashing sound and try not to cringe.

Arrow raises an eyebrow at me. "Your girl bulimic?"

"She's not my girl. Not by a long shot. And, no, I think she's just getting over the flu."

Liar, liar, liar. I grit my teeth against the fit my conscience is throwing. Sure, my conscience is about the size of a pea, but the little thing is devoted to my band. Lies don't work well in our musical family.

But I can't just blurt out the truth: that Ali doesn't have the flu, that she's terrified and worried and hurting. I recognize that expression she was wearing earlier, the one that probably just looks stressed to most people. But not to me. I can see the pain in the lines of her small frown, the anxiety in the way her eyes squint just a little. The expression screams of abuse, and years of it.

But it's not my place to start blabbering about that. Chances are, Arrow will know I'm lying the moment he sees Ali and realizes how completely freaked out she is. But, for now, I'm not going to say a single word more about her abuse than absolutely necessary. Earlier, she'd seemed embarrassed when I mentioned that the band knew why she was running away, and I don't want to make her feel any worse.

I glance toward the bathroom, wondering if I should go check on her. If she's secluded herself in there, she probably doesn't want to be bothered. But I also don't want her to feel alone. I get the feeling she's dealt with too much loneliness already.

Arrow grunts, bringing me back to our conversation. "Great. You brought a sick girl on board. What happens if she gives it to us all, and we miss the next concert?"

"Stop being a pessimist," I snap.

"I'm just taking over for you," Arrow says. "You're always Mr. Worst Case Scenario, but that seems to have flown out the door since this girl showed up. That and your logic."

I stand from the couch and head toward the bathroom. "I'm going to check on her."

When I reach the bathroom, I gently knock on the door. "Ali? You okay?" I immediately feel like an idiot. She's deaf. What am I expecting, for her to actually hear me? I knock harder, sending vibrations through the wall. A long second passes, and then the lock clicks, and Ali opens the door just a crack.

"Are you okay?" I repeat. "I heard you throw up."

"I'm fine." Her response is mumbled and scratchy.

"Liar," I say.

Hypocrite, my conscience replies.

I sigh and lean against the doorframe, resting my head against the cool paneling. Then I raise my hands and sign, *"Can I get you anything?"*

"No."

"You're sure you don't want a drink or something? I have a glass of water for you out here."

"I'm fine."

"You already told me that. And I already called you a liar."

"Just go away."

"You know, you're in my RV. You can't exactly start bossing me around."

She bites her lip and looks down, and immediately, I feel like a jerk. Scratch that; I *know* I'm a jerk. What's my problem, anyway? There must be something wrong with me, if I keep upsetting this girl. Not that I wasn't aware of that before, but being a jerk has never felt bad. It's felt comfortable and vital to survival. Now it just feels . . . *wrong.*

I shake away the thought and ask, "Do you want to go take a nap? You look like you haven't slept much."

She blushes in embarrassment and quickly rubs at her face, as if she's trying to brush away her obvious exhaustion. She looks cute like that, all flustered and freckly. I've never liked freckles before, but hers are pale and sparse, and they're kind of . . . adorable, I guess.

It's a strange contrast to the rest of her. There's nothing adorable about her oval face and refined features, or her dark auburn hair. No, not adorable. Just beautiful.

I take a step back. No, no, no. I'm not going to do this. I'm keeping this relationship completely, utterly platonic. Period.

"I'm fi—" She cuts off and sighs. "I'm good. I can just, um, hang out by the couches. Or the kitchen. Wherever I won't get in the way."

I push the door the rest of the way open, and Ali shuffles her feet so she faces the door of the RV, like she's considering bolting. I step in front of her and do my best to offer a small smile. Her expression stays scared, telling me that the Friendly Jace look has failed. Time for tactic number two.

"Look, I told you that I was going to help you get to safety. Remember? And that means I'm not going to hurt you, and I'm not going to let anyone else hurt you. Got it?"

Her eyes grow wide, and for a moment, I think she might actually go along with it. Then her eyes narrow and she says, "Why are you being so nice to me?"

I shrug.

She sidesteps away from me. "I'm about to travel across the country with you, Jace. I want more than that."

For a brief moment, I consider telling her everything. About the pain and the fear and the anger, and how I understand in the most unfortunate way possible. But I shake away the thought. I don't ever talk about that shit, and I'm not going to start now. "Well, you're not going to get it," I say.

Her lips purse into another frown, and I groan without moving my mouth. Damn it. Why can't I just be nice for once? But, no, it's like I'm hardwired to be a jerk.

I gently grasp her shoulders, and this time, she hardly flinches. I turn her around until she's facing the short hallway leading to my bedroom in the very back of the RV. I point to it and step forward so she can see my hands clearly. *"You should go take a nap. You look like you're about to collapse."*

She eyes the door hesitantly. *"Is that your room?"*

"Yes."

"Then no thanks."

I roll my eyes, not even hiding it this time. Then I sign, *"I'll take Cuddles out, and you can lock the door. We'll all stay out here."*

She stares hard at my bedroom door. *"Promise? You promise to stay away?"*

"Yeah," I say quietly. "I promise."

She nods, but her eyes narrow a little, and I know she's thinking the same thing I am: all she has to protect her is the word of a random dude she barely knows. A random dude publicly known for being a jerk and a player.

But it's the best she's going to get, and she seems to realize this, because she hesitantly shrugs in what I assume is resignation. I jog to the door and open it, finding Cuddles lying in the doorway, staring up with a pitiful expression. She's used to being the center of my attention when we're on the road, and she's probably not very happy about having Ali onboard. But my dog is going to have to buck up, because Ali is sticking around, as long as I have a say in it.

I shoo Cuddles out of the room, and she trots off toward the kitchen. Ali cringes away from my dog, but then she turns to me and gives a nod of thanks. I shrug and walk back toward the couches, leaving Ali to nap. She disappears into my bedroom, and as she closes the door, I hear the lock click into place.

My chest starts hurting again.

14

ALI

WHEN I OPEN my eyes, everything is wrong. The ceiling isn't the right shade of white, and it's too low. The walls are painted bright green, instead of the soft beige of my bedroom. Even the scent is wrong; my room is supposed to smell like pencil shavings and laundry detergent and that unmistakable odor of an overheated computer. This room smells like cologne and some sort of wood varnish. It smells like a . . . guy.

Then it hits me:

The concert. Tone Deaf. Running away. Jace.

A sudden burst of anxiety hits me, and my chest feels impossibly tight as the reality of my situation strikes me. I'm on the run with a guy who's practically a stranger. And if that's not bad enough, any minute now my dad is going to be figuring out that I'm gone, and he's not going to give up on finding me.

I close my eyes, concentrating on slowing my frantic breaths. There's nothing I can do now to make things better, so I just need to focus on staying hidden away and out of my dad's reach. I'm way too far into this to ditch my plans of escape.

I glance over to the door and find it still locked, which gives me a little relief. Jace kept his promise to leave me alone in here. As I toss the sheet off, I look down at my clothes and grimace. They're damp with sweat, probably from the nightmares I was having. Definitely time for a change.

The room shakes a little, and I throw out an arm to steady myself. We must be moving. I mean, this *is* an RV after all. As my heart calms down a little, I notice the steady flow of vibrations running through the floor, probably from the engine. It's official: we're on the road, and I'm actually running away.

I gulp in a deep breath and decide I can second-guess myself and freak out about the situation later. For now, I'm sweaty and thirsty and hungry, and I need to do something about that.

I creep outside the room, relieved when I don't see anyone. They must still be in the front of the RV, where those couches are. Should I join them? Or should I wait for Jace to come get me, to make sure I don't intrude on anything? I shuffle my feet and peer around, hoping for some sort of clue about what to do. My breath catches when I glance out the tiny window above the front door and see the setting sun. Have I really been asleep all day?

The RV jostles as it hits a pothole, making me stumble and bump against the wall. I curse and then bite my lip. Did anyone hear that? One of the worst parts about being deaf is not being able to control my volume level. It's hard to tell how loudly I'm talking when I can't hear myself, and my anxiety isn't making it any easier.

I give a frustrated groan—not too loudly—and then rush into the bathroom. Relief courses through me as I spot my duffle still tucked in the corner, undisturbed.

I grab the bag and dig through for another change of clothes, quickly settling on a pair of ripped jeans and a T-shirt. I take a deep breath and stare into the mirror, cringing at the mess that looks back at me. My hair is all ruffled, and without makeup to hide it, my skin is freakishly pale, except where it's blotched with dark bruises. I curse again, unable to stop myself, and do my best to quickly fix my hair. Cleaning up further will have to wait until I get something to eat. I'm starving and my mouth is totally dry, reminding me of my long trek to the stadium.

I hesitantly undo the lock and step out of the bathroom. The RV feels strange under my feet as the floor rocks softly, the rumbling engine creating a steady stream of vibrations. I glance out the window and see desert rushing past—sand and rocks, and more sand and more rocks. It seems endless.

New York has never felt farther away.

I shudder and tread down the short hallway leading to the room with the couches. Killer is sitting at the desk in the far corner with a laptop. He's wearing nerd glasses and squinting at the screen, and the way his wrist expertly flicks around the mouse tells me he's experienced with computers. Strange. I didn't think rock stars could be geeks.

Killer doesn't notice me, and I nervously shuffle my feet as I consider what to do. I could just nonchalantly say, "Hey," and pretend I belong here. Or I could introduce myself properly, which I never got a chance to do earlier. Although I'm not even sure how I'd do that. *Hello, I'm Ali, a random chick who will be stowing away here for a bit. Pleasure to meet you. Sorry I've never listened to even a second of your music.* Yeah, there's nothing I can say without being awkward.

Before I can force any words out of my mouth, more vibrations move across the floor, and I look up to find Arrow striding out of the kitchen and toward me. Heat instantly floods my cheeks, and I grit my teeth. Last time I saw Arrow, it was when Jace had flipped me off. Not the most elegant of introductions.

Arrow seems about as happy to see me as I am to see him. He tries to smile, but it comes off as more of a grimace. "Well," he says, "if it isn't Jace's little sailor."

I'm about to ask him what he means, when I remember my curses from before.

Oh. Right.

"Where's Jace?" I ask. I try to keep my feet still, but they just keep shuffling, giving away my anxiety. Arrow's posture remains rigid and unfriendly, and I can't help noticing that he has quite a bit of muscle. I watch his fists carefully in the corner of my eye as I wait for his reply, unable to stop myself from the habit.

Arrow inclines his head toward the front of the RV. "Jace is taking a shift driving."

I nod and force in a deep breath. Okay, so I'm stuck with two strangers in a small, isolated room that Jace definitely isn't in. I can handle this. After all, if Jace is going through all this trouble to help me, it's not like he's going to leave me alone with guys who are actually a threat.

I edge toward the couch facing the desk, and Arrow moves toward the one opposite of it. We both sit at the same time, me barely touching the cushions, and Arrow falling back heavily into them. The message is clear:

He belongs here. I don't.

Killer finally tears his attention from the computer and toward me, spinning his chair away from the desk as he offers me a wide smile. Relief trickles through me, slowing my pounding heart. At least *someone* is happy to see me.

Killer pushes his glasses up his nose in a practiced way that tells me he's been wearing them forever, and doesn't use them just for style. Then he strides over to me and extends his hand. "We haven't properly met."

His lips move slightly differently, and I can tell that he has a pretty strong accent. Which just makes him all the more interesting. Now that he's not hungover, I'm surprised to find that he's far from shabby looking. I can't tell what race he is—maybe Asian, maybe African American, maybe both. Whatever he is, he's drop-dead gorgeous. Not really a handsome type of gorgeous, but a more delicate type, the kind that would make most girls jealous.

"Hi," I say and hesitantly give him a little wave. But I don't take his hand. My nerves still feel overloaded with anxiety, and touching people is the last thing I want right now.

Killer doesn't skip a beat when I reject his handshake. He just sticks his hands in his pockets and settles next to me on the couch, sitting way, *way* too close. I frown at him and scooch away. It's not his fault that I don't like being close to people, but still, this is definitely uncomfortably close, even for normal people.

Again, Killer hardly seems to notice my reaction and just keeps smiling. He's wearing a black T-shirt with the silhouette of a white bow tie at the top. In bold letters, the shirt reads, BOW TIES ARE COOL. My frown disappears as I recognize the saying from my favorite TV show. Yeah, Killer is definitely a geek-in-disguise.

"So," Killer says, "what's your name, little stowaway?"

I'm guessing he already knows my name, and is just trying to be polite by asking, but that just makes me like him even more.

"I'm Ali Collins."

A smirk tugs at his lips, but it's merely amused and not at all scathing. "Ali Collins? Come on, can you get more generic than that?"

I roll my eyes. If anyone else had asked that, I would have bitten their head off—Collins is my mom's name, and one of the last things I have left of her. And she chose the name "Alison" for me, which somehow makes it special, even if it *is* generic. But I can't get mad, not with Killer's goofy shirt and smile so close. "It's not like I got to choose my name," I say.

He laughs a little. "Well, I guess that makes it more acceptable."

"Acceptable?" I repeat. "You're one to be talking. Who names their kid 'Killer'?"

"I was really bad at keeping my pet goldfish alive when I was little."

On the other couch, Arrow cracks a small smile. But it's strained, and as he stares at me, I avoid his harsh gaze. He nods to Killer. "Don't listen to him. His real name is Kilimanjaro."

I raise my eyebrows at Killer. "Wow. That's almost worse."

He sighs and holds his hands up, like he's surrendering to the terrible naming skills of his parents. "Totally not my fault

I was adopted by hippies." He points to his boyfriend. "Arrow started calling me Kilim when we were like sixteen."

"Which Jace quickly turned into Kill 'Em, and then to Killer," Arrow explains.

"And it stuck," Killer says.

It's kind of cute how they keep finishing each other's sentences. They sound like an old married couple, which I guess they pretty much are. Well, not *technically* married, and definitely not old. But according to Avery, Killer and Arrow have been boyfriends since the very start of their band.

Damn, I wish I could talk to Avery. It hasn't even been a day, and I already miss her excited babbling about Tone Deaf, something I never thought I'd want to hear. I think she was already asleep when I sent that message last night, otherwise she would have come over and demanded to speak to me. But I'm sure she got the message this morning, and I cringe as I think of how worried she must be.

"Your band seems to have a thing for unique names," I say, continuing the conversation to distract myself from thinking about Avery. "Why do you guys call yourself Tone Deaf?"

Killer smirks. "We used to practice in Jace's garage, and his neighbor was this grouchy lady who hated our music. So one day she comes over and tells Jace that having a deaf father is no excuse for having zero musical talent. He tried arguing back, but she just kept cutting him off and saying, 'Well *you* might not be deaf, but your band is tone deaf!' We were looking for a name at the time, and yeah, that's how we became Tone Deaf."

Interesting—Jace has a parent who's deaf, which explains why he knows ASL. I try to cover my surprise by nodding to

Arrow. "What about your name? Is Arrow short for something?"

The curve of Arrow's smile grows sharper. "Yeah. It's short for Poor Fool With White Trash Parents."

"Oh," I mumble.

I must look as uncomfortable as I feel, because Killer gently places a reassuring hand on my arm. I deftly remove myself from his touch, doing my best not to grimace.

"You were sleeping for a long time," Killer says, his smile fading just a little. "Do you want some food or something? Maybe something to drink?"

"I'll, um, get something myself. If that's okay?"

"Of course." He nods toward the kitchen and hops up from the couch. "Come on. I'll show you around."

I follow him into the small kitchen, where he proceeds to point out the refrigerator and cupboards full of health food. Whole-grain cereal, sunflower seeds, protein drinks, and fruit seem to be Jace's staples. Whatever happened to young guys living off junk food?

Killer is chatting excitedly, and I quickly lose track of his words. He doesn't seem to understand the concept of lip-reading. Namely, that it involves me looking at his *lips*, and not watching him twirl around the kitchen as he fetches me a cup of some natural energy drink that looks like pee. Apparently, he's not going to let me get a drink for myself, which is kind of annoying and kind of sweet.

I sit at the counter, which has two little stools pulled up to it. Killer plunks the drink beside me and sits on the other stool, once again way too close. But he's still smiling, not at all put off by the fact that I haven't replied to a word he's said in like two minutes.

"Here," he says, shoving the drink toward me. "It's lemon-lime. No caffeine, so it's good for dehydration."

I take a long gulp of it and find out a moment too late that it's carbonated. I start coughing the moment I pull the cup away, but can't stop myself from taking another gulp. After I've chugged half the glass, I realize that Killer is staring at me, his eyebrows raised in amusement.

"Sorry," I mumble.

He laughs a little and says, "So much for Jace taking care of you, hmm? Eight hours in, and you're already dying of thirst and pale as a ghost."

I blush as I look down at my arm, finding he's right. My skin is still totally white. It's going to take more than a few sips of energy drink to make up for my dehydration and lack of food.

"Sooo." He props his head up in his palm, leaning his elbow against the counter. "How's your road trip been so far?"

"Um, good?"

"You don't sound very sure of that."

I bite my lip as I struggle to think of a way to deflect this conversation, but Killer just shakes his head.

"Don't worry, sweetie," he says. "Jace can be a jerk, but he's not the type to back out of promises. If he says he'll help you stay safe, he means it."

His smile is soft and a little pitying, which probably means Jace told him more about my situation than I would have liked. Although I imagine it couldn't be helped. Jace told me he doesn't keep lies from his bandmates, and I doubt they would have been okay with me being here with zero explanation.

"Thanks," I murmur hesitantly.

Killer winks and quickly moves the conversation along. "You got a phone?"

"Not with me. Why?"

He rolls his eyes, but in a playful way, not a mean one. "Why do you think? I want your number."

"Oh."

He stares at me for a long second, his face crumpling into a puzzled expression. Then he throws his head back and laughs.

"What?" I demand.

Killer just keeps chuckling. "You just gave me the least enthusiastic response I've ever gotten from asking for a girl's number."

His hand flies toward me, and I nearly topple off the stool trying to dodge it. But he just lazily tosses his arm over my shoulder and pulls me into an awkward hug. Killer considers me for a moment, then reaches into his pocket with his free hand and pulls out his own phone. Popping up a blank text, he quickly types a message and tilts the screen so I can see it:

You have nothing to be sorry for. It's refreshing to not have a girl freak out when I ask for her number.

"Oh." I cringe, realizing I've just given another lame answer, and try to slip out from under his arm. Thankfully, he lets me.

Killer cocks his head, his smile fading as his gaze locks on my bruised cheek. He types a little more on the phone and then shows it to me again. *You're not exactly the huggable type?*

"Um, not really."

He shrugs and pulls his arm back toward his side and away from my personal space. *That's OK,* he types, keeping the screen tilted so I can see. His fingers glide across the screen impossibly fast as he adds, *I think I'm starting to understand why Jace likes you so much.*

Likes me? Yeah, right. He pities me, sure, but that's a far cry from *liking* me. But I keep all that to myself and say, "What do you mean?"

Jace isn't into hugs either.

I frown, trying to come up with an appropriate response other than "bullshit."

Killer catches my skeptical look and types, *You mean Jace actually tried to hug you?*

"Well, um, yeah. Um, he did." I wince at how stupid I sound. I'm seventeen; I should know how to talk properly by now. But it's like my brain doesn't realize that and is determined to make me sound like an idiot.

Killer's eyes grow wide and he leans forward a little, staring right at me. He must be looking for some hint that I'm joking, and when he doesn't find one, he slowly pulls back and frowns. "Wow," he says, and I'm not sure if he means for me to read his lips or not. "That's a first."

I blush, not sure how to reply. A first? Definitely not. There's no way I'm Jace's first *anything.*

He really likes you, Killer types.

I look down at the counter, pretending to study the granite. "I don't think so."

Killer nudges at my side until I look back at his phone. *No. Jace likes you. I'm sure of it.*

"Okay . . . thanks?"

Killer quickly changes the subject again. *So you don't have a cell phone?*

"No, I had to leave it." I don't elaborate on why: because my dad will never just let me go, because he could use it to track me, because I can never, ever let him find me.

I'll fix that for you, Killer types. Before I can reply, he jumps off the stool and leaves the kitchen. He gives me a little wave before disappearing into the next room.

I roll my cup back and forth between my palms, unsure if I should follow him. Probably not. Even if he's being nice to me, he didn't sign up to have me trailing along after him like some sort of puppy. I take a little sip of the energy drink, even though I'm not really thirsty anymore; my spinning thoughts have completely ruined my appetite.

The drink tastes too sweet, like it's made purely of sugar. But I ignore the taste and chug down the last few drops. As I set down the glass, I stare into it. It reflects my face, paleness and bruises and all. *What am I doing?* I mouth, watching my lips in the glass as they move with the words. Then I add, *I don't belong with these people.*

But just as I mouth the words, the RV hits a bump in the road, tilting the cup over and ruining the reflection.

15

JACE

I COLLAPSE ON the couch and bite back a groan. After an entire day of driving, my shoulders are aching from their old injuries. Usually when I get like this, I go on a run and let adrenaline numb my pain. But I'm hesitant to leave Ali, who still looks nearly as stressed as she was when we met up this morning.

She sits on the other couch, staring out the window into the darkness. With the shades drawn, there's only a little sliver of the night sky exposed at the top of the window. Ali has an opened magazine in her lap, but she seems too anxious to focus on reading, and she keeps nervously crinkling the corner of one of the pages.

Night fell about an hour ago, and our caravan stopped at a rest station right outside this dusty little town called Blythe.

With our first day of travel behind us, we're perfectly on schedule. Thank god, because when we *aren't* on schedule, Tony throws hissy fits that scare pretty much everyone.

A scratching sound comes from the other end of the RV, and I recognize it as Cuddles trying to get out of my room. Usually, I take her for a long run in the evenings; she needs the exercise, I need the physical challenge, and fans need a giant pit bull to get the message to stay the hell away from me. It's a good setup for all of us.

But Cuddles is going to have to wait for a run, because I'm not going to leave Ali when she's wearing that scared expression. I wave my hand a little, pulling Ali's attention to me. I have zero clue how to comfort her, but I'm pretty sure awkwardly ignoring each other isn't the ideal option.

"Tell me about yourself," I sign. I'm still a little surprised at how easily ASL is coming back to me. Technically, it's my first language, but I haven't signed in years. And I never thought I would again. Amazing how that's changed so quickly.

She raises her eyebrows. *"What about me?"*

"Anything. Like, do you have any pets?"

She shakes her head.

"Any sort of job?"

Another head shake, and another thing that makes us different. I glance out the window behind me, using the movement to hide my groan. Is there anything we have in common, besides parents who aren't overly fond of us?

"Friends?" I sign. *"Come on. You've got to have one of those."*

Her expression brightens just a little, a small smile playing at the corner of her lips.

"*A-v-e-r-y,*" she finger spells, and I assume this is her friend. "*She's the one who dragged me to your concert.*" She blushes as soon as she signs that, and I can tell she's regretting her word choice. Too bad. I think it's cute that she had to be dragged to see me perform. It's kind of refreshing, actually.

"*We've been friends since we were ten,*" she rushes on. "*She lives across the street from me. She's like my sister.*"

As soon as she says that, her expression falls again. I raise an eyebrow and sign, "*She didn't want you to run away, did she?*"

"*She wants me to be safe,*" Ali signs, her hands moving a little slower now. "*But I'm not sure she'd think this is a good way to go about it. So I didn't tell her exactly where I'm going or who I'm with. I know my dad is going to ask her questions, and I don't want to put her in a bad situation.*"

"*You're a good friend for that,*" I sign.

She nods and looks away, but I can tell she's still upset by the way her jaw clenches.

Then she signs, "*Thanks.*"

"*For what?*"

"*For saying that. I needed to hear that I'm doing the right thing for her.*" She takes a deep breath and then signs, "*How about you?*"

"*What about me?*"

"*Who are your friends? Other musicians?*"

I laugh, not even trying to hide it. She cringes, but I ignore it and say, "*Rock stars don't make friends. The band is my family, but aside from them? No. I make fans and haters, but not friends.*"

She purses her lips. "*But you have to have some.*"

I shrug. "*I've got my band, and that's all I need.*"

She nods and then signs, "So . . . *what do rock stars do for fun?*"

"*Play music. Write music. Perform music. What else?*"

She shakes her head. "*That's your career. What do you do when you have time off?*"

"*Like I was just saying, I don't have much time off.*"

"*You have to have some time off,*" she insists.

"*A little.*"

"*So,*" she signs, giving me an expectant look, "*what do you do with that time?*"

I roll my eyes. "*You're kind of relentless, you know that?*"

"*Yep. Now, come on. Tell me what you do in your free time.*"

"*I like to read.*" I gesture to the small end table, where I have a stack of fitness magazines and some books. Ali tilts her head sideways, reading the titles on the spines.

"*You like mystery novels?*" she signs.

"*Yeah.*"

She gives me a small, knowing smile. "*Because the bad guy always gets caught.*"

It's not a question, so I don't bother with an answer, aside from a small shrug. I'm not sure I like her being able to understand me so easily.

She gestures to the fitness magazines stacked next to the books. "*You're an athlete?*"

"*Not really, but I work out a lot. I like to stay healthy.*"

"*Okay. So what else besides reading and working out?*"

"*Sometimes I sketch random stuff.*" I shrug. "*You know, like scenes from my songs. Killer's trying to teach me how to use Photoshop—so I can draw digitally with that—but I kind of suck at it.*"

She laughs a little. *"I can't do Photoshop, either. There are way too many buttons. I mean, why not just use a pencil?"*

I tilt my head, considering her. *"You draw?"* I don't know why I find it surprising; her hands are delicate and precise when she signs, so I guess it'd make sense for them to make art along with words.

Ali nods. *"Yeah. It's kind of my hobby. Well, that and . . ."* She trails off and gives a shy smile.

"That and what? Frisbee golf? Cat training? Knitting hats?"

She tries to cover a laugh with a scoff, but totally fails. Her laughter seeps through, and it's just as pretty as she is, the sound high and soft. *"No!"*

I smirk. *"So then your hobby is all three?"*

"No, you jerk." She flinches the moment she signs that, but I just keep calm and shoot her an amused smile. As soon as she realizes I'm not going to get angry, she hesitantly adds, *"My other hobby is coding."*

"Coding?" I repeat. *"Like with computers?"*

"Yeah. I design websites and stuff."

"That's cool."

"You don't have to say that. I know most people think it's lame."

"Not me. Killer's really into that. I don't understand it at all, but he seems to enjoy it." I jerk a thumb over my shoulder, motioning to the laptop on the desk behind me. *"He has some coding programs downloaded on there, if you want to check them out."*

Her eyes light up, like I've just offered her a free sports car. *"You'd let me use your computer?"*

I lift one shoulder in a shrug. *"Yeah, sure. Just . . . don't mess with the desktop background, okay?"*

She quickly shakes her head. *"No. Of course not. I won't change a thing."*

She looks all anxious again, like she's honestly worried about upsetting me by simply using my computer. And here we go again. Excited Ali is gone, replaced by Cautious Ali. The fear in her eyes is gut-wrenchingly familiar, and I hate knowing I've just accidentally caused it.

I rub my temples, trying to clear my head. Her fear shouldn't matter, because she's not actually in danger right now. My job is to get her safely to NYC, not to be her personal counselor. As long as she's physically safe, she's okay.

"We need to figure out sleeping arrangements," I mutter abruptly.

"Um," Ali says hesitantly, "I . . . I can just sleep here." She pats the couch.

"Cool," I say. "I'm going to turn in early. I'll be in my room."

With that, I stand from the couch and head toward my bedroom. As I glance back at her one more time, I can see Ali frowning. She's probably wondering what just happened, but I'm too rattled to stop and explain things: The more I get to know her, the more I like her. And the more I like her, the more I want her to like *me*. Which was never supposed to be a part of this. My goal was to get her to safety, not to dredge up a bunch of memories and emotions I've shoved away for years.

I press my bedroom door firmly closed and collapse on my bed. My pillow smells like Ali. Kind of sweet, like apricots or something. Maybe plums. I think back to the duffle bag she brought and wonder just how many things she was able to fit in there. Should I offer to buy her some soap and stuff, so she doesn't have to worry about sharing mine? Or is it just going to embarrass her if I bring it up?

I groan and squeeze my eyes shut. I know what happens when people make an effort to care about others: they get taken advantage of, and then they get hurt. Ali is already bumming a ride with me, so I should draw the line there. There's no need for me to do anything else for her.

But I want to. I want to help her in every way possible, and that can only lead to trouble.

Although, if the trouble came in a form as sweet as Ali, it might be worth it . . .

16

ALI

IT'S BEEN THREE days since I left Los Angeles, but it feels like an eternity has passed. Jace has been strangely quiet since our awkward, bumbling conversation the first evening of my escape. I keep catching him frowning at me like I'm some sort of baffling jigsaw puzzle, but every time I try to talk with him, he shuts down the conversation the moment it starts to get personal. With the adrenaline of my escape wearing off, and with no one to talk to, boredom is starting to gnaw at me.

I click on the desktop's coding icon, bringing the program to life on the computer screen. Ever since Jace told me I could use the computer, I've been madly coding every moment I have. All my works in progress are trapped on my computer back in Los Angeles, but I'm almost glad I have to restart all my projects. It means I'm going to have to spend hours re-creating things, and the intense work is a welcome distraction from the monotony of traveling.

There's a tiny window right next to the desk, and I've opened the shades just a sliver, so I can watch our progress as we travel. We're still in the desert and surrounded by rocks, rocks, and more rocks. There's not much sand anymore. The RV caravan is stopped at a rest station for its usual afternoon break, and even though we've only been here for ten minutes, I'm already itching to get moving again. We're only seventy miles outside of Albuquerque, the city Tone Deaf will be stopping at for the next three days, and the city where I'll branch off and start traveling on my own.

I give up on the coding program, having made no progress since we stopped. I'm thinking too hard to focus on something as difficult as this. I click on the little Internet icon, silently cursing Jace for using Internet Explorer instead of Google Chrome. I hate Explorer, but it's easy enough to pull up a search engine and type in "A–X Lyrics Database." Aside from coding, that's the other thing I've been doing to keep busy: surfing the Internet and reading Tone Deaf's lyrics. About two-thirds of the songs aren't half bad; they're typical, cliché pop-punk songs about relationships and parties and other stuff I have no experience with. But they're catchy, and I can see why so many fans love them.

Then there's the remaining third. They're songs like "Criminal," and they're probably what made Tone Deaf famous. Dark and depressing, the lyrics would fit death metal songs better. But, somehow, Jace manages to make the lyrics beautiful and haunting, almost like a well-written eulogy at a funeral. His style is a huge variation from the normal pop-punk stuff, but, put to music, I can see the lyrics being enchanting, in an oddly morbid way.

A hand taps my shoulder, and I give a little yelp of surprise as I whirl around. Killer stands there, although I'm not sure exactly when he came inside the RV. He peers over my shoulder at the screen, and, even with his nerd glasses, he has to squint.

Killer nods toward the laptop. "What'cha doing on a lyrics site, darling?"

Without any invitation, he sits on the edge of the desk and leans in to get a closer look at the screen. I take a deep breath and resist the urge to shove him away. Killer seems to take the hint, because he backs off like half an inch, which I have a feeling is a pretty big move for him. Then he proceeds to nudge my hand away from the mouse, click on the History bar, and scroll through my latest page visits. He turns and grins at me, like he's not doing something totally invasive and annoying.

"Sooo," he says, drawing out the word. He clicks open a blank text document and tilts the keyboard toward himself, his fingers flying across the keys as he types out a message: *You like Jace's lyrics?*

I shrug. "They're all right."

He rolls his eyes and types a little more, then spins my chair so it faces the screen directly. *Millions of girls don't fall in love with "all right." Jace's lyrics are phenomenal. The dude's got talent.*

I raise my eyebrows. "You do realize you're calling your own band talented, don't you?" Killer just busts out laughing, like my response is the funniest thing he's ever heard. Then he squeezes my shoulder in an awkward little hug. "Darling, I like you," he announces.

"Um, okay?"

You're cute, you know that? he types, turning back to the screen. *I forget how cute girls can be. It's just not cute at all when they're strangely obsessed with you. But you're not obsessed, and that makes you cute.*

I have no idea what he's talking about, but I just nod. Killer smiles in return and, to my relief, backs away another inch.

Then he wags a finger at me, like I'm a puppy who's peed on the carpet, and types out another message. *And Jace is a fabulous musician. His lyrics are awesome, and his music is awesome, and you can't deny it.*

"Okay?"

He sighs, and his glasses slip to the tip of his nose as he stares down with an exasperated look. *Can't you sound a little more enthusiastic about his awesomeness?*

"Yippee?"

No. Try ditching the question at the end.

I give him my best you've-got-to-be-kidding-me look. "Jace is awesome. Hooray."

Much better! Now add some excited arm flailing.

Jace strides out of the kitchen and turns to me, a frown on his lips. "Why are you talking to yourself?" he asks, and heat floods my cheeks as I realize how crazy our half-typed conversation must sound. Then Jace sees Killer and the messages on my screen. "Oh."

Killer waves him away. "I'm just teaching Ali how to get excited over something," he says out loud. "I don't think she's quite grasping the concept, but with a little coaching, she'll have it down eventually."

"I'm sitting right here, you know," I snap. "And I can read lips."

Killer winks at me, his mouth lifting in a playful smile that tells me he's just teasing. Oh. I try to smile back a little, making the expression apologetic. I might have good reason for mistrusting guys, but I guess I shouldn't assume Killer is the type to intentionally cause harm.

Jace's chest moves up and down in a groan. "Excuse him," Jace says to me as he strides over to the desk. "Killer is socially inept and an idiot and very rude to company."

I cross my arms over my chest and look Jace right in the eye. "I like him."

"Well, then you can keep him," Jace says. "Seriously, keep him with you when you get to New York. It'd solve a lot of problems."

Killer turns to rattle off some retort. I can't see his lips from this angle, but judging by Jace's amused expression, Killer's language is getting pretty colorful.

Turning back to the computer screen, I leave the two to their bickering. I close the text document and the Internet browser, before Jace can read anything and start asking why I'm so interested in his lyrics. Not that I'd answer him. It's like I keep finding a little piece of myself in each of his songs, and some part of me thinks that maybe if I read all his lyrics, then I'll understand myself. But that sounds stupid even to me, and I'd never admit anything like that out loud.

As I click out of the browser, I find myself staring at Jace's desktop background again. When he asked me not to change it, I figured it would be some sentimental picture. I should have known better. Instead of a picture, the desktop is a plain white box with the words *Serva me, servabo te* written in it.

"What does that mean?" I ask before I can stop myself.

"What does what mean?" Jace asks.

I point to the computer. "Your desktop. What do those words mean?"

"It's an old Latin saying," Jace says. Then he hesitantly adds, "My mom used to always wear this locket with those words engraved on it. It was a family heirloom. My dad lost the locket, but I like to keep the phrase around."

"But what does it *mean*?" I insist.

He bites his lip and stares hard at the screen. Then he murmurs, "It means hope."

Okay, that's not exactly helpful. But I just shrug, like I really don't care about his cryptic explanation, and turn to Killer.

"Are you going to stick around until the next rest stop?" I try to keep my tone neutral, and not at all pleading. But if Killer stays, then I'd have someone to talk to and help fend off my boredom. I've given up on engaging Jace in a conversation that's not awkward and stunted.

"We're not heading to the next rest stop until tomorrow," Jace says. "We're done driving for the day."

"What?" Killer says. "But I thought Tony wanted us to get to Albuquerque by tonight."

Jace shakes his head. "Check your phone. He just texted. One of the trucks is having engine troubles, so we're stopped until that gets fixed."

Killer curses at this news, and then says to me, "Sorry, sweetie, but you're on your own with Jace for the evening. I promised I'd spend some time with Arrow." He offers me an apologetic smile and adds, "We'll catch up tomorrow, okay?"

I have no idea what we need to catch up on, but I nod anyway, even though I don't plan on doing any hanging out tomorrow. By the time we get to Albuquerque—hopefully in the late morning—I'll have hundreds of miles between me and Los Angeles. It should be far enough away to make it safe to find an airport and travel the rest of the way by plane. No one is going to know to look for me at an airport in New Mexico, and if I have Jace buy the ticket under his name, it should be completely safe.

Killer says a quick good-bye and leaves, and I sigh as I feel the rattle of the front door closing. Jace strides away from the desk area and collapses on the couch. With Killer gone, I guess we're back to normal: Jace awkwardly avoiding conversation with me, and me pretending I don't notice.

I glance back at the desktop screen one more time, trying to find meaning in the words. Googling the phrase would get me an easy answer, but I don't want to give Jace the satisfaction of knowing I care enough to bother researching it.

Jace waves at me to get my attention, and then scowls at the computer as he signs, *"I'm going to need to use that for a bit."*

"Are you going to write?" I ask. After reading most of his lyrics, I'm curious about his process for creating them.

He shakes his head. *"I only write lyrics freehand. I never type them until they're finished."* He grimaces at the computer. *"I'm just going to be working on marketing. My manager set me up with a bunch of social media accounts, so now I'm supposed to spend a few hours every week charming fans with my delightful personality."*

I raise an eyebrow. *"You're sure you shouldn't hire a new manager? Because you are neither charming or delightful."*

He shrugs, but doesn't bother protesting. *"I just respond to the messages about my music, and try to ignore all the other ones."*

"Ignoring people is also not charming or delightful," I sign, giving him a pointed look. I'm not exactly sure why he's been avoiding me the last couple days, but if he gets the hint that I'm annoyed, he doesn't show it. Instead, his eyes suddenly widen, like he's been struck with an idea.

He points to me. *"But you are."*

"I'm what?"

"Charming. Delightful." He raises his eyebrows. *"And hopefully merciful enough to take over my social media duties."*

I shoot him a skeptical look. *"You want me to post on your accounts?"*

"Yes," he signs. *"It'll be easy for you, I promise. Just reply to messages from fans and pretend to love everyone and be super excited."*

As I consider this, my stomach lets out a growl. I haven't eaten in a while, but I don't even want to go into the kitchen and grab food. All Jace has to eat are things like sesame seed crackers and seaweed sticks and carob chips. In other words, disgusting stuff I'd never touch in a million years.

"I'll make you a deal," I say out loud. "I'll do your social media stuff if you get me a bowl of mac and cheese. And not some gross healthy version. I mean the good stuff with ten thousand carbs and chemical cheese."

He cringes at the thought. "I'm not going to let you poison yourself as part of our deal."

"Too bad. Either get me mac and cheese, or do your social media on your own."

Jace lets out a relenting sigh and signs, *"Jon always keeps like ten boxes of that stuff around."*

"So do we have a deal?" I ask.

He smiles a little, and it makes me remember why I decided to trust him in the first place. His smile makes him seem real and genuine, not to mention extremely handsome. I realize I'm staring at him, and glance away, my cheeks flushing with heat.

He chuckles and signs, *"I'll get you your mac and cheese. It's a deal."*

17

JACE

ALI TURNS OUT to be a natural at social media. Her responses to fans sound personalized and thoughtful, and to keep things interesting, she throws in quite a bit of self-deprecating humor. Or, at least, it would be self-deprecating if I was the one actually writing the messages. Coming from Ali, I think it's subtle payback for flipping her off when I first met her, but it's not like I have any right to complain.

She spends the whole evening answering messages and shooting me victorious looks as she munches on her mac and cheese. I hang out on the couch and practice one of our newer songs, although my attention keeps drifting away from my guitar and back to Ali. Sitting there at the desk, her slim legs crossed and her head tilted in concentration, she looks more attractive than ever. Not just cute, not just beautiful, but confident and intelligent.

I keep wandering over to peer at what she's doing, and she doesn't move away from me as I look over her shoulder at the messages on the screen. She's obviously at ease working with computers, and it gives her a sort of calmness I haven't ever seen before. It's getting late, and I pack away my guitar, but I don't suggest she stop for the night. Ali seems to be enjoying herself for once, and I don't want to ruin that.

I grab the TV remote resting haphazardly on the couch's arm. From the bedroom, Cuddles lets out a bored whine, and I know I should probably take her out on a run. But I turn on the TV instead, deciding that bringing out Cuddles is just going to make Ali nervous.

I flick to the news channel and let myself zone out. News stories flash by on the screen, one by one, some of them happy, but most of them depressing as hell. Then a red banner appears at the bottom of the screen, along with the words "AMBER ALERT."

I turn up the volume just as Ali's face appears on the screen. It looks like a school photo, her hair carefully styled, her make-up carefully applied, but her smile fake and strained.

"According to authorities, Alison Collins went missing three days ago from her home in Los Angeles," a woman reporter says. I stare at the screen, too shocked to react.

What the hell? The girl is seventeen, and they're putting out an Amber Alert? She's almost a legal adult, so no one should care if she's gone, at least not enough for an emergency alert to be raised. Unless there's some other reason they're concerned about her safety?

As if answering my question, the reporter says, "Alison, who goes by Ali, has been diagnosed with multiple mental health disorders. Her father states that she has a history of self-harm, and it's urgent that she be found quickly."

I blink a few times, hoping I'm dreaming, that I'm about to wake up from a nightmare. Mental health disorders? *Self-harm?* Ali sure as hell didn't mention any of this. She led me to think the exact opposite—that she was running from someone hurting her, not doing it to herself. Is everything she's told me some sort of sick lie?

I whirl toward the desk, opening my mouth to demand answers, but stumbling uselessly over the words. The report has to be a mistake. Ali's face goes pale as she flicks her gaze between me and the flashing red banner on the screen. She jumps up from the desk, and I wait for her to launch into some explanation that'll clear everything up.

Instead, she runs. Ali slips out of the room, and a second later, I hear the bathroom door slam closed and the click of a lock. I curse and jump up from the couch, my bones screaming in protest, my heartbeat crashing against my chest as I race after her.

She lied. I believed her, I trusted her, I tried to help her, and all she gave me in return was lies.

I hear muffled crying from inside the bathroom, but Ali doesn't come to the door when I knock. I grab the emergency master key from the top of the doorframe, using that to pop the lock open.

Ali sits in the corner of the bathroom, tightly hugging her knees to her chest, like she's trying to put a barrier between us. She stares up at me, her eyes wide and terrified. Or is she really even scared? Is her fear even real, or is it just another lie?

"I'm sorry," she signs.

Is her sign language a piece of her act? Is she even *deaf*? My head pounds as I try to sort out the truth, and I reach up to rub my forehead.

As soon as my hand moves, Ali lets out a strangled yelp and draws closer to the wall. Her cheeks grow paler as more tears join the initial rush. One drips down from the tip of her nose, and she flinches as it brushes against her chin.

Shit. Maybe she could pretend to need help, and maybe even pretend to be deaf. But she can't fake fear like that. Her gaze flicks wildly between my face and my hands, and I know that sort of terror can only be the result of one thing.

I take a deep breath and hold up my hands in a gesture of innocence. It doesn't do anything to calm her, and my thoughts keep whirling in confusion. What the hell is going on?

I crouch beside Ali, ready to voice the question, but she cringes and rips her gaze away from mine. I remember that so well: *Don't look him in the eyes, don't make him mad, don't make things worse.* Those words were my personal mantra for years, and now . . . now those same words are probably running through Ali's head.

Because of me.

I shudder and stumble back a few steps, giving her space. Then I just freeze in place and wait for her to look up so she can see my words. It takes a long time. Maybe a minute, maybe an hour; I'm not sure. All I know is that it feels like an eternity. Tears stream down her face, landing with soft plops on the linoleum floor, creating a quiet beat that sears into me. Then Ali runs a shaking hand across her eyes, clearing them of tears, and finally looks up.

"Explain," I say, keeping my voice soft, even though I know she can't hear me.

Ali bites her lip and stares at me for a long second. Her teeth cut through her chapped skin, and a tiny drop of blood leaks out. She doesn't even seem to notice.

Then she raises her hands, and the story comes tumbling out. *"My mom died when I was ten, right at the same time I lost my hearing. I was sent to live with my dad, and . . ."* She shudders at some past memory. *"And he didn't like having me around."*

"He hit you," I murmur.

She shakes her head. *"Not at first. I think he always resented having to take care of me, but for a long time, the worst thing he did was ignore me."*

Her expression hardens, and she brushes away a tear. *"And he was even good to me in some ways. My school district put me in lessons to learn to read lips and sign, and he was supportive of that. He even learned some signing himself. But he pretty much just avoided me most of the time, and I was happy like that."*

"But you're not happy now," I sign. She hesitates, and I add, *"Don't try to tell me that's how it ended, Ali. People don't run away just because their parents ignore them."*

She sniffs a little and signs, *"When I was about thirteen, he starting getting really angry and drinking a ton. I'd always hear him lecturing the younger cops in his department about getting counseling if they developed PTSD. But I guess he couldn't take his own advice. He's a mean drunk, and . . ."*

Ali takes a deep breath and looks away from me. I can tell she's trying to be calm about this, but little tremors keep running through her hands, and her lips purse tightly. *"That's when he started hitting me."* She glances at me hesitantly, her cheeks flushing with shame as she blurts out loud, "He never . . . you know. He just struck me—a few punches and that sort of thing."

"Just punches?" I repeat. *"Ali, there's no such thing as 'just punches,'"* I sign. *"They're punches. Period. They're abuse. They never, ever should have happened to you."*

"I'm sorry," she whispers, her eyes focusing on the floor again.

I tap her chin, tilting it up so she looks at me. She breathes in sharply and jerks back from my touch, but her attention is on my hands.

"Don't apologize," I sign. *"Do you understand? You didn't do anything wrong. Nothing. I don't care what you think you did, it's not your fault. No one deserves to be treated like that, no matter what. Got it?"*

She gulps hard and nods. I sigh and lean back a little, giving her a bit more space as I desperately try to sort out everything she's telling me. *"I'm still confused though,"* I insist. *"What mental health issues were they talking about?"*

Her hands start signing again, but now they're a little slower, a little more hesitant. *"At first, I didn't want to tell anyone. My dad helped a lot of people during his career, and everybody thought he was a hero. Then his PTSD started getting totally out of control. He'd have a flashback, and it'd leave him so angry, he'd just lash out at whoever was nearest. Which was usually me.*

"That was when I tried reporting him. But right before then, one of my teachers insisted I start seeing the school counselor. She meant well, she was just worried since I wasn't talking much

and my grades were slipping. But my dad used the mandated counseling to his advantage. He said it was obvious I had emotional issues and was just crying out for attention, and that all my claims about his abuse were lies."

I stare at her hard. "And Child Protective Services bought that?"

She nods tightly. "My dad had worked with CPS probably hundreds of times during his career. They had no idea about his PTSD or his drinking, and they all thought he was a great guy. Plus, all my relatives backed him and told CPS he'd never hurt me. So of course they believed him."

I let out a small groan and pinch the bridge of my nose, trying to hold back the headache creeping up on me. Either Ali is a pathological liar, and a damn good one, or she's actually telling the truth.

"I still don't get how you got diagnosed as crazy," I sign. "Crying out for attention and crazy aren't the same thing."

Her hands freeze and she glares at the ground, like everything is the floor's fault. Then she signs, "I kept trying to report him, but CPS was totally convinced I was just some needy kid. My relatives all said I was fine, and my teachers said they didn't see any signs of abuse. I guess no one wanted to get in a fight with someone like my dad. So by the time he started hitting me hard enough to leave bruises, CPS thought I was doing it to myself. I got diagnosed with some self-harm disorder, and from then on, no one would listen to me."

Her eyes cast down in shame and her shoulders sag, and right then, I know she's telling the truth. She doesn't expect me to believe her, just like no one believed her before.

Just like no one ever believed me.

I stroke my thumb gently over her cheek, brushing away a tear. I hate seeing those tears there, knowing I caused them, knowing she's in pain. Whatever happened to me being her rescuer?

She looks up at me. "I'm sorry," I murmur. Ali shakes her head, jerking away from me, and stands on unsteady legs. She grabs her duffle bag, which still sits in the corner of the bathroom, and then edges past me, careful not to make contact.

A sharp pang hits my chest, and it just gets worse as she starts toward the door. I reach out and take her hand, careful to make my grasp gentle. It still makes Ali flinch, but at least she doesn't bolt. Instead, she freezes in the doorway and glances over her shoulder at me.

I release her hand and sign, *"Where are you going?"*

"Away. Isn't that what you want?"

"No."

She ignores me and walks out of the bathroom. I curse and jump up from my crouched position, ignoring the pain that flares up as I move too quickly. Right as Ali grabs the knob of the main RV door, I slide in front of her, blocking her way out.

Her suspicion nosedives back into fear, and she retreats a few steps. My instincts scream at me to back off, to give her some room and calm her down. But I can't make myself move. She's obviously planning on marching right out of here, and it's going to get her caught. And if she's taken back to her dad . . .

No. That won't happen, because I won't let it.

"Don't go," I sign.

"Why wouldn't I?" She makes an angry gesture toward me. *"I'm not going to stay with anyone who doesn't believe me."*

"I believe you," I quickly sign. *"And I want to help you."*

Her eyes narrow with suspicion. *"I'm getting really tired of you saying that and not explaining why."*

I rake a hand through my hair as I struggle to come up with an answer. Why should I care about Ali? Logically, it doesn't make sense. She's just one of thousands of girls who want something from me.

But I guess it's the *way* she asks for what she wants. So tentatively, so hesitantly, like she's betraying herself by asking someone else for help. She's determined to get by with only herself, and that makes her so strong, it's both beautiful and sad.

"It's late," I sign slowly. *"And we're in the middle of the desert. It's not safe for you to go."*

Damn it. Why can't I just speak my mind around her? I usually say whatever the hell I want, not worrying about consequences before I blurt out what's on my mind. But with Ali . . . I don't want to hurt her. And I don't want to give her any fuel to hurt *me.*

She takes a step forward, her hands trembling as she balls them at her sides. *"I want to know why, Jace,"* she signs, her fists unclenching just long enough to form the words. *"Why do you want to help me? And don't you dare give me some Good Samaritan bullshit. You don't just do people favors, and we both know it. So why are you doing one for me?"*

"Because I want to," I reply, my voice much closer to a growl than I'd like.

Ali shakes her head disgustedly. *"You won't even talk about how you learned ASL. How do you expect me to trust you when you keep hiding stuff from me?"*

I don't offer a response to that—as much as her suspicion hurts, it's still not enough to make me want to talk about my

Deaf parents. Ali grits her teeth in frustration when I don't reply and reaches for the door handle again.

"I want to help because I understand you."

"You don't know me, Jace," she says, and her spoken words are sharp and filled with scorn.

"Maybe not, but I know the pain. I've been there before."

She actually laughs at that, but it's a ruined sort of laugh that screams of brokenness and loneliness. "You know pain? What's that supposed to mean? Did your parents forget to buy you a Lamborghini for your sweet sixteen?"

I flinch and look over my shoulder, pretending to study the wall behind me. It's a weak cover for the truth: I don't want her to see my expression. Because right now, I'm hurting, and I'm not the type to hurt. I don't care enough about anyone to let simple words cause me pain.

And now I'm angry, too. It's infuriating that people think I was born into this life, that I didn't work for it, that I'm not capable of controlling my own future.

I take a shuddering breath, trying to calm my bewildered and shaky nerves, but my skin feels like it's on fire, and I think I might put a hole through the wall. I clench my fist, letting my fingernails dig into my skin, and resist the urge to destroy something. That would terrify Ali, not to mention break all my promises to her.

I can't lose it, or I'll lose her.

I slowly unclench my fist, one finger at a time, and turn back to her. She's still glaring at me.

Before I can think better, I reach for the hem of my T-shirt and quickly shrug it off. "Look," I say, pointing to my chest. I tap the long, jagged scar that runs from my right shoulder down to my left ribs. "You see this? This was my dad's parting gift when he kicked me out for forming a band."

A shudder quakes my skin as the memory comes hurtling back. My yelling, my dad's furious signing, and then me trying to storm out the door.

Sometimes, I try to tell myself he didn't mean to injure me so badly. I have no idea if that's true, but believing that makes it easier to deal with. My dad was high out of his mind, and he grabbed the first thing he could find to hit me with—an empty beer bottle. The first blow I dodged, and half the bottle shattered on the door. I didn't get so lucky with the second blow. It hit me right in the chest, and the broken glass sliced through my skin like butter.

My dad got five years in prison, and I finally got my freedom. Supposedly. When the memories come rushing back at me like this, it makes me wonder if I'll ever actually be free of his hold over me.

I wait for Ali to give one of the usual reactions to my scar: wincing, or gasping, or even turning away. But all she does is slowly shake her head, like she can't believe what she's seeing. Like she doesn't *want* to believe it.

She takes a hesitant step forward, and another. I've had girls show worry when they see my scar, but it's always been fleeting. Ali is the first to stare at me with this sort of concern—the kind that not only cares, but *knows*. It's a haunting expression, and I want to look away.

Ali brushes her fingertips along the very top of the scar, where it marks my shoulder. Her fingers are smooth and gentle, and as she touches me, heat spreads out across my skin. It reminds me that I can still feel, and that as much as I regret it sometimes, I'm still *alive.*

Her touch is feather-light and slow, but she never breaks contact from my skin. It's like she knows that if she does, this weird trance we're both in will end.

My muscles tense and itch with the urge to pull away, but I make myself stay still. When she reaches the base of my ribs, where the scar ends, she hesitantly retracts her hand and stares down at her fingers. She rubs the tips of them together, the movement slow and thoughtful, and then looks back at me.

She shakes her head again, and I cringe, knowing I've made a mistake. She probably thinks I'm trying to one-up her, like my abuse is somehow worse than hers. But, before I can apologize, Ali leaps forward and throws her slim arms around my neck.

I'm too shocked to react. I just stand there as she squeezes me into a hug, her cheek resting against my chest, right where the scar slashes over my heart.

She's short. The thought drifts through my mind as I struggle to find an appropriate reaction to her hug, other than jerking away. I'd almost forgotten how tiny she is. She's so strong, so brave, it's easy to forget she's hardly five feet tall.

I finally get my arms to work and wrap them around her shoulders. For once, she doesn't flinch, and just lets me press her closer.

"I'm so sorry," she mumbles into my chest.

I rest my cheek on top of her head and breathe in. Her hair smells like a sweet blend of plums and honeysuckle, and I gently smooth the locks that fall over her shoulder.

"Don't be sorry," I finally whisper back. I know she can't see my lips, but I'm not ready to let go of her.

We stand there for a long moment, just holding each other, until Ali slowly pulls away and offers me a shy smile. For the first time since I've met her, her smile seems completely sincere, without any wariness or suspicion weighing it down. As soon as I see that, I know I did the right thing showing her my scar. As painful as it is to bring up my past, it's worth it to see the trust in Ali's expression.

"Thank you," she signs.

I smile back a little and sign, *"Don't thank me yet. We still haven't gotten to New York."*

I hold my breath, half expecting her to resist my words and say she's not coming with me anymore. She shakes her head, and my stomach drops.

Then she signs, *"No, I mean thank you for believing me."*

She hesitantly looks down at her arms and rubs them, and I can tell she's thinking the same thing I am: did we really just hold each other like that? I've done more than holding girls—a hell of a lot more. But, somehow, that felt almost more intimate.

Before either of us can freak out, I gently take her hand, lacing my fingers through hers and pressing our palms together. Her hand feels so tiny and delicate in mine, but it's warm, and her grasp is surprisingly strong. I gently tug her toward the bedroom at the back of the RV.

"Come on," I say. "You should get to sleep."

She freezes for a single moment and then yanks away from me, her expression suspicious. I raise my hands in a gesture of surrender.

"I'm not going in there with you," I sign. *"I'll sleep out on the couch. You take the bed tonight."*

She purses her lips. *"You're sure?"*

"I'm positive." I nod toward the bedroom. *"I'm going to go get Cuddles out, and then you can crash in there. Okay?"*

I reluctantly let my hand slip away from hers, glad that she wasn't the one to pull away first, and retreat to my bedroom. Cuddles is waiting just inside the door. My dog cocks her head to the side and stares up with a highly perplexed look, like she can't imagine what could possibly be important enough to keep me distracted from her. I kneel beside Cuddles and wrap an arm around her thick shoulders. She wiggles her stump of a tail, happily accepting the hug as she tries to lick my face.

By the time I have Cuddles fed and put away in the bathroom, Ali is already fast asleep on the couch. I consider waking her up, so she can move to my bedroom, but decide it's not worth disturbing her. As she sleeps, Ali's expression is troubled, but it's not at all fearful. I think this is the first time I've seen her like that, and I'm not going to mess it up.

I grab a few blankets and lay them over her, careful not to wake her.

"Sleep tight," I murmur as I retreat to my room.

18

ALI

WHEN I WAKE up, my muscles are so tense they hurt, and my throat is strained from screaming. Something slams repeatedly against my chest, and it takes me a moment to realize it's my frantic heartbeat. It's not a fist, like it was in my nightmare.

Arms wrap around my shoulders, and I open my mouth to scream again. But before I can make any sound, a hand gently cups my face and tilts my chin up. I find myself staring into blue eyes, their color clear and sharp like gemstones. Despite their boldness, there's something soft about them, gentle.

"You're okay," Jace says, his other hand stroking my cheek. His fingers are calloused from all the years he's spent playing the guitar. "You're okay," he repeats, and then he says it again and again and again. I watch his lips closely, not wanting to tear my eyes away from the words.

I can tell from his nervous expression that he doesn't know what else to say, but I don't want him to say anything else. I just want him to be here.

Jace swallows hard and finally stops repeating the words. His gaze drifts away from my eyes, focusing instead on the place where his hand touches my cheek. He pulls away and stands from where he was crouched beside me. Then he runs both hands through his hair, making it stick out at all sorts of angles.

He stares at me. *Hard.*

My face heats up as I realize how pathetic I must look. I'm seventeen, way too old to be screaming from a nightmare, and definitely too old to need any kind of comfort. I've dealt with these bad dreams on my own for years, and I've never run to anyone for reassurance. So why should that change now?

Because he ran to me. The answer is so simple, but it still makes the air whoosh out of my lungs. I didn't go to him; Jace came to me.

He stands there, still unsure what to do, and then edges toward me without meeting my eyes. He sits on the couch next to me and takes my trembling hand in his own. My entire body shakes, like it's trying to dislodge the last remnants of the nightmare. I remember my dad coming closer, his fist clenched, his expression stormy, his footsteps—

Jace nudges my shoulder, jarring me from the memory and making me gasp. He pulls me close to his chest, and the moment his arms wrap around me, panic sears through my veins. I shove at him, yanking out of his embrace.

Jace frowns, his eyebrows furrowing into an expression that's both confused and rejected. He leans away and signs, *"Sorry. I didn't mean to scare you."*

I can't breathe, and my lungs burn with a mix of relief and gratefulness and painful uncertainty. Before I can stop myself, I throw my arms around him and press my face against his chest.

He doesn't react, and I tense, but just as I'm about to pull away, he slowly wraps his arms around my waist and starts rubbing the small of my back. I smile shakily as I realize this is the second time in just a few hours that we've ended up like this. But it's not like I'm going to complain. His touch is light and soothing, like he's trying to brush away the fear leftover from my nightmare.

I press closer to him, not even caring that he's only wearing boxer shorts. I close my eyes and rest my cheek against his warm chest. His scar is rough against my skin, but his rhythmic heartbeat is soothing. It pounds fast, and his muscles are so tense that I know he's uncomfortable being this close. But he doesn't move away, and just holds me, his arms warm and strong.

Soft, steady bursts of air brush against my ear, and I guess that he's murmuring words, probably something to comfort me. I relax into him, and after a few minutes pass, my shivering stops, leaving me drained and exhausted. My breathing slows. The adrenaline is gone, and the memories are all that's left.

I squeeze my eyes shut, trying not to think of the fists and pain and tears. Jace just keeps whispering to me, his breath warm against my neck, his hand still rubbing slow circles on the small of my back. Part of me hates him being this close, but the other part needs him. I think I've actually needed him for years, and now that I finally have someone to comfort me, it feels strange and scary and right.

I soak in his presence, trying to memorize the feel of his touch so I can remember it the next time I have a nightmare. Finally, when my breaths slow to a more reasonable rate, I gently push away from him. He lets go of me, but slowly, and I can feel his reluctance as I slip away.

I look up at him and give a sheepish smile. *"Sorry,"* I sign, unsure what else to say. My hands falter, and then I hesitantly add, *"I have nightmares sometimes. I guess I should have warned you."*

He shakes his head. *"Don't be sorry. You didn't do anything wrong."*

My embarrassment makes me want to disagree, but before I can, he stands and glances toward his bedroom.

"I'll leave you alone now," he signs. But he doesn't move, and just stands there, skimming a hand through his tousled hair.

Alone. That's the absolute *last* thing I want. My expression must drop at the thought of it, because Jace takes a hesitant step toward me.

"Unless . . ." His hands freeze mid-air, and he swallows hard. *"Unless you want me to stay?"*

I nod before I can stop myself. A small smile flickers across his lips, and he sits next to me and pulls me close, until my head is resting on his chest again. For the first time, I'm acutely aware that he's only wearing boxers, and I try not to blush. I must fail pretty miserably, because he chuckles a little, sending vibrations through his chest.

Jace just pulls a couple of blankets over us, which I apparently kicked to the floor during my nightmare. Then he snuggles close to me, until I'm completely wrapped in his arms, and rests his cheek on top of my head. We both relax into each other.

His heartbeat thuds against my chest, his breathing is warm against my cheek, and I can't help but to feel safer than ever before. I close my eyes, giving into sleep.

19

JACE

I FEEL CONTENT. I blearily open my eyes, wondering what the hell is wrong. Am I high? Drunk? Dead? I always wake up to pain ricocheting through my body as my old injuries scream their complaints. But now . . . well, the pain is still there, that's for sure. But there's also this bizarre feeling of contentment.

I blink a couple times, clearing my eyes of sleep, and find that I'm looking at Ali. She's snuggled into me, her head resting on my chest, her arms tangled around my neck. This is weird. Really, really freaking weird. When I sleep with girls, I don't *sleep* with them. We don't cuddle or snuggle.

But now I'm wondering why I've never done this before. Ali's arms feel good wrapped around me, and her weight on my chest makes me feel secure and even a little protective. The steady rhythm of her breathing threatens to lull me back to sleep.

I'm about to drift off when I hear the hum of a vibrating cell phone. Shit. I must have left mine in my room. I groan, knowing I'm going to have to get up and answer it, or else someone is likely to come barging in here and find us together.

I carefully extract myself from the couch, moving slowly so I don't wake Ali up, and head to my bedroom. Cuddles scratches at the bathroom door as I pass, and I open it, letting her out. She shoots me an offended glance and stalks off toward the kitchen, probably so she can curl up on her doggy bed and mope. I shake my head and make a mental reminder to take her on a long run later. If I don't, she'll get upset and chew on stuff. Stupid dog. Or maybe it's me who's stupid for liking her so damn much.

I shove open my bedroom door just as my cell phone goes off again. I snatch it from my nightstand, and a new message blinks on the screen:

Jace??? Answer!!

It's from Killer, and there's another notification at the bottom of the screen: *Fifteen Unread Messages.* Wonderful. Only the band and Tony have this number, which means someone I actually give a crap about is having some sort of panic attack. And there's nothing to panic about, unless . . . unless someone saw Ali on the news last night.

Shit.

I open the message inbox and read over the newest texts near the top, mumbling curses under my breath as I scan over them. There are more messages from Killer, and Jon and Arrow, too.

You see the news?
ur chick is nutso
We have a maaaajor problem.
cops r after her
Nevermind. YOU have a maaaajor problem.
U brought a crazy chick on tour? What the hell is ur issue????

When I reach the last one, I hesitantly start typing a reply to all. What am I even supposed to say? *Everything's fine, Ali didn't actually lie about anything, she's not crazy, and I slept with her last night. But not that kind of sleeping, so don't worry.* Yeah, that wouldn't go over very well . . .

I rub my face, trying to think of a reasonable response, when someone knocks on the front door. Actually, it's more of a frantic bang, and I know it's Arrow. The dude sounds like a cannon when he knocks, especially if he's pissed.

"Just a sec!"

I grab a T-shirt off my floor and shrug it on, yanking at the hem harder than I need to. Scrubbing my hands over my face, I take a deep breath, trying—and failing—to relax. Another bang echoes down the hall, and Arrow's muffled voice calls out something that's royally pissed. I roll my eyes and grab a pair of jeans out of a drawer, pulling them on and immediately hating them. Back home in Denver, jeans are always a welcome barrier against the cold. Here in the Southwest, they're just annoyingly hot and really not improving my mood.

I jog to the front door, throwing it open and making sure my scowl is obvious, even though it lost its effect on Arrow years ago. He stands on the doorstep, his hands interlaced behind his neck, his foot tapping out a nervous rhythm. Behind him, the sun rises over the desert horizon, making me squint. What's Arrow doing here so early, anyway? It's like six o'clock, and definitely not the right time for a confrontation.

Arrow nods to the open door. "Can I come in?"

I close it just a little, so only my face shows. "No. Ali's sleeping."

Arrow shoves past me, clearly not giving a shit about my excuse. I cuss at him, but don't put up a struggle as he barges into the RV and heads for my bedroom. Arrow flops down on my messy bed and throws one arm over his face, leaving me to stand in the doorway.

"Dude," he grumbles, "why the hell weren't you answering your phone?"

"I didn't hear it go off until a minute ago."

He grunts. "Did you see my message?"

"I just read it."

"And?"

"And what?"

He abruptly sits up and pins me with a glare. "And I told you so. I *told* you there'd be issues if you brought that girl along. And now look at the mess you're in. We're in the middle of a tour, and you've got a psycho in your RV that half the country is now looking for!"

"She's not psycho," I hiss.

Arrow scoffs. "What sob story did she tell you to make you believe that?"

"It wasn't a sob story. And I don't have the right to just spill everything she told me."

Arrow shakes his head and throws his hands up in disbelief. "Seriously, Jace? We don't keep secrets from each other. That's rule number one, and you know it."

"No, that's *not* rule number one," I snap. "Rule number one is that we trust each other. And, right now, I need you to trust me, okay? She's not a liar. She has a severely abusive father and some really shitty luck. She deserves my help. *Our* help. And you can't just walk away from her." Arrow has always been my right-hand man, and he can't just ditch me like this.

Arrow's eyes narrow. "Yes, I can."

"You can what?"

"I can walk away. I don't have to do anything you say, Jace. You might be our lead singer, but you're sure as hell *not* our leader. None of us have to listen to you."

I let out a string of cuss words. Arrow just stares at me, his green eyes evaluating me with eerie calmness. When I finally run out of insults, I pause for breath and glare at him, waiting for whatever retort he's cooked up.

"But I'll still help her," he says.

I'm too shocked to say anything for a long moment. Then I swallow back my surprise. "What?"

"You heard me. I said I'll help."

"But you said . . ."

He scoffs. "I said you can't force me to do anything. And you can't. But I want to help you, and you want to help Ali, so . . ." He shrugs. "I'll help her. It seems like the best way to keep you out of trouble, if you're going to be too stubborn to kick her out."

I just stand there and struggle to figure out a response, not quite believing I heard him correctly.

"I don't trust that girl, Jace," he says. "But I do trust you. You're right, that *is* rule number one. And you trust Ali, so . . . yeah. Actually, I guess I do trust her."

I stumble over my reply a couple times, but finally manage, "Thank you. Seriously, just . . . thanks."

He shrugs, like it's no big deal. "You've always had my back. I'd be a total jerk to not have yours. And you've already filled the position of Chief Jerk, so there's no room in the band for another one."

I scoff and throw a mock punch at his arm. "Don't make me regret thanking you."

His expression turns serious again. "As long as you don't make me regret not turning Ali in. I hope to god you know what you're doing, Jace. Keeping around a chick who has an Amber Alert out on her is just asking for trouble." He doesn't give me a chance to respond before moving toward the door, gesturing for me to follow as he says, "Now, come on. Tony wants to meet with us at seven, and if you don't want him barging in here to find you, we'd better go find him."

20

ALI

I FLIP THE page of one of Jace's fitness magazines, even though I have zero clue what I just read. Something about an abdominal workout, I think, although the pictures looked more like a runway model being tortured. Either way, I couldn't focus on the article, just like I haven't been able to focus on a single thing in the past hour since I woke up.

It only took me a quick search around the RV to realize Jace wasn't here, and even though I know he'll probably be back soon, I wouldn't blame him if he decided to stay away longer. What was I thinking, falling asleep in his arms? He's here to help me get to New York, not to act as my teddy bear.

I drop the magazine beside me on the couch and rub my tired eyes. Maybe I should have left when I got the chance yesterday, although the Amber Alert has completely ruined my plans to take a flight to New York. Traveling by plane would have been risky to begin with, but now that I've been broadcasted nationally as a missing person, it'd be downright idiotic to walk into an airport. Which leaves me still dependent on Jace for my escape, and which really doesn't make me feel any better about him avoiding me this morning. It probably means he's regretting what happened between us last night. Whatever *that* was. His comfort felt like more than simple pity—a lot more. But with Jace missing this morning, I'm starting to think I completely misinterpreted it.

Something taps my shoulder, and I yelp, looking up to find Killer hovering above me. I glance toward the door, but it's already closed, and it looks like Killer is the only one who came in.

"Rise and shine, sweetie," he says. Or at least that's what I *think* he says. He's using what I guess is a sing-song voice, and his lips are moving all weird, making them hard to read. He quits the singing and adds, "The other guys are going to be in here in just a second, and I don't think you want to meet Jon while you're in . . . *that*." He gestures to my crumpled T-shirt and wrinkles his nose.

"Um, thanks." I stand up, my arms crossed over my chest, and mutter, "I'm going to go change." As annoying as Killer's warning is, I should probably be grateful for it. Facing Jace is going to be awkward enough without me looking like hell.

Killer chuckles and nods. "Good idea."

I jog to the bathroom and rush inside. My duffle bag is still in the corner, but it looks scrunched, like someone's been sitting on it. I pick it up and find dog hair covering the top of the bag and some of the clothes inside. Great. Not only has Jace's pet grim reaper decided to use my belongings as a bed, but now I'm going to smell like a dog all day.

I shake away the thought and fish out a pair of jean shorts and a T-shirt. I'm about to pull them on, when I realize I smell like sweat, probably from last night's nightmare. Ick. Double ick, since I was cuddling with Jace while I stunk like this. I cringe, trying not to dwell on that fact, and start the shower in the corner of the bathroom.

Once I'm out of the shower, I throw my hair up into a loose bun. I didn't have enough room to bring my own shower products, so now I'm going to smell like dude shampoo *and* dog hair. I bite back a groan and shrug on my clothes, silently hoping that Jace owns a lint roller.

As I step out of the bathroom, I can't help shooting the window a glare. The desert stretches as far as I can see, and even though we're just a few miles outside of Albuquerque, I feel hopelessly far from civilization. I'm not sure when we're going to travel the final stretch to the city, but I sure hope it's soon. Being cooped up in the RV is bad enough without being surrounded by such a miserably empty landscape.

I pad toward the front of the RV, all too aware that I probably don't look much better than when Killer first found me. I usually don't recover from my nightmares very fast. It's strange—when my dad hits me, I can walk away and pretend like nothing ever happened. But when I have nightmares, it's different. It's like the pain has infiltrated my subconscious, and at that level, there's no ignoring it.

As I enter the living area, four heads turn toward me. Killer and Arrow sit on the far couch, snuggled close to each other.

Killer beams at me, while Arrow gives me an appraising look, and I can feel him judging me.

I quickly turn to Jace, who sits on the opposite couch. He regards me with a completely neutral expression. Heat creeps into my cheeks, and I grit my teeth to keep my expression from tumbling into one of pain. How could I have thought last night meant anything? I'm someone for him to pity, and nothing more.

I try to ignore my embarrassment as I shift my attention to the fourth guy, who I assume is Jon. He's lounging on the couch, both arms thrown over the back of it. Jon is shorter than the others, but muscular, and his right arm is covered in tattoos. They're gorgeous, with bold colors and real artwork.

"Hi," I say, deciding to break the silence when no one else does. "I'm Ali."

"Nice to meet you," Jon says, offering me a hesitant smile. His teeth are just a teensy bit crooked. It's his only real physical flaw, and I make myself return the smile, forcing away the feeling that I'm woefully inept.

I shuffle my feet, waiting for someone else to say something. They don't. They're all staring at me, and I have the distinct feeling that I've just interrupted a conversation about myself.

Killer breaks the stillness by waving at me and patting the couch next to him. "Come sit down," he says.

As I sit next to him, my muscles automatically tense from the closeness, and I silently remind myself that Killer is a nice guy I should have no issues with. But he doesn't make things any easier when he slides his arms away from Arrow and tosses one over my shoulders, giving me a little hug. He says something to me, but I'm too focused on pulling away to properly read his lips.

Jace waves to get my attention and then signs, *"Killer just asked how you slept last night."*

Is he for real? I watch Jace's expression for any hint of humor, but his face remains deadpan. I bite my lip to keep from cussing at him. What's his problem, anyway? He's all hot and cold, and I can't figure out any pattern his mood is following.

"I slept fine," I say, hoping my tone is as nonchalant as I mean for it to be. I gesture to the window, which shows tiny slats of desert through the closed shades. "Are we leaving soon?"

"No," Jace says with a shake of his head. Then he switches to sign language and quickly explains, *"We've got three vehicles out of commission. Some idiot tried to replace the oil and put it in with the antifreeze, so all the RVs and trailers are stopped while that gets fixed. But since we're so close to Albuquerque, we're going to take a car and head into the city. I've got an event I'm scheduled to attend, and the others"*—he pauses to gesture to his bandmates—*"are going to take the day off."*

I nod stiffly, knowing that my frustration will show through if I give an actual response. It makes sense that Jace isn't offering for me to join them—it's really not safe for me to leave the RV. But that doesn't stop me from feeling jealous at the thought of them hanging out in the city while I stay cooped up in here.

Killer nudges my ribs, making me flinch. As long as I'm trying to figure out Jace's issue, I'd like to know Killer's, too. What is so damn hard to understand about the no-touching concept?

"You need something to eat before we go," Killer declares. "You're skinny as a stick."

He jumps up and grabs my hand, tugging me toward the small kitchen. "Come along, sweetie," he says. "I think there are still some pancakes in the fridge, but they're some weird bran thing, so you might be poisoned. But all of Jace's cereal is bound to turn you into a raging health-hippie, so—"

I quickly lose track of his words, and I don't even try to focus on his lips after that. He's talking too fast and not looking straight at me, which makes it practically impossible to know what he's saying. But he doesn't seem to mind the fact that I'm not responding to a word he says, and he continues chattering as he runs around the kitchen retrieving a plate of pancakes for me.

I try to help him, not wanting him to have to serve me again, but he shoos me back to the counter and points at the stools. I take the hint and sit down, letting him continue his little pancake-fetching frenzy.

My stomach grumbles as he opens the microwave and pops in a huge plate of pancakes. They're dark brown and grainy-looking, and I can practically hear my taste buds sobbing over the lack of carbs and sugar. But at least I got my mac and cheese last night, so I guess I can't complain too much about eating a healthy breakfast.

Something brushes against my arm, and I turn to find Jace sitting beside me on the other stool. He's sitting so close our forearms touch, his tan skin a strange contrast against my pale freckles. His touch is a warm comfort, and as uncertain as I am of him, it feels good.

I'm not hungry anymore. My stomach knots as I stare down at our touching arms, wondering what the hell is going on. Does Jace like me? Well, yeah, if he's helping me to this extent, he has to like me at least a little. But does he *like* like me?

Ugh. I'm thinking like a third grader.

Jace rests his hand on my knee. I freeze. Part of me wants to snap at him to back off and make up his mind about how he's going to treat me. But the other part is too satisfied with his touch to bother pulling away.

Before my instincts can sort out themselves out, Killer slides the plate of pancakes in front of me, and Jace pulls away. I pick up the fork on the side of the plate and start picking at the meal, my appetite gone.

Jace walks to the refrigerator, leaving me alone at the counter. Killer quickly fills his spot, and I'm not sure if I should be relieved or resentful. I settle on relieved. It's probably a good thing Jace isn't next to me anymore, because his touch does weird things to me, and I'm getting close to . . .

To what? Falling for him? No, I'm not letting that happen. Jace is a player—a player with a very long, very public track record of breaking hearts—and I'm not going to let myself get swept up in his fleeting touches.

So why can't I take my eyes off him? I watch as he leans over and grabs a water bottle from the bottom shelf of the fridge. There's something about the way he moves that's almost hypnotic. He's all grace and power, wrapped up in a package of complete nonchalance, like he's not even trying to look hot. Which he's not, of course. He has no one to show off for in this room.

Killer nudges me in the side, making me cringe and effectively getting my attention. "So Arrow and I saw you on TV last night," he offers. "I had no idea you were planning to outdo us in the fame department."

I raise my eyebrows at Jace, hoping he'll save me by changing the subject. After all the stress of last night, I have no desire to talk about this anymore. The Amber Alert doesn't immediately change anything—traveling with Jace is still my safest option, so I'll just have to keep lying low and staying out of sight.

Jace catches my glance and pins Killer with a glare that would melt me into a puddle of shame. But Killer doesn't even react, and I get the feeling he's used to this grumpy side of Jace.

"Now really isn't the right time to be making jokes, Killer," Jace says.

Killer rolls his eyes. "You just have no sense of humor."

Before Jace can retort, Arrow strides into the kitchen. He nods to Jace and Killer, but doesn't bother acknowledging me. Jace tenses a little, and I wonder if it's because Arrow is being rude, or because he's anxious to get out of here before Killer annoys him any more.

Arrow lays his hands on Killer's shoulders, then leans over and kisses him on the cheek. "Jon's ready to go," he says. "You want to take off?"

Killer nods. "Yeah, just one sec," he says as he pulls out his phone. He quickly types out a message and tilts the screen so only I can read it:

Jace is trying to pretend he has no emotions, which is always a sure sign he's feeling too many. Sorry he's being a grump. Just give him some time. He'll eventually work up the nerve to talk about whatever's going on between you two.

I give him a grateful smile, and Killer winks before hopping down from the stool. He grabs Arrow's hand and pulls him away from the kitchen, his lips moving at the speed of light while he plans their trip into the city. As Arrow is tugged along, he looks back and flicks his gaze between Jace and me. His expression tightens with uncertainty, and he says to Jace, "Don't do anything stupid."

Jace just rolls his eyes and sticks up his middle finger. Arrow doesn't get a chance to return the gesture as Killer pulls him away from the room.

As soon as they leave, Jace turns to me and signs, *"Sorry. Arrow's still worried you're going to get the band in trouble. But he'll warm up eventually."*

I nod and try not to look too relieved. As awkward and quiet as Jace has been this morning, I was starting to wonder if he was still okay with me traveling with them. Apparently he is, but I'm also guessing that Killer is completely right. Jace isn't going to open up a discussion about last night unless he absolutely has to.

Jace sighs and rubs at his temples. "And sorry for Killer being insensitive," he says, although he looks away a little, and I get the feeling he's not apologizing for just his bandmate. "I swear he's the dumbest human being to ever get accepted into Mensa."

I try to hold back a laugh, sure that I read his lips wrong. "Mensa?"

Jace nods. "As ditsy as he acts, Killer is technically genius. Mensa is a high-IQ society he tested into."

"Yeah, I know what it is. I was—" I snap my mouth shut, cutting off the words about to emerge. Because none of that matters anymore. My life as a musical genius is done, over, finished, kaput. And there's no going back.

Jace leans against the counter and cocks his head. "You were . . . ?"

I sigh, realizing it's too late and I'm going to have to give him an answer. "I was in Mensa."

"Isn't it like a lifelong thing? Like, once you're in, you stay in?"

I shrug. "Yeah. I guess."

"So shouldn't you say you're in it, not you *were* in it?"

"Why are you suddenly so interested in grammar tenses?"

He holds up his hands, as if warding off my sharp tone. Then he signs, *"It's just, most people like to brag about that stuff. And you're not. I'm just wondering why."*

"I don't really belong in it anymore," I sign.

He raises a skeptical eyebrow. *"Why not? Did you get a bad grade or something?"*

"Just drop it, okay?"

Jace nods. Apparently, he's one of the few people in the world who can actually drop a subject, because he snags his water bottle off the counter and starts walking out of the room. He pauses at the exit to sign, *"I'm heading out to a local studio for the day. They're doing some promo thing, and I'm supposed to be their poster boy. You stay here and lie low, okay?"*

He looks a little hesitant, and I wonder what he's worried about. *"Sure,"* I reply.

He flashes me a quick smile, which makes my stomach do one of those little butterfly-dances. I quickly look away, knowing I'm about to blush and not wanting him to see my reaction. Jace just waves at me and quickly signs, *"Catch you later."* Then he walks out of the kitchen, and a few moments later, I feel vibrations run through the RV as the front door closes behind him.

My stomach finally quits its tap dancing, but I decide to give up on breakfast. I toss the last of my pancakes and clean up my plate—along with the syrupy mess Killer made on the counter—and then pad into the living area. It's empty, so I assume Jon left with the others.

I let out a long breath and collapse on the couch, and something hard pokes at my scalp. I snatch up the pillow and find a notebook that looks just like the kind I use at school. On the marble-print cover, someone has scrawled in messy handwriting, THE PERFECT SONG.

I know it'd be rude to read it, but I'm more than a little curious. I like most of Tone Deaf's lyrics, and if they have a perfect song . . . ? Well, it might be worth being caught snooping to read some perfect lyrics.

I peer around, making sure no one else is in the RV, and crack open the notebook. When no alarms go off, I flip to its first page. There's a little printed box that says, *This notebook belongs to . . .* In scrawled handwriting, the line under it reads, *Jace B.*

I turn to the second page, which is wide-ruled and smudged with pencil lead and eraser marks. Lyrics fill the page, one song repeated over and over again, with little tweaks on every line. Sometimes there's a different starting sentence, sometimes a different ending word, sometimes different musical notes scribbled above the lyrics. That one song goes on and on, filling almost the whole notebook. I watch as Jace's handwriting slowly grows different, changing from boyish scrawling to the nearly illegible mess of a professional writer. It's clear he has been working on this one song for years.

I brush my fingertips over the last page with writing, which is filled with pen smudges and crossed out sections. The lyrics on this page are very similar to the ones from a few pages back, so Jace must be pretty happy with how they turned out. But the pattern of musical notes above the words keeps changing, and I read the line closest to the bottom of the page:

AADDCFG

That doesn't sound right. But it sounds . . . *close*. Not quite perfect, but not far away.

I strain my memory, trying to remember the sound of each note and how they work together to create harmonies. It's been so long since I thought about music in this way, and I wait for the bad memories to come crashing down. Memories of the surgery, of the accident, of the loss.

But, instead, there's just *now*. I'm stuck in the present with familiar adrenaline racing through me as the notes play song after song inside my head, trying to find the patterns they like best. I'm not sure how long I sit there, just staring at the page, struggling to figure out this puzzle with no solid answer.

Then it hits me. Not really an answer, but a solution that just might work. Before I can stop myself, I grab a pen from the small stand next to the couch and start scribbling.

21

JACE

I WANT TO punch something. Hard. The studio that hired me as Mr. Promo Boy ended up being a dinky little place with a broken AC and a jackass manager. I spend the entire day in the sweltering Albuquerque heat, sweating through my T-shirt and forcing smiles for all the fans that showed up. Add that to the guilt I feel over leaving Ali alone all day, and my frustration is ready to boil over. I swear, if I hear one more squeal come out of the mouth of a teenage girl, I'm going to dissolve Tone Deaf and move to a secluded island.

I shove open the door to the RV and take a deep breath as a blast of cold air hits me. "Ali?" I call out, and then roll my eyes at myself for forgetting she can't hear.

Despite that, I can't help the nervousness that runs through me when she doesn't respond. After seeing the sheer panic in her eyes last night, I didn't want to leave her today. I wanted to spend the day with her, apologizing for not being there when she woke up in the morning, making sure she was okay, and assuring her that she'd make it safely to NYC. I wanted to spend the day . . . *with her.*

As I walk toward the living area, I hear a scratching and a low whine come from my bedroom. Poor Cuddles. My dog is going to disown me if I keep locking her up like this.

Cuddles lets out another whine, but I don't hear anything else as I head toward the couches. The TV is flicked on, with no volume coming out of the sound system and subtitles flitting past on the bottom of the screen. Ali has changed the channel away from the news station, so now it's tuned to some boring cooking show.

She's curled up on the couch, her head tucked close to her knees. She breathes softly, and I watch her chest rise and fall for a long moment, making sure she's not hyperventilating like she was last night. I cringe as I think of her nightmare; her expression had looked so freaking terrified. How could I not have stayed close to her afterward? I mean, maybe the whole cuddling thing wasn't necessary, but it's not like I could have left her.

I back up a few steps, figuring it's best to leave Ali alone so she can rest. Besides, Cuddles needs a walk, and it's not like she can go out by herself.

As I leave the living area, I glance back one more time at Ali. She shifts slightly in her sleep, letting out a tiny whimper, and the sound is like a shard of glass trapped in my chest. Is she having another nightmare? Maybe I should wake her up. I don't want her to have a freak-out episode while I'm gone.

I walk over to her, but as I reach out to shake her shoulder, I notice the notebook. *My* notebook. I let out a loud curse as I see it sitting on the armrest next to Ali's head. It's open, and I didn't leave it that way.

No one reads my notebook. Ever. Never, never, *ever*.

I snatch up the notebook, holding it protectively against my chest and wishing it would stanch the pain blooming there. It feels like a part of me has been ripped away and destroyed. That song was mine. *Mine.* I swore not to share it until it was perfect, and it was so close.

Now it's ruined.

Then I notice the pen marks scratched across the page. What was she thinking? Doodling in my notebook, on the same page I was writing my almost-complete lyrics? That's just *wrong*.

I peer down at the notebook, wondering what the hell could be so important that Ali felt the need to draw it on my lyrics. What I see . . . they're not doodles. They're letters and words, musical notes and lyrics. I blink a few times, wondering if maybe I wrote this last night and just don't remember doing it. But, no, the handwriting is curly and neat, the cute sort that belongs to a girl. It's the first half of my song, but it's definitely not my handwriting.

I think back to what she told me when I first met her: *"I used to play."* I'd just assumed she was messing around, but she must have been telling the truth.

I shake my head and hesitantly trail my finger down the blue lines of the notebook, reading the song our words have combined to create:

Close Your Eyes

When clarity's gone and logic is done and love flees out the doorway,
When kisses hurt and your heart is cursed and so carelessly cast away,
When life's tumbling down, down, down,
And nothing's there when you look up,
Except the innocence you let life corrupt.

Just close your eyes,
Feel my hand in yours and know you're alive,
Just close your eyes,
Feel my lips on yours and know you'll survive,
Oh, close your eyes,
And in the darkness of the hour,
Know that I'll be here forever,
Forever yours,
I'll never go.

I'm not sure how long I stand there staring down at the notebook, reading her lyrics over and over again. In my head, I hear the notes she's neatly written above the words, and they flow together seamlessly. They're complex but effortless, in a haunting sort of way. Ali has only written adjustments for the beginning half of the lyrics, but it still feels like the closest my song has ever been to completion.

I glance around the room, looking for my guitar. I'm desperate to try out these lyrics, so I can see if they're as good as they sound in my head. I hear a slight rustling and look down to find Ali peering sleepily up at me. Her eyes grow wide as she sees the notebook in my hand, and she looks like a kid with her hand caught in a cookie jar. She blushes, making her freckles pop.

"Hey," she signs uncertainly.

I set down the notebook next to her and sign back, *"Hey. I read your adjustments."*

She looks down and purses her lips. *"Sorry. I really didn't mean to write that much. I kind of got carried away."*

"Yeah. I can tell."

By the way she presses back against the couch, I can tell she's trying to disappear, like she's expecting me to be pissed. Which I *should* be. And I was. But I can't bring myself to be upset anymore, not when my song is finally starting to sound right.

I kneel next to the couch and tilt her chin up, so we're eye-to-eye. *"You weren't lying when you said you played, were you?"*

She shakes her head. *"I played piano for years."*

"And you still haven't forgotten how music sounds?"

A small, sad smile plays at the corners of her lips. *"I'll never forget."* She hesitantly tilts her head up until she's directly looking at me. I take in her hazel eyes, which are so beautiful, so pained.

"How did you end up like this?" I gesture to the notebook. *"This is brilliant, Ali. Freaking brilliant. You've got talent, and you say you belong in Mensa, so . . . what happened?"*

Her expression wavers between hurt and anger, and she swallows hard, like she's trying to gulp back painful memories. "*I started playing when I was three. My mom inherited this old piano, and I just sat down one day and banged around on it until I figured out how to play 'Twinkle Twinkle Little Star.' I had perfect pitch, so I could replicate pretty much any song I heard.*"

I raise an eyebrow in surprise, but don't say anything. I don't want to interrupt her.

She takes a shaky breath and says, "When I was about four, my mom enrolled me in lessons. We were totally broke, but I loved playing, and she didn't want to keep me from my passion. She was the best mom ever. I mean, she gave up so much for me, and . . ."

She clears her throat and shakes her head, like she's trying to shoo away the past. She sits a little taller and continues. "My instructor called me a prodigy the moment he saw me first play. He had me get an IQ test, and I scored within the ninety-ninth percentile. I was admitted into Mensa, and from there, things just took off.

"I started with little performances, but I quickly started getting into larger venues. People were interested in seeing someone as young as me perform. Within a few years, I managed to get invited to play at Carnegie with a group of other students who were considered prodigies. After that, I could pretty much get into any venue I wanted."

She's breathing fast now, like the memories are starting to overwhelm her. Without thinking, I slip my hand into hers. Ali jumps, startled by the contact, but she doesn't pull away. I've never noticed it before, but she has the hands of a musician—wide palms and long, delicate fingers.

"I loved it. And my mom was awesome about the whole thing," Ali murmurs as she runs her thumb over the back of my hand. "I mean, she could have exploited me to make money. But she only let me perform when I wanted to, and she made sure I also focused on things like school and Girl Scouts. You know, normal stuff for kids. She didn't want me getting a big head."

A long moment passes, and she doesn't say anything else.

"What happened?" I ask again.

"Right about the time I turned ten, I started getting really bad headaches," Ali murmurs. "My doctors figured out I had a brain tumor. It was benign and not all that dangerous, but it was right against my temporal lobe—the part of the brain that lets people hear.

"If it got any bigger, it would have destroyed my hearing, and my mom didn't want that to happen. We didn't have insurance, but she still decided to pay for an operation to have it removed right away."

I hold her hand tighter, silently encouraging her to finish the story.

Ali takes another deep breath and then says, "When I woke up from the surgery, I couldn't hear a thing. Ends up, the tumor was worse than they'd thought. They had to cut away part of my brain to get it all out. Chances are, the tumor will never come back, but the surgery left me permanently deaf."

A tear slips down her cheek, and she quickly brushes it away. "A nurse wrote all this down for me to explain what had happened. All I remember is sobbing, and thinking how creepy it was that I couldn't hear my own crying. I just kept asking for my mom, but she wasn't there."

"She left you?" I say, trying not to show my surprise.

"No," Ali says, shaking her head fiercely. "It wasn't her fault. She was so stressed about my surgery, and she'd barely gotten any sleep, and . . ." Another tear escapes, and this time Ali's hand trembles as she scrubs it away. "There was a café right down the street from the hospital, and my mom walked there to get some coffee. A drunk driver hit her. It was a freak accident, but by the time my surgery was over, she was in critical condition.

"My mom was in a coma for a couple of weeks after that, and then she died, and . . . well, you know the rest. I was sent to live with my dad. And here I am now."

I shake my head, having no idea what to say. How the hell am I supposed to reply to that kind of story? Saying sorry doesn't cut it.

Ali shakes her head just the tiniest bit. "Sometimes, I still want to blame myself for it. If I hadn't needed that surgery, my mom never would have been on that street, and she never would have gotten hit."

You can't believe that, I quickly sign. *Fate's a bitch, but that's not your fault. And I think that if your mom had to die, that's probably exactly how she would have wanted to go. Taking care of you. Loving you.*

A fresh flood of tears trickles down her cheeks, but she doesn't break eye contact with me as she signs, *You know, you're the first person to ever tell me that.*

I clear my throat uncertainly.

"So," she says slowly, "did I answer your question?"

"Yeah."

"Are you regretting asking?"

"I don't know." I leave it at that, unsure how to say the rest of what's going through my mind: that it's thrilling to finally understand her better. But, at the same time, I'm hurting from the pain I imagine she feels every day.

Ali lets her gaze wander to the notebook I dropped next to her. She stares at it for a long moment, and her smile takes on a slightly impish look. "So did you like my adjustments?"

I cup her face in both my hands, stroking my thumb over her cheek. For once, she doesn't pull away, and I swear the pain fades from her eyes. Now there's a gentleness in her expression, timid and hesitant, but trusting. She's let her guard down because of me. Maybe even *for* me.

I lean forward, until the gap between us is closed, and press my lips against hers.

At first she freezes, unsure how to react to my kiss. But then she kisses me back. Her lips are soft and delicate, but there's a strength to her kiss that surprises me and makes me want more. More of the kiss, more of her lips, more of Ali.

I twine my fingers in her hair and gently press her closer. I half expect her to pull away, but instead she reaches out and wraps her arms around my neck. Her skin is warm and smooth against mine.

Our kiss seems to last forever, but I'm still not satisfied when I pull back. I rest my forehead against hers and smile at her, brushing a strand of hair out of her face. She smiles back, the kind of smile that says she's happy. Not just satisfied, not just content, but *happy*. She quietly murmurs, "Can I assume that means you liked the changes I made?"

I pull her close to my chest, so that our hearts are pressed against each other, and I can feel the rapid pattering of her heartbeat. Her breath is warm against my collarbone, and her fingers trace the edge of my scar.

"They're perfect," I whisper in her ear. I kiss her forehead and then pull away a little so I can sign, *"Absolutely perfect."*

22

JACE

KILLER COMES BOUNDING into the RV shortly after Ali drifts off to sleep. I'm a little worried about her sleeping so much, but I guess it's to be expected. She probably hasn't gotten a full night's sleep in years, not if she's been living in an abusive home. I still remember trying to force myself into fitful sleep, holding my breath as I listened for any sign that my dad had woken up from his drug-induced stupor. And then there was the first time I spent the night at Killer's place—I'd slept for fifteen hours straight, and had only woken up when Killer tried taking my pulse to make sure I wasn't in a coma.

"Dude!" Killer says as he comes skidding to a stop in front of me. "Seriously, what is *wrong* with you?"

I pull Ali's sleeping form a little closer. What's his problem? If anyone needs to be more discreet, it's him and Arrow.

I open my mouth to say this, but then I realize Killer isn't talking about Ali. He's pointing to my mouth and gaping at me with an exaggerated expression of shock. Typical Killer.

"What?" I mutter, even though I know exactly why he's surprised.

"You're actually *smiling*. Do I need to call 9-1-1 or something? You're not going to drop dead on me, are you?"

"You don't need to act so damn shocked," I say. "It's not like you haven't seen me smile before."

He ignores me and points excitedly at Ali's sleeping form. "Are you two together now?"

I nod and brace myself for the wave of uneasiness I'm sure is about to hit me. I'm not the type to "be" with a girl, at least not for longer than one night. Being with someone means handing my emotions over to them, and that never ends prettily.

But the uneasiness doesn't come. As hesitant as I am to believe it, I think a relationship with Ali might actually be worth the potential pain.

Holy shit. Did I just use the "r" word?

Ali stirs in my arms and nuzzles closer to me in her sleep, a soft smile on her mouth. I trail my fingertip along her full lips, tracing the contours of her smile. I've had hundreds, probably even thousands, of girls flash me smiles. But none of them have been as pretty as Ali's. Hers is hesitant, like she isn't used to happiness, and it's hard not to share her good mood when I know I'm the reason for the gentle expression.

The RV door opens and slams shut, and Arrow walks into the room. The second he sees Ali curled up in my arms, his expression darkens. I instinctively tighten my grasp on her.

He shakes his head in disbelief. "What . . . ?"

"Don't even start," I snap.

He throws his hands up in defeat and sits right next to Killer on the other couch. "I'm just saying—"

"That they're absolutely adorable together!" Killer interrupts, clapping his hands together excitedly.

I raise an eyebrow at Arrow. "You let Killer have caffeine, didn't you?"

"Two mochas," Arrow admits with a grimace. Then he points back at Ali. "But we're talking about your mistake, not mine."

"She's not any kind of mistake, Arrow," I say, doing my best to keep my tone calm. I'm pretty sure I fail, because his eyes narrow a little.

"I'm just saying this is happening awfully fast," Arrow says.

"It's not like this is random," I argue. "I've been around her constantly for a full week."

"Which is much longer than he knows most girls," Killer chirps.

I ignore him and continue, "Plus, I'm not sleeping with her or anything."

Killer nods enthusiastically. "Which just shows how special this one is."

I grit my teeth and shoot Killer a glare. "Dude, you're not helping."

He holds his hands up in an innocent gesture, but the smirk on his lips tells the real story. I flip him off and then say to Arrow, "You have no reason to not like her."

"No reason?" Arrow runs a hand through his shaggy hair and shakes his head. "Jace, you're being delusional. I mean, taking her in is one thing, but being in a *relationship* with her? That's practically begging for the cops to accuse you of kidnapping, or worse."

"I've already told you, I don't care."

"Clearly," Arrow says with a scoff. "If you cared, you'd stay away from her."

"Not everything in my life has to revolve around the band," I snap.

"I'm not talking about the band. I'm talking about Ali. I think we all know you're not healthy for her. Hell, you're not healthy for *any* girl."

I open my mouth, waiting for a retort to come springing out. But there's only my stunned silence. He's right. Of course I'm not healthy for her, and of course Arrow is so annoyingly, stupidly *right*.

But it's still not enough to make me give her up. "I can change," I say slowly, finally finding my voice. "I can figure out how to make a relationship work. But I'm not changing the fact that we're together. So get over it, Arrow. Either that, or get out of here."

"I already told you I'm not just going to leave you," Arrow says with a sigh.

"I know."

He points an accusing finger at me. "Then don't make me do anything I regret, okay? I've already promised that I'll stand by you for this, but if you hurt that girl or the band, it's over."

"What's over?"

"Everything," Arrow says. "You walk a fine line between jackass and unredeemable, and if you cross that line, I'm not going to put up with you anymore."

My eyes widen. Is he actually threatening to ditch? To leave the band, leave our careers, leave *me*? I glance down at Ali, and for a brief moment, I wonder if she's worth all of this. Then I shake my head and grit my teeth.

"I understand."

Arrow gives a short nod. "Good." With that, he lets out a tired sigh and throws an arm over his boyfriend's shoulders.

There's a long, awkward silence. Then Killer hesitantly asks, "Does this mean we get to double-date?"

Arrow and I manage to stretch out the silence about three more seconds, as we stare incredulously at Killer. Then Arrow bursts out laughing, and even I can't help but chuckle a little. Trust Killer to take *that* away from our conversation. I shake my head at my bandmate, wishing I could be as carefree as he is.

But then who would worry about Ali?

23

ALI

I SPEND MOST of the next day hiding out in the RV's living area. With all the vehicles back in commission, Tone Deaf's caravan travels into Albuquerque in the morning and gets settled at the stadium they'll be performing at. They were supposed to have a rehearsal of the concert yesterday, but thanks to the traveling delays, it didn't happen.

Which means Jace and other members of the crew have been scrambling around all afternoon, squeezing in a rehearsal and last-minute equipment checks before their concert tonight. The room with the couches is the comfiest spot around, so I hang out in there and just try to keep out of sight and out of the way. I fill the morning by working on Jace's social media profiles, updating his links and answering a few fan messages. But then I notice a tweet linking to a news article about my disappearance, and I quickly close out of the browser, not even wanting to think about all the people searching for me. I find a blank notebook to distract myself with and spend the afternoon sketching the cityscape outside the window.

Around four o'clock, Jace comes into the RV carrying a bag of Chinese takeout in one hand and his guitar in the other. I join him in the kitchen and scarf down a plate of orange chicken and noodles. Jace doesn't say much, and he only picks at his vegetable stir-fry before he grabs his guitar and starts practicing chords. He's clearly nervous, which is kind of cute. Here he is, the lead singer of a renowned band, and he still gets stage fright before concerts.

"You should eat more," I sign, pointing to his plate.

He strums his guitar, his long fingers finding a chord with casual precision. "I'm not hungry."

"Then you should at least rest before the concert," I sign. *"You look like hell."*

A smirk lifts his lips, although his expression remains haggard and stressed. "How is it that I ended up with the one girl in the world who thinks I look like hell?"

"Because you value honesty in a relationship," I sign, giving him an overly sweet smile.

He sticks his tongue out at me, but finally puts down the guitar. With a flick of his hand, he gestures for me to follow him as he heads for the living area. *"Come on,"* he signs. *"We could both use a nap."*

"I've been resting all day."

"And it's clearly given you way too much time to worry about me. I'm fine. I just always get nerves before I perform. But if you really want to make me feel better, come take a nap with me."

I give a relenting sigh and trail after him into the living area. I pause by the couch, but he grabs my hand and tugs me toward his bedroom. A flare of panic rises in my chest, and I try to calm it by taking a deep breath. I place my hands on my hips and do my best to put on a fierce expression. Jace's smirk tells me that I fail miserably.

"I'm not having sex with you," I snap.

He holds up his hands innocently. Then he quickly signs, *"I wasn't expecting you to."*

I cross my arms over my chest. "You're trying to lead me into your bedroom."

"I wasn't going to make you nap on the couch. Believe it or not, I'm a big boy, and sometimes I actually share things. Like my bed." I give him an accusing look and he chuckles, a mischievous glint showing in his pale eyes. *"I can share a bed without having sex."*

If I've learned anything about Jace in the short span I've known him, it's that he's honest. Probably too honest for his own good. And he gave me no reason not to trust him when we slept together on the couch, so I take his hand as he offers it to me again. He keeps his grasp gentle as he leads me into the back, and I'm struck again by the unique smell of his bedroom—faint cologne and wood varnish. I decide I kind of like it.

Jace leads me over to the bed. It's been made, but judging by the way the blankets are all rumpled in the corners, I have a feeling it usually isn't. Which is actually a little surprising, considering how pristine the rest of the RV is. Actually, now that I take the time to really look around, I realize there are a lot of things different about this room. It's pretty messy, with dirty clothes kicked into the corner, and his nightstand littered with notebooks and novels.

Jace has a stack of mystery books there, and I almost laugh as I notice a sci-fi novel resting next to them. Killer must be rubbing off on Jace more than he thinks. Under the sci-fi book is a romance novel, which makes my eyebrows raise. Jace rolls his eyes again and tugs me onto the bed, where we both sit on the edge.

"Romance books?" I sign, unable to keep an amused smile from my lips.

He blushes. Actually *blushes*. I laugh a little as I watch his cheeks redden. *"They're good for songwriting,"* he explains. *"Popular songs are all about romance, and I kind of fail in that arena. So I try to learn from books."*

I gently kiss his cheek. *"You don't always fail."*

He shrugs, like he isn't sure how to respond to that, and I lean into his warm shoulder and close my eyes. His arms wrap around my waist, and for a moment, I'm able to pretend that everything is okay. That I'm not on the run, that I don't have to be scared of my dad, that my hearing is still intact and my mom is still alive.

He lies down on the bed and tugs me down too, so I'm lying beside him. I rest my head on his chest, and he gently strokes my hair, lulling me close to sleep. Just as I'm about to drift off, I feel warm breath and vibrations close to my ear. I open my eyes and look up, finding Jace smiling down at me sheepishly.

"Did you say something?" I ask.

He nibbles at his lip, clearly debating whether or not to repeat what he'd said. "I said you're beautiful."

I blush, and he laughs gently. I think back to the first time I watched him laugh, and how contemptuous and angry it had felt. Now it just seems . . . happy. I smile as he brushes his thumbs over my reddened cheeks.

"You're so freaking adorable when you blush." Before I can come up with any kind of response, he gently kisses the tip of my nose and presses his forehead against mine. "But I really should leave soon. Tired or not, my concert is going to start in just a couple hours."

I bite my lip to keep from frowning. Jace tips my chin up and brushes his lips against mine, not quite a kiss, but teasingly close. And suddenly I feel sad.

"What's the matter?" he asks.

"Nothing," I mutter, even though it's not true. Knowing I'm going to be alone all evening makes me feel just a tiny bit lonely, which reminds me that as soon as I get to New York, I'll be completely on my own. And, hell, I've survived for years with hardly anyone to lean on. I know I can do it. But now that I have a glimpse into a life that isn't so lonely, I don't *want* to do it.

He gently traces my frown with his fingertip. "That doesn't look like nothing."

I sigh and shake my head. "It's just . . . I'm going to miss you when we get to New York. That's all."

"Who says I'm going to leave you?" he asks.

My eyes widen. Could he actually plan on having me around for longer than just the tour? I mean, it will never work out, but still . . . that's sweet. Probably the sweetest thing anyone has ever said to me.

"Thank you," I murmur, unsure what else to say.

"You don't have to thank me. I *want* to be with you."

My cheeks flush a little, but I can't stop myself from smiling. I reach up and run a hand through his hair, messing up his fauxhawk. He leans in a little closer, and I take the opportunity to kiss him.

His lips are firm and warm against mine, and he holds my face gently in his hands. This close to him, I can smell his sharp cologne and the woodsy scent that clings to his skin. He runs a hand through my hair, pressing me closer to him and intensifying the kiss.

After a long minute, Jace pulls away and gently strokes my cheek. *"If I don't leave now, someone is going to come looking for me, and they might find you."*

All the warmth rushes from my body, leaving cold nervousness. In Jace's arms, it's easy to believe I'm safe. But his words bring reality crashing back down—I'm still thousands of miles from New York and a long way off from being truly safe at all.

Jace frowns at my nervous expression and wraps his arms back around me. His hand rubs soft circles against the small of my back, and I close my eyes, leaning into him.

I stay there for a moment, but then pull away to sign, *"What do I do if someone does find me?"*

He lets out a long, slow breath as he considers this. Then he presses a gentle kiss against my forehead and signs, *"We've worked well together getting you away from your dad. So if someone tries to force you to go back, we'll deal with it the same way. Together."*

24

JACE

WHEN I FINALLY make it backstage, I'm swarmed by the stage crew. The rest of the band is already onstage waiting for me, and the crew buzzes around frantically, speed-talking through last-minute prep. I was planning on actually being on time for once, but I couldn't bring myself to leave Ali. Usually, concerts turn me into a ball of energy and nerves, and I'm always anxious to jump onstage. But I would have preferred to spend this evening with Ali, who was peacefully dozing by the time I left.

The stage crew is officially freaking out as they recite instructions I already know by heart. Once I have all my mics set up and my guitar in hand, they all stop panicking and direct me toward the stage. Tony is waiting for me by the steps. He rushes forward and grabs both my shoulders in a vise-like grip, and I quickly shrug his hands off, shooting him an impatient glare. He pins me with a similar expression, but lowers his hands to his sides.

"You're forty-eight minutes late," he snaps. Tony gestures toward the front of the stage, where the rest of the band waits with all our equipment. Killer catches sight of me and waves. I don't wave back.

"I got sidetracked," I say, and start making my way toward the stage.

Tony walks beside me, his footsteps heavier than usual. "Jace, you can't be late to your own concert."

"I always am."

"Yeah, five or ten minutes. This is different. You kept fans waiting for almost an hour. People are getting restless, and it's your fault. Some people have already left."

"Then they're not true fans, and I don't need them."

I jog toward the steps leading to the stage. Before I reach them, Tony grabs my arm and yanks on it, stopping me. I curse and whirl toward him, my fists automatically clenching. He backs away a step, but his tone is sharp as he says, "Those people out there are your livelihood. And not just yours, but all of ours. Don't screw things up."

"I won't."

"You already are. You haven't been acting like yourself lately, Jace. Something's off, and I want to know what."

"Nothing. Everything's fine."

"The manager at that studio called to complain that you left early yesterday. He said you were rude to fans, which doesn't surprise me, but he also said you ignored them. Since when do you ignore people? And then there's that poor deaf girl you flipped off the other day."

That poor deaf girl. I flinch at the memory. Flipping off Ali definitely qualifies me for the Jackass of the Year Award. If I'd just known what she was really like . . .

No, that's not an excuse. I never should have treated her that way. Period.

Tony doesn't seem to notice that I haven't given a response and continues his rant. "That, plus you've been holed up in your RV all the time, and you're acting all secretive." He steps toward me, until his face is right in mine, and says in a softer voice, "If you're hooked on something, let me help. Please."

What the hell? He thinks I'm on drugs? *Me?* I shake my head, unable to form any words, and kind of glad I can't. I'd just say something I'll regret. But does Tony *really* think I'd follow in the footsteps of my dad? Tony knows I'm far from angelic, but I thought he also believed I'm not a monster.

Tony takes my silence as an answer—the wrong type, of course. He looks down and shakes his head, and for some reason, that hurts. Even as he glances back up and forces a small smile, the pain stays. I've obviously disappointed him, and . . . and, dammit, I don't *want* to disappoint him. For once in my life, I want someone to be proud of me. I want for them to tell me that I'm a good guy, that I do the right things, that . . .

. . . that I deserve Ali.

Tony pushes his glasses back into place and puts on his usual businesslike expression. "We'll talk later. Okay? For now, you've got a show to put on."

I nod tightly and walk up the steps to the darkened stage, stomping a little harder than I need to. At the sound of my footsteps, Arrow turns and shoots me a glare. But I pick up on the concerned edge to his expression, which is the only reason I don't explode right then and there.

Jon raises his eyebrows at me, and from behind his drum set, he mouths, "It's about time."

I flip him off and stride over to the microphone at the center of the stage. Usually, this is the part when my adrenaline takes over, and everything hazes out into a blur of raw energy and music and applause. Today is different. My thoughts are still back in the RV and concentrated on Ali. That's where I want to be—relaxing alone with her, not putting on a show for strangers.

But I'm here, and there's not much I can do to change that. I'm about to cue the beginning of the show, when Killer jumps up from behind his keyboard and rushes over to me, an anxious look on his face. I open my mouth to tell him to mind his own business, but he cuts me off by whispering, "Is Ali okay? You look worried."

I try not to show my shock. He seems genuinely concerned about her, and in any other situation, I probably would have thanked him. But I give him a warning glare, nodding to the small mic clipped to his shirt. He taps it and shakes his head. "It's off."

Letting out a long breath, I quickly double-check that my own mic is off and murmur, "She's fine. Um . . . thanks for asking."

His usual grin springs back onto his lips. "Great. And, yeah, no problem." With that, he runs back to his keyboard, but not before stopping to give Arrow a kiss on the cheek. Arrow playfully swats at him and "accidentally" smacks his butt, which results in Killer laughing and tackle-hugging his boyfriend.

I hold my hand up briefly, giving the cue for the show to begin. The main lights come on, fully illuminating the stage and revealing us to hundreds of waiting Tone Deaf fans. They scream in excitement, and only grow louder as Killer throws his arms around Arrow's neck and kisses him fully on the lips. Applause and whistling breaks out, and Killer finally pulls away, laughing from the excitement and adrenaline. Arrow grins like a maniac, and I roll my eyes at them, shooting Killer an exasperated look.

"All right, all right," he mouths to me. As Killer retreats back to his keyboard, the crowd slowly quiets. I switch on my mic and plaster a smile on my face, but it doesn't feel right. I've always felt happiest onstage, having hundreds of people watching me and knowing they're here for my music.

But now I'd rather be with Ali. She might not be able to fully appreciate my music the way others do, but she appreciates me. I'd always thought those were the same thing, but as I fight off the longing to ditch the concert and spend the evening with Ali, I realize how much more precious her offering is.

I force in a deep breath, exhaling it slowly so it doesn't cause static in the mic. Then I force my smile to grow and look up at the crowd in front of me. "Good evening, ladies and gents!" I call out. There's a resounding response as the crowd breaks out in cheering and screaming. I strum my guitar, effectively quieting them. "My name is Jace Beckett, my band is Tone Deaf, and tonight we'll be performing just for *you*."

The crowd erupts in excited applause, and my smile feels a little less fake as the sound washes over me. My heart starts pounding, just like it always does during a performance, and adrenaline spreads through my body. I strum my guitar again and then pick delicately at the strings, sending music surging out the stereo system. It surrounds me, fills me, envelops me.

Just like that, the music and I are one, and the show begins.

25

ALI

I PAD DOWN the short hallway, using one hand to rub sleep out of my eyes and the other to rub my cramped neck. After I woke up from my nap last night, I tried staying awake until Jace came back from his concert, but I gave up around three in the morning and crashed on the couch. It didn't quite seem right to sleep in Jace's bed without him there, but now I'm regretting the couch. My neck muscles feel like someone's wrung them out.

I'm not really sure where Jace went to—he's probably with one of the other band members, or maybe still out partying. That's what rock stars do after a performance, right? They party wildly? It's strange thinking of Jace doing that—he's so tightly wound, I can't picture him at a party at all.

I jump in surprise as I step into the kitchen and find I'm not alone. Jace leans against the counter, munching on a toaster waffle as he peers down at his smartphone. I have no idea when he got back, although it was probably pretty recently, because his eyes are bleary and dark with exhaustion. But he must be in a good mood if he's willing to eat something as unhealthy as a waffle, even though I'm sure it's whole-grain and low-fat.

Jace waves at me with the hand holding the waffle, takes a bite out of his breakfast, and then goes back to typing on his phone. His hair flops into his face, and as he brushes it away, I realize with a touch of surprise that this is the first time I've seen his hair unstyled. Usually, it's in that fauxhawk, but now it hangs loosely around his face. It's kind of cute like this, with the dyed tips almost reaching his chin.

The smartphone is the same one I've seen him with before, only now it has a bright-pink case. Huh. I didn't take Jace to be a pink guy.

Jace types for a couple more seconds and then winks. "Catch," he mouths, and tosses the phone to me. A yelp strains my throat, and I hastily snatch the phone out of the air right before it hits the ground. I glare at Jace, showing him the full brunt of my annoyance. What if I'd dropped the thing? There's no way in hell I could ever pay him back.

Then I notice the phone has little purple present bows stuck all over the back of it. I blink a few times, sure that they're going to disappear any second. They don't. Flipping it over, I glance at the screen and find that it's open to the contacts page. There are only five programmed in: Arrow Beckett, Jace Beckett,

Kilimanjaro Johnson, and Jon McKinley. My breath catches as I read the fifth entry: Avery Summers.

Clutching the phone to my chest, I turn to Jace. "This is . . . for me?"

He smiles, and it's an unrestrained expression that wipes the tiredness straight off his face. *"Killer grabbed it for you on his day off. We don't want you to have to strain to lip-read all the time, so we figured this would make things easier. I was just programming in the numbers you'll need. You'll have to add in Avery's yourself, but I'm guessing you probably have it memorized, anyway."*

I nod dumbly. "Thank you." There are probably a dozen other things I could say, but none of them could even begin to express my relief and gratitude, so I don't even try. I miss Avery more than I ever imagined, and my fingers are already itching to send her a text message.

Jace chuckles at my expression and signs, *"I'm glad you like it."*

I rush over to him and throw my arms around his neck. As always, he stiffens at first, and it takes a moment for him to relax. When he finally does, he hugs me back, pressing me close to his chest. He kisses my forehead and smiles at me.

I blush and look down. Again. That seems to be my unconscious reaction to anything sweet Jace does—blush and look away. I wonder if I'll ever break that habit.

Jace tips my chin up—his own habit—and gently strokes my cheek with the back of his hand. "I'm leaving again today," he murmurs, but he's staring right into my eyes and doesn't seem all that focused on his words or our conversation.

I take it as a chance to more closely examine his eyes. I think they're really the only gorgeous part of him—the rest of him is handsome and masculine. But his eyes are so expressive, and with his thick lashes framing them, they're beautiful in the best of ways.

I lean into Jace and press my cheek against his soft cotton shirt, realizing I have a conversation to finish. "Where are you going?"

"*Some local music festival that's happening downtown. Arrow and Killer wanted to check it out, and I said I'd come.*"

Vibrations run through the floor, and I glance down the hallway to see who it is. Killer waves as he approaches us, his typical dorky grin on his face. "You like it?" he asks, pointing to the phone still in my hand.

I return the grin. "I love it."

Killer pulls me away from Jace and into a tight hug. I feel slight vibrations in his chest as he chatters away, but as usual, he doesn't seem to notice or care that I can't read his lips while smushed against him. He finally releases me and holds me at arm's length.

"Sorry you can't come with us today," he says. "You must be going crazy being cooped up in here."

I hold up the phone. "I've got this to keep me entertained. I'll be fine."

Jace raises his hands and signs, "*I put my personal cell number in your contacts, so if anything happens while we're gone, just call.*"

"Thanks," I sign. "*But I'll make sure nothing happens. I'm just going to keep lying low.*"

Jace nods and offers an encouraging smile. *"I'm sure you'll be fine. No one should come in here while I'm gone."*

Killer glances between us, a perplexed look on his face. He looks kind of like a lost puppy dog, with his head tilted to the side and his brows furrowed in confusion.

"You guys are making me feel left out with all this code talk," he says.

"It's not code," I protest. "It's ASL."

"You've got a freaking code name for it. How is that not code?" Despite his words, there's an amused glint in his eyes, and I know he's just teasing.

Reaching up, I feel the smile on my lips and try not to show my surprise. I haven't smiled this much in years. For just a moment, part of me tries to believe that everyone was right when they said I was crazy, and that Jace and Tone Deaf and my escape are all part of some hallucination. But the other part of me knows that can't be right—this kind of happy doesn't come from any sort of delusion.

I hold up my new smartphone. "So . . . do you think it'd be safe to text Avery?"

It's been a full week since I left, which should mean it's safe to contact her directly. I'm sure my dad has already questioned her, and at this point, he's probably given up on getting answers out of her. I know there's still a chance contacting Avery could get her in trouble, but just staring at her number makes my chest hurt. I can't leave her to panic over me for any longer—it just wouldn't be right.

Jace shakes his head and signs, *"It's probably not a good idea. If anyone figured out you were texting her, it'd be too easy to track you from that phone."*

"Oh." I try to keep the disappointment out of my voice, but I'm pretty sure I fail.

Jace fishes in his pocket and pulls out a small, cheap-looking cell phone. *"But I thought you might want to talk to her. So Killer had the idea of getting this one, too."*

He hands the other phone to me, and I brush my fingers over the flimsy keypad, trying not to let any confusion show on my face. It's not like I'm expecting Jace to spend a lot of money on me, but this is a strange contrast to the smartphone.

Killer taps my shoulder, gaining my attention. "It's a disposable cell phone," he explains. "Totally untraceable. You can text your friend using it, and as long as you don't say where you are, no one can use it to find you."

I clutch the disposable phone close to my chest. It suddenly feels like a better present than the smartphone.

"Thank you," I say to Killer. Then I turn and grin at Jace. "I totally owe you."

He shrugs, but he looks away for a moment, and I know he's hiding a smile. *"You don't owe me anything,"* he signs as he turns back. *"You're obviously close to your friend. You should be able to talk to her, whether you're on the run or not."*

I nod and sign, *"It means a lot. Thanks."*

Before the moment can get any more sentimental, Jace nods toward the exit of the RV and nudges at Killer. "Come on," he says. "Arrow's going to be pissed if we're late."

Killer heads toward the door and says over his shoulder to me, "You stay low, darling. I'll see you later."

Jace pulls me back into a quick hug and then signs, *"I'll be back this evening, okay?"*

"Have fun," I sign.

He gently kisses the top of my head and then points to my phone. *"You, too."*

I smile at his back as he strides out the door. The moment they're gone, I sit on one of the couches and flick open the disposable phone. Taking a shaky breath, I quickly enter in Avery's number and start typing out a message. How mad is she going to be? I've had a perfectly good reason for not contacting her directly—with my dad's experience as a cop, it's just too likely that he'd find a way to fish info from Avery. Despite that, I can't even imagine how upset she is right now.

I make my text simple: **Hey.**

Her reply comes only seconds later. ***whoever u r, u'd better have a good reason 4 waking me up this early.***

It's Ali.

omg r u ok?!?!?!

I'm safe.

ur sure???

Positive.

There's a slight lag after that, and I know she's fuming. Then the phone buzzes with a new text: ***where r u??***

I laugh a little. The truth is so bizarre, I don't think she'd believe it. But it's not like I can tell her, anyway.

Somewhere safe, I text back.

where?

I can't say.

tell me dammit!!!

I'm safe. That's all I can tell you. I wish I could say more, but it could get us both in trouble.

An entire minute passes without a reply from Avery. I start to feel dizzy, and I realize I'm holding my breath. I let it out in a whoosh just as another text comes in: *u freaking ran away. without warning me or letting me help. wtf?!*

I didn't have a choice.

There's another lag. Then, *i no. that's the only reason i'm gonna forgive u.*

I bite my lip. *Really?*

of course really. ur my bestie. i love u 2 much 2 hate u.

I read her text four times, relief spreading through me. *I love you too*, I text back.

u'd better. now i need an update on ur life. tell me every-thing u can.

I need to hear about you too. I miss you so freaking much it hurts.

me 2. now spill. what's going on?

I tell her as much as I can: that I'm traveling somewhere, that I'm protected, and that I'm happier than I've been in a long time. At first, her responses are short, and I can tell she's still upset at me for keeping so much from her. But by the time I get to the part about maybe-kinda-sorta falling for a guy, she replies with a bunch of OMGs and smileys. After that, the conversation flows just as easily as normal.

The time stamp on the texts says we talk for three hours, but I swear it's hardly three minutes. Avery fills me in on the details of the search my dad has launched for me—she says he's exhausted all the local police resources, but he still has no idea where I might have gone. Relief settles in me as I read that; if my dad's search has been so useless, hopefully he'll give up soon.

We're on the subject of Jace again when I glance at the phone's clock. It's already eleven o'clock, and it's a Saturday. I sigh, realizing what that means.

You have work today, right? I text.

I can practically hear her pain in the reply she sends: *ugggg-hhh. yes. damn u 4 reminding me.*

I can't help but laugh a little. I guess that's one good thing about being on the run—I don't have to worry about dealing with a crappy summer job, like the one Avery got waitressing at a local café.

TTYL, I text back.

ugh. yeah. bye. A moment later, another text pops up. *luv u! b safe! and hug ur mysterious crush 4 me. then remind him i'll chop his balls off if he hurts u. ;)*

I smile and lean back on the couch, closing my eyes. I probably should be going stir-crazy, having been cooped up in this RV for so long, but I'm not anymore. Things might be cramped in here, but everything is comfortable and slightly insane and strangely enjoyable.

Something taps my knee, and I snap my eyes open. Jon stands in front of the couch, his head tilted to the side as he stares down at me. I swallow hard as instinctual fear streaks through my veins, but I push it away with a deep breath. If Jace trusts Jon, then I can, too.

"Hey," I say. "I didn't see you come in."

He nods a greeting. "Sorry. I didn't mean to scare you."

I can tell by the way his lips move that his voice is almost a whisper. He looks hesitant, his feet shuffling a little, and he backs up a couple of steps.

"No, it's . . . fine," I say.

We just stare at each other for an awkward moment, but then Jon backs up and sits on the opposite couch. His muscular frame fills most of it, and as he tosses his arm over the back, I catch another glimpse of his tattoos. They're beautiful, even if I'm not quite sure what they mean. One is of a panther running up his bicep, another of a blood-red sparrow flying toward his heart. He has at least half a dozen more along his arm, each one as intricate as it is breathtaking.

He raises an eyebrow at me, and I realize I've been caught staring. "They're gorgeous," I say, gesturing to his arm.

Jon laughs, his pale lips turning up at the corners. "Thanks. It's not every day I get called gorgeous."

My cheeks flare with heat, and I shake my head. "The tattoos, I mean. *They're* gorgeous. I didn't mean you're gorgeous. But I don't mean you're *not*. You're, like, handsome, and . . ."

I trail off, giving up on my babbling response. His smile grows a little.

"It's okay, Ali," he says. "I get what you're saying. I was just teasing."

Somehow, it doesn't seem fitting for him to be teasing. He's at least six feet tall and has enough muscle for two people. But it's not just his physique that's intimidating—there's something about his expression that's totally serious, like he's never heard a joke in his life.

I wonder what his story is. And, as long as I'm wondering, I'd like to know the story behind all of the band. Tone Deaf has always kept quiet private lives, and as much as the media goes crazy over them, no one has been able to dig up much about their pasts. All I know is that they rose into popularity after winning a nation-wide contest for one of their music videos. Aside from that, their past is a mystery to me, and I don't think even their most hardcore fans know much more.

Jon shifts nervously, and I get the feeling he's not comfortable around me. Why? I hardly know the guy.

"Jace asked me to keep you company," he says. "He was worried you'd get lonely being by yourself all day."

I search for any trace of mocking in his expression. Most guys would start cracking jokes the moment their friend got all sentimental, but Jon doesn't seem to have any issues with Jace's concern. Jon's serious expression remains in place, and I offer him a small smile.

"Thanks," I say. "I appreciate it."

He shrugs, like it's no big deal, but I can see the tension in his shoulders. Something's definitely bothering him.

"Are you okay?" I ask.

He nods. "Fine."

"You're sure?"

"Yeah. I just, um . . ." He lets out a hesitant laugh. "I'm shy. You know, around girls."

I give him a skeptical look and wait for the punch line. But he just smiles a little sheepishly and shrugs again. That's the moment I decide I like Jon.

"Well, thanks for keeping me company," I say.

"No problem."

There's an awkward silence, and then Jon looks toward Jace's bedroom. His expression turns puzzled, and he says something, but I can only see half his lips with his head turned like that. I quickly pick up the smartphone and open up the contacts page, tapping on the number that Jace programmed in under Jon's name. I start a new texting thread and send a quick message:

Can you text me so I don't have to read your lips? It gets tiring pretty quickly.

It's not too bad with someone like Killer, who boldly enunciates every word he says. But Jon's voice is soft, and he keeps nervously glancing away when he speaks, which is going to make a lip-reading conversation difficult.

Jon nods a couple times as he reads the message on his screen, and I swear he looks a little relieved that he doesn't have to talk anymore. Then he texts back, *Sure. And I was just asking why Cuddles is locked in Jace's room. She's scratching at the door.*

I'm scared of dogs, I text.

His eyes widen in surprise. *You're scared of Cuddles?*

I don't think she lives up to her name.

He shakes his head. *Trust me, she does. She's just a big wuss.* Before I can protest, he jumps up and heads down the hallway. Vibrations run through the floor as he opens Jace's door and unleashes the pit bull. I scoot closer to the corner of the couch and tuck my feet close to me. This is what you're supposed to do to stop a dog attack, right? Look small and helpless?

. . . Or is that for bears?

Before I can figure it out, Jon comes back into the room with Cuddles at his heels. Her stub of a tail wags madly, and she keeps slurping his hand with her long tongue. He doesn't seem to even mind that she's taste-testing him.

Jon sits back on the couch and Cuddles finally notices me. Her muscles tense, readying to pounce. I squeeze my eyes closed. So this is it. After making it hundreds of miles from my home, I'm going to be mauled by a dog before I even reach NYC. Just my luck.

My heart thuds wildly in my chest, and my breathing comes in sharp gasps. A large weight dips the couch next to me. But a moment passes, and no teeth dig into my skin. I crack open an eye and find Cuddles on the cushion next to me. She's lying on her back, her stubby tail wiggling in excitement and her paws curled toward her stomach.

I scoot away from her and glare over at Jon, wondering what his problem is. He *so* didn't have to let the dog out.

Jon rolls his eyes at my expression, and then quickly blushes, like he's afraid of being rude. A new message lights up on my phone: **She wants a tummy rub**.

"No," I say out loud, not wanting to type my response. Any movement might be enough to set this dog off.

He frowns. "No?"

"I don't like big dogs, and I definitely don't pet them."

His expression is slightly appalled. "But she's so cute. How can you not love her?"

Okay, I'll admit those are the last words I expected to come out of his mouth. Who would have guessed the Hulk was so sentimental?

Jon cocks his head as he examines me and then sends another message. **You've been attacked, haven't you?**

I cringe and search for a defensive retort to snap back at him. Then I see his gaze flick over to Cuddles, and I realize he's talking about a dog attack. Oh. That changes things a bit.

Yeah, I text, moving my hands slowly and carefully as I type the word. Cuddles doesn't seem to care about the motion, so I add, **When I was twelve, my neighbor had a pit bull that escaped from her yard. I tried to catch it so I could bring it back, but it freaked out and bit my arm.**

I don't tell him about the real wound: How it was one of the first times I saw my dad's PTSD totally take over, how the sight of the blood made him go silent and brooding, and how he wouldn't even go back into the examination room when the ER doctor stitched me up. He never really talked about my injury—he just gave me a long lecture about not provoking animals. To this day, *those* wounds still haven't healed.

Jon nods slowly. ***I can see why you're afraid of dogs***. I wait for him to get up and put Cuddles away, but instead he just adds, ***But that's no excuse to be scared of Cuddles***.

I scoff and edge back from the gigantic dog. "Oh, really?"

He pats the cushion next to him, and Cuddles leaps off my couch. She trots over to Jon and jumps up next to him, rolling back over for a tummy rub. Her tail wags frantically as Jon scratches her stomach, and she reaches out a paw so it touches his shoulder. He pats her paw and says to me, "Here, have a look."

Jon rolls Cuddles over a little, so she's on her side. From this angle, I can see a mass of scars running up and down the dog's hide.

She belonged to one of Jace's neighbors, Jon texts, using one hand to type and the other to pet Cuddles. ***They were into dog fighting, and poor Cuddles lost a match***. Jon lifts up the dog's giant head, and I see a bunch more scars around her neck.

I swallow hard, trying to keep bile from rising up. That's just sick. Vicious or not, no animal deserves to be hurt like that.

Jon lets Cuddles's head drop, and he gently scratches behind one of her cropped ears. She opens her mouth, and I wait for her to bite at Jon's hand. But she just lets her tongue loll out and pants happily as he pets her.

Jace found her a couple of days later, he texts. ***She'd managed to escape before she was killed, and she ended up in his***

yard. Jace had been saving up all year to buy a new guitar, but he decided to use that money to take her to a vet. He pats Cuddles on the head. *And Jace has had her ever since.*

"So Jace saved her," I murmur.

Jon nods. *He's not always a good guy, but he has his moments.*

He's been good to me, I protest.

A slight smile lifts Jon's lips. *He has, hasn't he? You seem to take all the bad out of him.*

I don't know what to say to that, but I'm saved from having to respond when Jon's phone lights up with a message from someone else. He reads it and stands from the couch. *Sorry, but I've got to go,* he texts. He hesitates and then adds, *Tony wants to talk with me. I think he's getting really suspicious that Jace is up to something. So you two need to keep being careful, okay?*

Of course, I text back, and I keep my eyes locked on my screen so Jon can't see the worry on my face. *I guess I'll see you later.*

Yeah. Later.

He heads for the door, not making a move to put Cuddles away. Before I can protest, he waves at me and strides out the exit.

I groan and let my head fall back, all the time keeping an eye on Cuddles. She wags her tail and jumps onto the couch cushion right next to me. I stiffen, wondering how hard it would be to put her away myself. She's trained, right? Maybe she knows a command that will make her go away.

I point to Jace's bedroom and say, "Go."

She cocks her head and just stares at me.

I take a shuddering breath and say with more force, "Go!"

Cuddles barks at me, but doesn't do anything else. Then she opens her mouth in a huge yawn, announcing to me that she has extremely large teeth and is very tired. Without any warning, she plops her head in my lap and closes her eyes.

I freeze, not knowing what to do. If I shove her off, she could get mad, but I can't just let her stay there. No way is a pit bull using me as a pillow.

Cuddles reaches toward me with a paw and gently lays it on my knee. She keeps it there, her huge paw pressing against my fragile skin. I cringe and wait for her to claw at me, but all she does is start to snore, the deep noise vibrating against my leg.

Before I can think better, I reach down and tentatively pat her head. Her tail wags in her sleep, and her paw presses against me a little harder, but she doesn't react beyond that. I keep petting her, all the time ready to leap up and run if I need to. But a minute passes, and then two, and Cuddles just continues her nap.

"Hey, girl," I whisper, stroking the soft fur around her ear. "I guess you're not as vicious as I thought."

She shifts in her sleep and keeps snoring.

I scratch her neck and then softly ask, "You want to be friends? I promise to give you tummy rubs if you promise not to eat me."

My voice must be a little louder than I wanted it, because Cuddles blinks her eyes open and peers at me. After a moment, she licks my hand and closes her eyes, her tail still slowly wagging in her sleep.

I give her head another pat and the gently trace one of the scars on her shoulder. "Yeah, that's what I thought," I murmur. "We're going to be besties before you know it."

26

ALI

KILLER COMES INTO the RV in a flurry of smiles and rapid-fire chattering. I wave a greeting from the couch, where I've been sketching a drawing of Cuddles. She's taking our new friendship rather seriously and hasn't left my side all day. I even had to shove her out of the bathroom, and then she just waited for me by the door. At this point, I'm more concerned about her stalking habits than her teeth.

Cuddles wags her tail at the sight of Killer, and he kneels next to the dog, throwing one arm around her in a hug. His other hand is busy handling a to-go cup of coffee that could fit half the Pacific Ocean. Unfortunately, it's missing a lid and most of its contents. Killer on caffeine? Not good . . .

Jace and Arrow come trailing into the RV, both of them looking tired but content. As soon as Jace spots me on the couch, he sits next to me and pulls me into a hug. His lips move as he says something, probably a greeting. But I don't quite catch what he says as he leans forward and affectionately kisses the top of my head.

"How did it go?" I ask.

"Good," he signs. *"We did some autographs, and then just walked around the festival for a while. They had some good talent this year."*

Killer steps up to me, butting into our conversation. He blurts out something, but he's glancing between everyone in the room, and there's no way I can follow what he's saying.

"Killer, calm down," I say. "I can't read your lips when they're moving at the speed of light."

He rolls his eyes, like this is somehow my fault, and says more slowly, "We're having a sleepover tonight."

"What?"

I turn to Arrow, figuring that he'll know what's going on. He's Killer's second half, so surely he can explain everything to me at a reasonable pace. But he looks just as confused and repeats, "We're having a sleepover?"

Killer scoffs. "No, Ali and I are having a sleepover. You're bunking with Jace."

"What? Why?"

"Because we're going to have a *Doctor Who* marathon, and you laugh at all the wrong times whenever we watch it."

Arrow scowls and mutters, "You just don't want me to see you bawling like a three-year-old when David Tennant dies."

Killer nods agreeably. "That, too."

Jace signs to me, *"What're they talking about?"*

I shake my head and sign back, *"It's a geek thing. You wouldn't understand."*

Killer taps my shoulder so I'll look back at him. "Get your jammies and meet me over in our RV."

"Um . . . okay?"

Jace pulls me close to him. "Killer, I don't think she wants to watch your ridiculous show."

"I love *Doctor Who*," I say, partly because I really do, and partly because it's kind of fun watching Jace's confused expression. He looks cute with his face scrunched like that.

Killer jumps up from the couch. "Then it's settled!" he says to me. "You're coming over to watch the Doctor and his awesomeness." He turns to Arrow. "And you, sweetie, are going to have to sleep here on the couch. See where your lack of respect for geeks gets you?"

"Bastard," Arrow mutters, although I can see the small smile at the corner of his mouth. I wonder if any of Killer's antics ever truly annoy him. As grumpy as the dude is, Arrow seems awfully patient with his boyfriend.

Killer ignores the insult and points to me. "I'll see you in my RV in fifteen minutes. Okay?"

"How am I going to get to your RV without being caught?" I ask.

He shrugs. "It's dark and my RV is right next door. No one will see you. And, if they do, I'll just tell them you're with me, and I'm actually bi."

Jace struggles to hold back a laugh, and I feel my own mouth twitching into a smile. Killer cheating on Arrow? Yeah, right, no one would ever believe that.

But I get the feeling protesting would be useless, and Killer confirms this as he leaves the RV without waiting for my response, his lips moving in a flurry as he plans our sleepover. We all roll our eyes when he exits the RV, the door slamming closed behind him.

"Why do I date that idiot?" Arrow asks.

"Because you love him."

A jolt of surprise runs through me as Jace says that. I was expecting some sarcastic remark to be his reply. But I suppose I shouldn't be completely shocked—after all, Jace has a thing for brutal honesty.

Arrow turns and stares out the window in an attempt to hide his smile. I smirk up at Jace, but his expression quickly kills my amusement. His good mood from before is gone, and now a worried scowl tugs at his lips. As soon as he sees that I'm watching him, Jace jumps up and heads into the kitchen. "If you're going to stay over with Killer, you should go pack," he says to me over his shoulder.

What's with the sudden mood swing? I glance over to Arrow, ready to ask him this question, but he's still staring out the window and ignoring me. With a sigh, I head toward the back of the RV, where my duffle bag is. Knowing Jace, he'll explain his uneasiness eventually. For now, I'll just give him some space to sort through his brooding thoughts.

27

JACE

I SOFTLY HIT my forehead against the refrigerator door, not so hard it hurts, but enough to jar the unsettling thoughts trying to latch onto my mind. Hitting my head isn't the most practical way to fetch a water bottle, which was my original intent when I walked into the kitchen, but my stomach is too upset to drink anything, and my brain feels like it's about to explode. Which might be because I just smacked it against a very dense refrigerator. But no, that's not it, not really. It's because I just said what has got to be the dumbest sentence ever uttered.

"Because you love him."

Why the hell did I say that in front of Ali? I thought I wanted to keep her, for her to be with me for longer than just awhile.

But, apparently, my stupid mouth has different ideas. Sure, all I said was the truth: Arrow has Killer because he loves him, and because they love each other. And, yeah, that's all I meant to say. But instead, I said so much more. I practically screamed it, and even if Ali doesn't understand now, she'll get it later.

Love is what keeps relationships going. And I can't love. That part of me died off a long time ago, and I doubt anything could resuscitate it.

So where does that leave Ali and me?

As if reading my mind, I feel a soft hand rest on my shoulder. I flinch, partially because she scared me, and partially because her touch scares me. It makes my heart race, and my skin grow warm, and my breathing come faster. And nobody should be able to control me that easily . . . right?

"You look like you're going to be sick," Ali says softly.

I whirl around and sign, *"I'm never going to love you."*

Her eyes grow wide and she slowly backs away. Tears spring into her eyes faster than I thought possible. But they're quickly masked by a look of anger, and she grits her teeth and glares right at me.

Shit. All I meant was to give her a fair warning, but instead I just did exactly what I said I promised not to. I hurt her.

"Don't take it like that," I sign. *"Please don't take it like that."*

She lets out a harsh laugh. *"How else am I supposed to take it? There are subtler ways to tell a girl to back off, you know."*

I rush toward her, wanting her in my arms, but she sidesteps my embrace and just keeps glaring at me. I stare up at the ceiling, down at the floor, out the window. Anywhere to escape that glare, the evidence that I've hurt her.

"Ali . . ." A single tear drips down her cheek, and I switch back to sign language, knowing her watering eyes will make it hard to read my lips. *"I don't want to hurt you."*

She scoffs and starts walking out of the kitchen. I leap forward and grab her elbow, stopping her. For once, she doesn't look scared of me, even though my grasp is desperate. Instead, she looks furious.

I swallow hard and let go, launching back into sign language. I estimate I have about three, maybe four seconds before she walks right out that door and doesn't come back.

"Look, Ali, my life is pain. It hurts and it sucks and nothing can change what it is. Not even you."

I see her eyes narrow even more. Every bit of instinct in me screams that I should get ready to defend myself, but I don't. This is Ali, and she'd never lash out at me, no matter how angry she gets.

"Every time I look at you, I realize that I really don't deserve you," I sign. *"And that's more painful than anything."*

Another tear trickles down her cheek, and I gently kiss it away. Her sorrow tastes salty and slightly metallic. *"But here's the thing,"* I sign. *"You're the best kind of pain I've ever felt. I've always worked so hard to avoid pain, but as much as you hurt, I don't want to leave you."*

She looks a little shocked, and I get the feeling she never expected me to say anything so openly. I didn't, either. And if I didn't care about her so much, I never would have.

Her serious gaze settles on my eyes and stays there. Maybe she sees the desperation I'm feeling, or the sadness. Or maybe there's nothing in my eyes; they're supposed to be the window to the soul, and I'm pretty sure my soul died off a long time ago.

Whatever she sees, it makes her tears stop. Then she raises her hands and signs, *"Then you don't have to leave. Not as long as you keep caring about me. Because you do care, even if you hate to admit it."*

Her gaze flicks back to my lips, and for a moment, I think she's waiting for me to respond. But then she throws herself into my arms and kisses me.

Finally. That's the only word running through my head as I kiss her back. Maybe not the most romantic sentiment, but I can't help it. All those times we've kissed, she's felt so hesitant. Now she's just as desperate as I am, and her lips are sweet and incredible.

When she pulls away, we're both breathing hard. Ali reaches up and wipes away the last of her tears. I kiss her forehead and brush my fingertip over the hesitant smile on her lips, relieved to see it back.

"I have to get over to Killer's," she signs, taking a step toward the door.

I let out a small breath of relief. Ali seems to sense that I can only handle so many emotions at once. As good as it feels to get all this off my chest, I'm glad she's not going to draw out this conversation any longer. I need time to process my muddled thoughts.

"Yeah," I sign back uncertainly. *"He'll worry if you're late."*

She pulls away from me, and just as she's about to walk out of the kitchen, she says, "I'll wait for you. You can be a jerk, but I also really believe you care about people. And if you can do that, then I think you have more good in you than bad. So I'll wait for you to figure out how to love."

With that said, she grabs her duffle bag off the couch and walks out of the RV, not even giving me a chance to respond.

I don't think I could have come up with one, anyway.

28

ALI

KILLER AND I stay up until three in the morning, watching a grand total of eight *Doctor Who* episodes. Killer has most of the episodes memorized line for line, and he waves his hands around as he acts along with David Tennant and the rest of the cast. Unfortunately, I'm right next to him on the couch, so I keep having to dodge his flails when he gets too excited. Fortunately, I'm deaf, so I don't have to hear his attempts at mimicking the voices.

When the eighth episode ends, and Killer's caffeine high has officially worn off, I tell him he should have been an actor. He grimaces and says, "But then I would have had to kiss *girls.*" He smiles sheepishly. "No offense, darling."

I laugh and let my head fall back against the cushion, my gaze roaming around the room. Killer and Arrow's RV is different from Jace's. Some of it's technically the same—there are the band posters, the bright colors, the comfy couches. But there's no denying it's totally different. It feels . . . alive. Like it's been lived in so much, it's actually absorbed some of that life. It practically radiates the message *Happy Couple Lives Here.* There are pictures all over of Killer and Arrow together, some of them with the rest of the band.

Next to the couch is a picture I keep studying. It must have been taken when the band had just started; they all look impossibly young, and they're standing in front of less-than-professional music equipment. In the photo, Killer wears a shirt that says, KEEP CALM AND DON'T BLINK, a pair of jeans that look designer brand, and that dorky grin of his. So he's been a Doctor Who fan and fashion aficionado since the very beginning of the band—it's not at all surprising, and neither is the trademark smile.

Arrow stands behind him, his arms wrapped around Killer's waist and a sheepish smile on his face. Jon is missing from the picture, except for his thumb. At least I'm *assuming* that's what the pinkish-tan splotch is in the corner.

As interesting and cute as the picture is, it makes me sad. Because standing next to Arrow and Killer is Jace. His arm is in a sling, and he has a black eye that just makes his glare at the camera look all the more severe. Jace's good arm clutches an electric guitar—it's beaten up and scratched all over, but polished to an impossible shine. He holds onto it like he'll simply dissolve into a pile of dead dust if he ever lets go.

Something taps my arm, startling me back to the present. I turn to Killer, but his eyes are on the picture and his lips turned down in a frown. I've never seen him look so serious and sorrowful, and it's such a drastic contrast to his usual expression that I want to look away from him.

Killer nods to my new smartphone in my lap, which he's been texting me on all evening so I don't have to focus on reading his lips. There's a new message on my screen: *He's never been happy, you know*. My fingers hover over the keyboard, not sure how to respond, but then Killer taps out another message before I get the chance. *You've seen his scar?*

Yeah.

Killer shakes his head, like he's trying to dislodge a memory from his skull. *I thought he might show you that. He usually doesn't even mention it to anyone, but you're special to him.*

I smile uncertainly, but Killer just sighs and shakes his head.

You shouldn't be smiling about that.

His words do the trick—my smile disappears. *Why not?*

Because this is Jace we're talking about. He's messed up. I love the dude like a brother, but I still don't think he's healthy for a girl like you.

A girl like me? I text back, shooting him a challenging look to go along with the message. *You think a musician shouldn't date a deaf girl?*

No. I think a whole shouldn't have to date a half.

What's that supposed to mean?

It means you came out all right, even though some bad shit has obviously happened to you.

I snap my attention up from my screen and glare right at him, my eyes narrowing. Killer just holds up his hands innocently, then types out another message.

Don't give me that look. Jace hasn't told me hardly anything about your past. I'm just speculating here.

I nod slowly as he keeps typing.

Jace didn't turn out like you. He came out broken.

So I'll fix him.

Killer smiles, but it's sad and longing, a far cry from his usual expression. *I wish it was that easy.*

I'm quiet for a long minute, absorbing his words, examining his expression, trying to find some way I can refute everything he's telling me. But no argument can stand up against the look of pain in Killer's eyes.

What happened to him? I ask. *You say he's broken, so what broke him?*

The obvious answer would be what Jace told me—the time his dad attacked him. But there has to be something more than that, because Jace is strong. Sure, he's evasive, but even more than that, he's stubborn and determined and passionate.

Killer nibbles at his lip uncertainly. *I don't think I can tell you that. You'll have to ask Jace.*

I narrow my eyes in my best tell-or-die expression, but that just makes him chuckle. *Although I do understand why Jace likes you so much. You've got spunk.*

That makes me blush, and Killer smirks at my red cheeks. He's been teasing me about them all night, saying that if I keep blushing so much, I'm going to wake up one day in the body of a lobster. I playfully slap at his forearm, and he cringes like I've actually hurt him. For a quick moment, there's that gut-instinct panic that always invades me when I see pain, but then I realize he's just kidding around, and I roll my eyes at him.

From then on, the topic of Jace is dropped. Killer rattles off a list of questions he wants to know about me: what's my favorite food, movie, animal, memory, friend, family member. He doesn't ask what my favorite TV show is; our six-hour marathon makes that answer pretty clear.

And Killer lets me ask a bunch of questions about him. I find out he grew up in London, although he moved to Colorado by the time he hit middle school, leaving him with the accent of a highly sophisticated country bumpkin. He hates the cold, especially snow. He and Arrow have been friends since sixth grade, when they bonded over the fact that they both had bizarre names. He thinks cats are way better than dogs, although Cuddles is an exception. He's been out of the closet since twelve, and his parents are totally cool with it. He's anxiously expecting Arrow to propose, and sometimes Killer likes to introduce Arrow as his fiancé, just to bother him.

It's almost four in the morning by the time we decide to actually get some sleep. This whole night has been kind of strange—chatting with a rock star about mundane things, laughing with him, playfully smacking his shoulder when he gets too rude. But I like it, and I like Killer. I think he might actually be a friend now.

I drift off with a smile on my lips and that thought in my head: I have a new friend. And, as soon as I get to NYC, I'll also have a new life.

29

JACE

A SIGH OF relief whooshes out of me as I hear the RV door open. Ali's back. I knew she'd be safe spending the night over with Killer, but that didn't stop me from worrying all night about her getting caught. I thought that fear would lessen the further we got from Los Angeles, but instead, it's just gotten stronger as she and I have grown closer.

Ali strides into the living area, smiling despite the tired bags under her eyes. It's amazing to see her like that, so happy and confident. It's only been a week since she left that hellhole of a home, but being away from it has already changed her.

"No one saw you?" I ask, gesturing out the window.

She shakes her head. *"Nope. The lot is pretty much empty, and I was really careful sneaking back over here."*

She sits next to me on the couch and wraps her arms around me, letting her head rest against my shoulder. I set down my guitar, which I've been absently strumming while I waited for her to return. I made a few mistakes at the last show, which is totally unlike me. Usually, I'm spot-on with every note, but having Ali around has infringed on my practice time.

Not that I'm complaining, of course. Although Tony did. He's convinced that something serious is distracting me, and if I'm going to keep him from investigating, I need to stop giving him reasons to worry. That means extra practice and putting on a flawless show next time.

I smooth Ali's hair, which is still slightly ruffled from her sleepover. Even like this, it looks gorgeous; it's a perfect shade of auburn, half red and half brown. I guess it kind of fits her sometimes fiery and sometimes sweet personality.

"Good morning," she murmurs. Her warm breath seeps through my cotton T-shirt and brushes against the skin of my shoulder. I shiver, but try to conceal it by wrapping my arms around her. A small smirk lifts the corners of her lips, telling me that I'm not very good at hiding how much her touch messes with me.

I kiss her forehead and sign back, *"Good morning."* And it definitely is, now that she's with me and safe. I pull her into my lap and rest my cheek on top of her head, and we stay that way for a long time. I'm not sure exactly how long, because having Ali this close does a weird time warp thing to me. It's like time stops, and all that matters is this brave, feisty, beautiful girl in my arms.

I kiss along the side of her jaw, stopping every once in a while to teasingly brush my lips against her mouth. She closes her eyes and tilts her head back, capturing me in a deep kiss.

Then she slowly pulls away and picks up my electric guitar I'd left leaning against the couch. She runs her hand along the smooth varnish, pausing to trace the small scratches that mar it after years of use. Usually, I hate it when other people touch my guitar, but Ali's grasp on the instrument is delicate and reverent, and I don't mind it at all.

"Killer has a picture in his RV of you guys when you first started the band," she says. She softly strums a simple chord. "You're holding this same guitar in it."

"This was the first one I ever owned," I sign. *"It's still my favorite."*

"You use a different one when you perform," she notes.

"Yeah." I reach over and run my hand along the neck of the guitar. *"It's my favorite, but the sound quality is honestly not that great. So I have to use a more professional one for performances."*

She nods and carefully picks at a couple strings, and I smile as I recognize the notes she wrote to go along with the lyrics in my notebook.

"It sounds a lot better with your adjustments," I sign. *"I've been playing what you wrote all morning."*

She blushes a little at that, but a smile upturns her lips. "So do you think after all these years of working on it, your song might actually turn out perfect?"

"No," I sign. *"But if you help me write it, I think* our *song might turn out perfect."*

Ali's smile grows, but then she looks up from the guitar and stares me right in the eye. Her lips tighten into a thoughtful expression, and she looks just as intense as she was when we had that serious discussion yesterday. I shift back a little, unsure where this conversation is going.

"*I'll make you a deal,*" she signs.

"*You promise to help me finish the song, and then I'll kiss you again?*"

She scoffs at my suggestion. "*Not quite. You answer one question of mine totally truthfully, and then I'll help you with the song.*"

"*That's not fair.*

"*Welcome to life.*"

I don't like it when she talks like that, all bitter and realistic. Ali is the type of girl who deserves to live in a fairy tale world full of happily-ever-afters. The fact that she never got that—that instead she's been struggling through hell—makes my chest ache. I peck her on the cheek and sign, "*Fine. It's a deal.*"

She smirks triumphantly, but the expression quickly melts into a hesitant frown. She brushes her fingers along my jaw, then drops her hand and trails it along the scar on my chest. Even though my shirt separates our skin, a trail of heat follows her fingertips.

"Tell me about your family," she says.

I pull away from her, but she keeps her gaze steadily on mine, her hazel eyes concerned and curious. I swallow hard and hesitantly sign, "*That's not a question.*"

She sighs. "Must we get into specifics?"

"We made a deal. I'm supposed to answer a question."

"Fine." She rolls her eyes and asks, "Would you please tell me about your family?"

"No."

She cocks her head a little. "*What?*"

"*I said no,*" I sign, switching back to ASL to make sure she gets the message. "*There, I answered.*"

Her lips purse into a tight little frown. *"That's not fair."*

I pick her up off my lap, depositing her next to me on the couch. Anxiety crawls over my skin, and I don't want to be near anyone, not even Ali. I stand up and repeat what she signed before. *"Welcome to life."*

I head into the kitchen, needing some ice water to cool me down. My blood feels like it's suddenly boiling, and I'm breathing too fast, and I need to escape these feelings. Scratch that—I need to escape the past. And talking about it is *not* going to help.

As I reach for a glass in the cupboard, a small hand snatches mine out of the air. Ali tugs me around to face her, and as I stare down, I'm once again amazed at how such a tiny girl can have so much power over me.

Ali pulls me close to her, until there's just enough room between us for our hands to sign. *"It's okay,"* she signs. *"I don't care what you tell me. I'll be okay with it."*

She smiles up at me softly, and I'm pretty sure this is the moment when I'm supposed to break down and admit every horrific detail of my past. But I've never been very good at the whole "supposed to" thing, so I just step away from her and snatch a cup from the shelf.

I grab some ice out of the freezer, and I'm about to drop it into the cup when Ali says, "I told you about my past. Now you tell me about yours."

The ice starts to freeze my hand, but I just tighten my grip on it, taking in the pain. It's so familiar that it's almost comforting. "It doesn't work that way, Ali," I mutter, turning my head just enough for her to read my lips.

"Then how does it work?"

The pain becomes too much, so I let the ice cubes fall one by one, watching them hit the bottom before I reply. "It works like this: you stop asking questions about my life, and leave me the hell alone."

There's a long pause, and then I feel her arms wrap around my waist, and her warm breath whisper in my ear, "But I don't want to leave, and I don't think you want to be alone. Not really."

I'm pretty sure her arms are the only thing keeping me standing. I turn around and grab her hand, firmly entwining our fingers. Brushing a strand of hair from her face, I lean close to her and say, "My story isn't pretty, Ali."

She stares up at me, her eyes open wide, asking me to tell her more. I groan and let my head fall back. Memories claw at my brain, and I just want to collapse somewhere and close my eyes, to block it all out. I dump my cup in the sink and lead Ali to my bedroom. I tug her onto the bed, and she lies down, letting me wrap her in my arms and press close to her. Her sweet scent calms me, and I breathe in deeply, reminding myself that even if I don't have her forever, I have her now.

We stay there for a long moment, wrapped in each other's arms. I soak in her presence; I've never felt this close to someone. Her warm breaths heat my neck, and gradually they slow, until I'm sure she'll fall asleep. But her eyes stay open and locked on mine, still waiting for an answer to a question I never discuss.

I untangle my hands from hers and slowly sign, *"My dad killed my mom when I was ten."*

I wait for her to recoil and run away, but all she does is reach up and brush her fingers against my cheek. Her touch is firmer than usual, like she's trying to brush the memory straight out of my head, and I close my eyes, appreciating the contact more than I thought possible. There are no sparks like before, but there's warmth in her touch that fights off the cold chills I always get when I think about this.

"So you grew up in the foster system?" she guesses.

"No. I wish I had, but no."

Her gaze turns inquisitive, and I hesitantly go on. *"He didn't physically kill her. I mean, he wasn't the one to give her the pills. But she had psych issues, and she was suicidal. Instead of helping her, my dad drove her off the edge."*

"So you blame him for her death."

I nod. *"Of course."*

She doesn't judge me, or tell me I'm wrong, or try to change my mind. She just holds me closer, wrapping her arms around me so tight that I don't think I could leave if I tried. But, strangely, I don't want to leave. Somehow, it feels right to tell her all this, like our relationship wouldn't be real if she didn't know the truth about me and my past.

My vision blurs, and it takes me a moment to realize it's from tears. This is the second time she's made me cry since I met her, but this time, I don't feel ashamed. She wipes away one of my tears, just like I did for her. "Tell me everything," she says.

I swallow hard. *"Both my parents were deaf. I learned to speak English because my mom insisted on it, but as soon as she died, my dad wouldn't let me talk around him. He always resented having a kid who could hear, so he insisted I use sign language.*

"I had a lisp all through elementary school, because I didn't speak enough. I got picked on for it, but that didn't even begin to compare to my home life."

I squeeze my eyes shut, and Ali brushes her fingers across my cheek and lightly kisses each of my closed eyes. After a long minute, she seems to realize that I don't want to admit to anything, so she says it for me.

"Your dad abused you. Like mine."

I nod and shudder, hating those words. Yeah, I was young, and yeah, there probably wasn't anything I could do about it. But . . . what if there was? What if I could have stopped it, what if I'd tried harder, what if I just wasn't strong enough?

Ali sighs, seeming to read my mind. "It's not your fault, Jace."

"But what if it is? He was obviously mentally ill, and I knew it, and I always went and pissed him off, anyway."

"If it is your fault, then everything you told me the other night is a lie."

"What's that supposed to mean?"

"You told me it wasn't my fault that my dad hit me. So if you're saying that it *is* your fault that your dad did the same thing . . . then I must be at fault, too."

My breath catches, and I snap my eyes open, staring right at her. I hurriedly sign, *"It's not your fault, Ali. Don't even suggest that. You did nothing wrong."*

She smiles gently. *"Then you didn't do anything wrong, either."*

Tears flow freely down my face, and Ali kisses each one away, her lips soft against my skin. I close my eyes, trying to figure out the emotions racing through me. There's anger, of course, because that's always there. But it seems subdued, and there's also something else: relief. Other people have told me before that I did nothing wrong. But it feels different coming from Ali, knowing that she's been through the same hell and believes I didn't deserve any of it. She's the first person who really understands.

She holds me for a long time, and I let her. We don't talk, and Ali doesn't try to counsel me or give me pity. She just presses me close to her, letting me absorb her warmth and strength.

Eventually, she holds up her hands and signs, *"Can I ask you another question?"*

"If you really have to."

"Is this why you hated me so much at first?"

I frown. *"I hated the fact that you were deaf and that you reminded me of my past. But I never hated you."* Guilt gnaws at me, and I add, *"I'm sorry. How I treated you when we first met was wrong, not to mention idiotic. My dad had issues because he was too selfish to take care of his mental illness. It had nothing to do with him being deaf."*

Ali gives a slow nod, accepting this. She stares at me intently, and I can tell she's trying to judge how fragile I am, and how many more questions I can take. I brush the back of my hand against her cheek, silently telling her it's okay.

"Your whole obsession with health," she signs, *"I mean, all the health foods and exercise and stuff. Is that why?"*

"Yeah. My dad had some sort of mental illness, and instead of getting real medication, he used meth to deal with it. He was always cruel, but when he shot up, he was downright vicious."

"I'm sorry. You never should have had to go through that." She hesitates, and then signs, *"Is he in your life at all anymore?"*

I shudder at the thought and shake my head. *"No. He went to prison after he gave me that scar on my chest. There was no way he could explain away an injury like that, and he'd already* been arrested before on a couple of minor crimes. So he got sentenced to five years."

Ali relaxes a little and signs, *"I'm glad he's locked away now."*

I nod, silently agreeing. Then I add, *"I guess the whole health thing is my way of making sure I don't turn into him. My dad never took care of anyone, including himself. So I guess I'm into all the health stuff because of that."*

She stares at me, her eyes so serious that I have a hard time meeting them. "You do know that it won't work," she murmurs. "Don't you?"

I freeze, stunned at her words. *"What do you mean?"*

"I mean that eating healthy and running won't ensure you don't turn into your dad."

I open my mouth to shout, to tell her she's completely wrong. But all that comes out is a hoarse squeak. I stare at her, longing for her to take back what she just said, but she just shakes her head. Then she presses a hand against my chest, right over my scar.

"This is what will make sure you never become your dad."

At first I think she's talking about my scar, and I'm confused. Then I realize her hand is pressed over my heart. Ali places her other hand against me so both her palms are pressed against my chest. Comforting warmth spreads out from her touch, and I close my eyes and cover her hands with my own.

"It's okay, Jace," Ali murmurs. "Everything's going to be okay."

How many times have I told myself those exact same words? *Everything's going to be okay.* But I've never been able to believe it.

At least not until now. Hearing Ali say those words changes them completely, and part of me latches onto them, believing what she says.

"Thank you," I whisper. I smile shakily and pull back so I can sign, *"So now that I've spilled my guts to you, will you help me finish our song?"*

She nods, but then hesitates and signs, *"With one condition."*

I raise an eyebrow. *"That wasn't part of our deal."*

"Too bad."

I try to give her an exasperated look, but I don't think I manage. The small smile on her lips is soft and caring, and it's impossible to get upset at her when she looks like that. *"What's the condition?"* I ask.

She leans over and tenderly kisses me on the cheek. *"It has to end on a happy note."*

30

ALI

OVER THE NEXT week, Jace and I fall into an easy routine. The early mornings we spend working on songwriting; Jace is due to submit four new songs to his label in just a couple weeks, and I agree to help with all of them. While he has natural talent, he's never had classical training, and his eyes light up excitedly as I teach him new concepts. He spends hours scribbling lyrics, testing chords on his guitar, and signing rapid-fire questions at me. His enthusiasm is contagious, and I find myself enjoying music in ways I haven't allowed myself to in years.

Our mornings together are always too short, and the days too long. Jace's tour schedule is crammed with events, so if he's not prepping or performing, he's traveling. I just keep hiding away in the back of the RV, staying safely out of view and only going outside for a few minutes at a time. Boredom eats at me, and texting Avery helps, but I'm growing more and more anxious to get to New York. After weeks of travel, we're stopped in Austin, Texas, and still so far away from my destination.

This morning, we sit together on the couch closest to the window. The curtains are drawn to keep anyone from seeing me, but other than that, everything seems perfect. I'm texting Avery, and Jace is testing out a series of chords I wrote for a bridge, occasionally pausing to kiss me.

I stand up and grab our breakfast plates off the small side table. In just a few minutes, Jace is going to have to leave for a rehearsal, and I can already feel boredom gnawing at me. I'm sick of drawing and coding to pass the time, and even managing Jace's social media stuff is starting to feel tedious.

I walk into the kitchen and dump the plates in the sink. There's a growing mound there, and I frown, deciding that someone needs to take care of them. I turn on the sink, but just as I'm about to grab the dish soap, Jace's strong arm wraps around my shoulders. He rests his chin on top of my head and uses his free hand to push the soap away from me. I turn off the water and face him, my eyebrows raised questioningly.

He gives me a chiding look and signs, *"I woke you up early so we could spend time together, not so you could be my maid."*

I roll my eyes and say, "I thought you were a health freak. Don't you know that dirty dishes build up bacteria?"

He shrugs and kisses me on the tip of my nose. That seems to be his favorite place to kiss me, aside from my lips, of course. It's such a sweet gesture, and it always takes me a little by surprise.

"I want to spend the morning with you," he signs. *"Is that really such a terrible thing?"*

"Of course not," I reply with a smile.

He pulls me into his arms and presses me firmly against his chest, and his breath tickles my ear. I have no idea what he's saying, but I know it's affectionate.

Jace suddenly freezes, every muscle in his body stiffening like he's been shocked. His grip on me tightens. Then he takes a giant step away from me, his eyes growing wide as he stares at something behind my back. I turn toward the entrance of the kitchen, and—

Shit.

Tony gapes at me, frozen in the doorway. He pushes his glasses up his nose and squints, like he thinks he might be seeing things. When I don't disappear, his eyes grow wide, and he opens and shuts his mouth a couple times as he struggles for something to say. Finally, he manages to sputter out, "What?"

Not good, not good, *not good.* I tense, unsure whether I should try to explain what I'm doing here, or follow my instincts and bolt for the door. Jace pulls me back to him, wrapping a protective arm around my shoulders. Tony takes a step toward me, his brows furrowed in a mixture of disbelief and anger.

"*What* is she doing here?" he demands, and the way his mouth mouths exaggeratedly, I know his words are sharp and loud.

I turn toward Jace, waiting to see his reply. Jace glances down at my nervous expression and then back to Tony. "Don't yell," he snaps.

"I'll yell however much I want to!" Tony gestures angrily toward me. "Don't you know the police are after this girl?

What are you *thinking* having her in here?" He rakes his hands through his hair. "How long has she been with you?"

"She's been with us since we left Los Angeles," Jace replies, his words clipped. He clutches me tighter against him, like he's afraid I'm going to run away. Which I might. I need to get away from here. Fast.

I lose track of their conversation after that—the movement of their lips is too harsh and frantic for me to follow. There's lots of yelling, and Tony gradually stomps forward, until he's right in Jace's face. And mine.

I breathe faster and faster, my muscles tense and screaming at me to run, my heart pounding a rhythm so fast, I feel like my chest is about to explode. Finally, Tony throws his hands up in the air in exasperation and stalks back a few steps. He leans against the counter and crosses his arms over his chest, like he's warding off any other argument Jace could make.

Tony speaks slower, and I'm able to follow his words as he says, "I'll tell you this for the last time. She needs to go. *Now*."

"She's not going anywhere," Jace growls.

"Yes, she is. Jace, you're legally an adult, she's legally a minor, and the authorities are looking for her. What part about this don't you understand? If you get caught with her, you are *beyond* in trouble."

There's a tense pause after that, and I hesitantly clear my throat and say, "Everything that Amber Alert report said isn't true. I'm not mentally ill, and I didn't make up the need to run away. I have a good reason for wanting to escape."

Tony shakes his head. "That is exactly what I would expect a delusional person to believe."

I wince and steel my expression into one of anger, refusing to show how much his words hurt. But how many times have I heard people deny what my dad did to me? Too many. Way, *way* too many.

I desperately try to think up some retort, but nothing comes out of my mouth. Jace strides to the other side of the room in three steps, stopping just inches from Tony. I can't see what he's saying from this viewpoint, but I watch as Tony's posture grows rigid and aggressive, and Jace clenches his fist. No, no, no, I'm *not* letting this happen.

"Stop," I say. They don't, so I raise my voice and shout, "Stop! Just . . . don't do this. Don't hurt each other."

Both of them turn to me, their expressions taut with frustration and anger. I swallow hard and add in a quieter voice, "Please don't fight."

Jace glares down at his fist, which is clenched so hard, his knuckles are turning a bright red color. He takes a shuddering breath, looks back to Tony, and then to me. There's rage in his eyes, so intense it makes his ice-blue irises seem darker. I automatically look away, shifting toward the exit. I hate seeing his eyes like that. *Hate* it.

A minute passes, but I keep my eyes stuck to the floor. I feel the vibrations of Jace's footsteps as he angrily paces in front of Tony. Then there's more pounding steps as they both move out of the room.

All the vibrations stop. I hold my breath, still not wanting to look up.

A warm hand touches my shoulder, and I finally tear my gaze from the floor, finding Jace standing right in front of me. He stares down, his eyes just as angry as before. I know

246

I should be scared—anger that strong leads to violence. But I can't be scared, because this is Jace, and because there's something more in his expression: protectiveness.

"Are you okay?" he asks.

I look over all of him, searching for injuries Tony could have dealt. But there's nothing. No blood, no welting bruises, no sign of any violence at all. The anger fades from Jace's expression, and when I don't answer him right away, a worried look appears in his eyes.

I reach out and trail my fingertips over his cheek. I don't know what I'm trying to do—maybe brush away the worry, or maybe comfort him. Whatever I'm doing, it seems to work, because he closes his eyes for a moment and lets out a long breath. A smile flits at the corner of his mouth, and when he opens his eyes, the worry has gone into hiding.

I know it's still there—once fear enters you, it can't just leave. But his eyes are clear again, not angry or scared, but instead . . . soft.

I realize I still have a question to answer, and I murmur, "Yeah. I think I'm okay." Or at least I am for the moment. As soon as Tony reports me, things will change.

Jace pulls me close to him and kisses the top of my head, his hand smoothing a stray strand of my hair back into place. I glance anxiously around, my stomach roiling as I wonder how Tony would react to Jace's affection for me. But we're the only ones in the kitchen, and a moment later, I feel the vibration of the front door closing.

I turn back to Jace and hesitantly ask, "Where's Tony going?"

"Away."

I swallow hard and grit my jaw, trying to keep tears at bay. My escape hardly lasted two weeks, and I'm already busted. I was half expecting this much, but the failure still makes me want to scream in frustration.

Jace quickly signs, *"Please don't look so sad."*

"But what about Tony?" I sign. *"He's going to report me."*

Jace shakes his head. *"No, he isn't."*

"What? But he said he was going to."

"And I convinced him not to."

I blink hard, not understanding. Tony had been so mad. There's no way he'd just walk away and not report me.

"What'd you say to him?" My stomach churns as I ask the question. I don't really want to know the answer, do I? The only way Jace could have scared away Tony is with some sort of threat, and probably a pretty severe one. And I don't like that angry side of Jace.

Jace chuckles at my nervous expression and kisses my forehead. *"Don't worry, sweetheart. I didn't threaten his life or anything."*

Sweetheart. I remember the first time he called me that, and how scathing and demeaning it had seemed. Now it seems the exact opposite, and the smile that forms as he signs it makes a little of my cold dread melt away.

"What did you tell Tony?" I repeat.

"I told him the truth."

I jerk back from him. Is he serious? He can't just go around blabbing about my abusive situation. *"What's that supposed to mean?"* I demand.

Jace shakes his head and gently wraps his arms around my waist, pulling me back to him. "I didn't tell him anything you wouldn't have wanted me to."

"Then what the hell did you tell him?"

Jace chews at his lip, his eyebrows furrowed with uncertainty. He releases me from his grasp, slowly raising his hands to sign, *"I told him that I'm going to do everything I can to keep you safe. I said that I'm going to stand by you, and that if he reported you, he'd take both of us down."*

I stare blankly at his hands, certain I've misread what he signed. But he's smiling at me now, and the tender look in his eyes tells me that I saw everything right.

"Thank you," I whisper. Then I hesitantly sign, *"You really think that will work? He won't report me?"*

Jace bites his lip. *"He promised not to report you today, since he wants tonight's concert to happen without any drama. And he wants to meet with me and the rest of the band tomorrow and discuss what to do. But we'll convince him not to tell anyone you're with me. I'm sure of it."*

He wraps me back in his arms, pulling me against his chest and pressing his lips against the top of my head. I squeeze him back tightly, silently hoping Tony keeps his promise and stays quiet for now. We stay there for a minute, until Jace hesitantly pulls away from me, freeing his hands.

"I need to go now," he signs. *"Tony is furious enough without me being late to our rehearsal."*

"When will you be back?"

"Not until really late," he signs. *"We're doing a publicity event at a club right after the concert. So I won't be back here until early morning."*

I nod and try not to show my disappointment. With the threat of Tony reporting me looming over my head, waiting around alone in the RV is going to be even harder than usual.

Jace frowns at my anxious expression and presses a firm kiss against my lips.

"*I meant what I told Tony,*" he signs, and then reaches out and brushes the back of his hand against my cheek. "*I'm usually no good at commitment, but this is different. You're different. I'm not just going to let you go. Not unless you want me to.*"

I shake my head. "*I don't want you to go.*"

He nods seriously and kisses my forehead. "*Then I'm not going anywhere.*"

31

ALI

JACE STUMBLES INTO the RV around 12:30, and I immediately know something is wrong. His steps are heavy and uneven, like he's drunk. Wasn't he supposed to get back way later?

He heads straight to the room with the couches, where I've been waiting all evening. He texted me earlier not to bother staying up for him, but I've never been very good at listening. I've been an anxious ball of nerves ever since Tony found me, and since there's no chance of me getting sleep, I want to spend every moment I can with Jace.

Those plans go flying out the window as soon as Jace steps closer. In the dim light of the lamp, his skin gleams with sweat, and the whites of his eyes are red. I jump up from the couch and run to his side, wrapping my arms around his waist to steady him a little. He's so unstable, I'm afraid he's going to topple right over.

"How many did you have?" I demand. It seems really weird that he's drunk; he never drinks. Never, ever. He's made that more than clear.

Jace blinks at me a few times and squints, like he can't figure out what I'm doing in his RV. "What? How . . . how many of what?" His words are slurred, and it's nearly impossible to read his lips.

I let out a frustrated sigh and guide him toward the couch. He's totally, utterly smashed. Tomorrow morning is so not going to be pleasant . . .

"Drinks," I answer. "How many drinks did you have?"

He frowns deeply. "Drinks? None. Never."

"Come on, Jace. You're beyond drunk. How did you even get back like this?"

"Taxi," he murmurs. He groans and squeezes his eyes shut as he leans back into the couch. "Light."

"What about it?" I ask.

"Off."

I roll my eyes, getting really sick of these one-word answers, but I flick the light off. "I'm going to get you some water. Just stay there, okay? You'll fall if you get up again."

He just squeezes his eyes closed tighter, and I have a feeling that I don't have to worry about him moving for a long time. Shaking my head, I head into the kitchen and grab a cup for him. I force in a couple of deep breaths, trying to ward off my urge to try to lecture Jace. Sure, I hate being around drunk people, and, sure, Jace knows that. But if he wants to pollute his own body with that crap, I have no right to tell him he shouldn't.

Although I *do* have the right to be upset with him. After our run-in with Tony, I could really use Jace's comfort, not his drunken mumbling. Why did he have to pick tonight of all nights to get smashed?

As I'm filling the cup with ice, a strong vibration runs through the floorboards. I curse in frustration and hurry back toward the couches. Jace must have fallen. Idiot. Couldn't he have just stayed put, like I asked him to?

I open my mouth to scold him, but choke on my words as I enter the living area. Jace is sprawled on the floor, convulsing. Every part of his body shakes violently. His eyes are open, but they're rolled back and staring at nothing.

For a long moment, I just stand there, unable to move. Horror takes over my body and freezes my veins, rendering me useless. But then I realize I can't be useless. I need to help Jace, and that means fighting my terror and doing something.

I step toward Jace and collapse on my knees next to him. Blood seeps from his mouth, and I realize his shaking has made him bite his tongue. I desperately rack my brain for any first-aid skills I know about seizures. Loosen clothing around the neck, don't try to hold the person down, and . . .

Call 9-1-1.

I swallow hard. If an ambulance comes, they'll see me, and they'll turn me over to the police, who will drag me all the way back to Los Angeles.

But it doesn't matter. I'm not just going to leave Jace like this. He needs an ambulance, and he needs one immediately.

I carefully remove his phone from his front pocket. His convulsing arm slams into my knee, and I shriek, shocked by how strong it is. Dammit. He's shaking a hell of a lot harder than I thought.

I pick up the phone, and for one uncertain moment, I almost try calling 9-1-1 myself. But I won't be able to hear the operator's questions or any medical directions she gives me. And I'm using a cell phone, so tracking the location on it would take time. Time I don't have. Shit, shit, shit. This isn't going to work.

I take a shuddering breath, forcing myself to calm down. I can do this. I know I can. I just need to get someone over here to make the 9-1-1 call.

Opening up Jace's messages, I quickly spot a group text thread that includes all the members of the band and Tony. My heart pounds desperately as I open up the thread and shakily type *Jace having seizure. We're in his RV. Call 9-1-1.*

After I make sure the text goes through, I turn my attention back to Jace. His shaking isn't stopping. My vision blurs, and it takes me a moment to realize I'm crying. I don't bother to wipe away the tears.

"It's going to be okay, Jace," I whisper. I don't know if he can hear me, or if he can even understand me through my tears, but I can't hold in the words. "It's going to be fine. Okay? Everything is going to be perfectly fine."

I repeat those words over and over again, just like he did for me that night I woke up from a nightmare. His shaking slows and then stops, but his breathing is weak, and his eyes remain glazed and unseeing. I reach out with a trembling hand and trace his scar from the tip to the base.

"I love you," I whisper. "I know it makes me crazy, but I love you. Okay? So hang in there. Please."

I'm vaguely aware of strong arms wrapping around me, and for a single moment, I feel relief. But then I realize the arms don't belong to Jace; they're too rough and too skinny. I struggle against them, but they just keep pulling me back.

I blink to clear my vision, and look up to find Tony staring down at me, his eyes wide with panic and horror. Tony yells something, his mouth moving exaggeratedly as his fingers dig into my shoulder. I keep struggling, wanting to be back at Jace's side. Then three men in paramedic uniforms burst into the RV with a stretcher. Flashing red and white lights seep in from the window, illuminating Jace's pale skin in sickly colors. The paramedics quickly load Jace onto the stretcher and hurry him out of the RV.

Tony stops trying to restrain me and strides after the paramedics, his face a mask of fear and confusion. I try to follow him, but then a police officer barges in through the door. Tony points to me and snaps something, and the officer's eyes grow wide as he recognizes my face.

I run after Jace. I can't think of anything else to do, and I make it outside just as they load him into the back of an ambulance. The vehicle seems huge, and the men around me are too big, and I want to run away to somewhere where I don't feel so small. I want to run to Jace. I never feel small when I'm with him.

A pair of hands grabs my shoulders and turns me around, and I find myself staring at the cop. He gives my shoulder a rough pat of reassurance and starts guiding me toward his police car, which is parked right next to the ambulance.

I struggle against his grip, and when he doesn't let go, I punch him in the stomach. That surprises him for just a moment, and I manage to wiggle out of his grasp. I sprint toward the ambulance, but just then the back doors slam shut, and the vehicle takes off toward the hospital. I'm left standing in the dust it kicks up, coughing and crying.

The cop grabs me again and hauls me to his car. He's talking to me and growing increasingly agitated when I don't answer, but my head is spinning too hard to read his lips, and my throat feels too tight to form any sort of explanation. I don't see Tony anywhere. He must have climbed in the ambulance with Jace.

I numbly allow the cop to guide me into the back of his car, and the moment I sit in the cold, metal backseat, I realize it:

Everything is over.

32

JACE

I WAKE TO the sound of beeping machines. Snapping my eyes open, I find myself staring at a white ceiling. What the hell? I blink a couple times, clearing my vision, and look around. I'm in a bed—a hospital bed— and there are a bunch of monitors and an IV hooked up to me. I reach over to rip out the IV, but a strong hand stops me.

"I know it hurts, but it'll hurt more if you tear at it," Arrow says. He stares down at me, and I wonder where he came from, and where he's been. And where the hell have *I* been?

The club, that's right. I was supposed to stay there for a few hours and do fan meet-and-greets, but then I started to feel dizzy, so I got out of there and went . . . to the RV. Yeah, that's right. I remember walking in and seeing concern on Ali's face, and hearing her pretty voice, and thinking it sounded a lot more beautiful than the music we played earlier. And after that . . .

Nothing.

"Where's Ali?" I ask. My voice is scratchy and hoarse, and it feels like someone scrubbed my throat with sandpaper. I try swallowing, but that just makes it worse.

Arrow doesn't reply, so I reach for the IV again. If he's going to be a jerk and not tell me, then I'm going to be a jerk and not listen to his instructions. Arrow tries to stop me from yanking on the IV, and I fight back, only to feel another pair of hands join in pinning me down. I look up to find Jon hovering over me. Behind him is Killer, ready to help keep me still.

"Ali," I repeat, my voice nothing but a small croak. "Where's Ali?"

They all exchange uncertain glances, and I start to panic. I sit up, and the world spins wildly. As I gasp in a breath, pain ricochets through my chest and limbs, tearing a groan from me. What the hell happened? And why don't I remember any of it?

The room finally stops spinning, and I manage to focus on the figure standing at the foot of my bed. It's a doctor in a white coat, and he stares down intently at a clipboard. He has salt-and-pepper hair and glasses with thick lenses, and I get the feeling that he's avoiding my gaze. The doctor shuffles uncertainly when he feels my stare on him, making me think he's not used to working on celebrities.

"You should try to rest, Mr. Beckett," the doctor says. "We were able to flush most of the flunitrazepam out of your system, but you're going to feel weak for a couple of days."

"Fluna-what?" I say.

"Roofie," Arrow says to me. "Someone drugged your drink in the club. You overdosed."

My skin crawls at the thought of having drugs in my body, and I blink hard, trying to remember what I'd even had at the club. I'd asked for bottled water, but when my order was forgotten, I'd accepted a glass of punch. It was alcohol-free, so I figured the worse thing in it would be the sugar. I should have known better.

The doctor shakes his head at my chart. "You can consider yourself lucky to be alive. Whoever put the flunitrazepam in your drink used a dose that could have knocked out ten people. The police are looking into it, but so far they haven't found a culprit."

And they won't—I know at least that much. Maybe it was a crazed fan targeting me, maybe the dose was actually meant for a girl, maybe it was some sort of prank. Doesn't matter much why the drug ended up in my drink, because the police aren't ever going to figure it out. The downtown club scene is just as tight-lipped as it is risky.

I close my eyes and let out a curse, wincing as the loud sound strikes my aching head. I'll probably never know who drugged me, but that's not going to stop me from hating their guts.

Killer rests a comforting hand on my shoulder, and I wait for him to make some crack about the irony of the situation—I always go out of my way to avoid alcoholic drinks, and I still ended up getting roofied. But Killer stays quiet. That's a first.

I swallow hard, and more pain burns my throat. "Why does my throat hurt so bad?" I ask. "And the rest of me?"

The doctor glances up from his chart and says, "Your throat hurts because we had to intubate you for a short period. You stopped breathing on the way to the hospital. The rest of your body is probably sore from the seizure you had, but there was no serious damage from it."

I stare at him incredulously. "My breathing stopped?"

He nods. "Like I said, the overdose was very serious."

"And what about Ali?" I ask, turning back to Arrow.

The doctor clears his throat and announces, "You're on a light dose of painkillers, and the IV saline will flush the last of the toxins out of your system. You should be feeling back to normal within a few days, but you need to stay in bed for now. We'll talk later about when you can be released from the hospital. Any questions?"

I shake my head, and the doctor quickly shuffles out the door, his nose buried back in his notes. My focus shifts back to Arrow, who is shaking his head. Oh hell. This can't be good. My pain is suddenly a hundred times worse, and my stomach clenches with nausea. I squeeze my eyes closed as I wait for his answer.

"The cops have her," Arrow says finally. "I called the local station and managed to talk to someone. He said they're putting her on a plane back to Los Angeles. Her dad will pick her up at the airport."

Something pokes at the back of my mind, a clouded memory I can barely grasp. It slowly comes into focus, and I hear Ali's voice whispering to me, *"I know it makes me crazy, but I love you."* She must have known at that point that she was about to get caught. But she still said she loved me, like it didn't even matter that I had completely failed to keep her safe.

I tear out my IV before anyone can stop me. It hurts like a bitch, but I don't care. I deserve the pain.

Clenching my fists, I stumble out of the bed. Dizziness slams into me, and Arrow yells at me to lie back down, but I ignore him and head for the door. I need to get to that police station and make them realize it'd be dangerous to send her back.

Something hard slams into my face, and I vaguely register that it's the floor. Voices erupt around me, and everything goes black.

33

ALI

WHEN MY PLANE lands in Los Angeles, I swear I feel the whole ground shake. Then I realize it's not the ground—I'm the one shaking. I wish my emotions were something innocent, like fear or terror, but that's not the case. What I'm feeling is pure rage. It eats at my insides until I can't keep it in anymore, and my whole body trembles.

As soon as the cops picked me up, they called my dad and made arrangements to transport me back home. No one has spoken to me in-depth about Jace, although one of the officers told me that Los Angeles authorities will be filing kidnapping charges against him. I still haven't gotten over the relief of hearing Jace is alive, but I'm choking on the guilt of knowing he's in trouble because of me.

Next to me, the airplane's deputy watches me with mild concern. He's the guy who was put in charge of monitoring me during the flight and getting me back "safely" to Los Angeles. He wears his gun and security badge on his right hip, so everyone walking down the airplane's aisle can see them. The deputy hasn't told me his name, and I haven't asked. I've kept quiet ever since I was handed over to his custody.

The deputy raises an eyebrow at me as the plane comes rolling to a stop. "Not fond of plane rides, huh?"

"Screw off," I snap, surprising both of us. I don't think I've ever said that to an adult. Maybe Jace is rubbing off on me in more ways than I thought, although I'm not sure that's a bad thing.

The deputy's brows narrow, and he opens his mouth to retort. But then the seatbelt light turns off, and a voice must come on over the intercom, because he stares at the speaker above us.

The next few minutes are quieter than ever before. My mind should probably be buzzing with angry thoughts, but it's not. All that's there is a simmering sort of rage, and the solemn knowledge that I can't simply go back to my old life. I made it so far. I almost escaped, almost started over. Jace gave me a taste of life—real, vibrant, free life. And now that I've had a taste, I don't think I can ever let it go.

I'm *not* going back to my dad.

The plane clears of people, and the deputy stands from his seat, gesturing for me to follow. I stand slowly. My legs are still shaking, and my heart beats too fast for my lungs to keep up with it.

We come out of the landing tunnel, and the vibrations of the noisy airport strike me from all sides. All around us are bustling travelers coming and going from various terminals, but no one seems to notice me.

To my right, I see a little girl run toward a man dressed in a suit. She tackles his waist in a hug, and the man laughs as he scoops her up into his arms. The scene should probably make me smile, but instead, it just inflates my anger. Why can't I have a dad like that? What did I do to deserve a father like the one I have?

No, that's not the right question. What I should be asking is: what did my dad ever do to deserve *me*? I'm a good teenager; I don't smoke or drink or cause trouble. And, if given half the chance, I'm more than capable of loving. Hell, most parents would consider me the perfect kid.

Nothing. That's my answer; my dad did nothing to deserve me. He *doesn't* deserve me. I should have no hesitations to fight his hold over me.

So then why is my heart beating so fast? And why is my head so dizzy, my palms so sweaty?

I swallow hard, gulping back the fear and replacing it with anger.

I can do this.

I *will* do this.

The deputy starts leading me toward the main hallway. I assume my dad is somewhere in this crowd, and that makes my gut twist and my blood burn. I've felt like this so many times before: terrified and filled with rage.

But now it's . . . *different*. Before, there was shame mixed in with my emotions, and that always stopped me from trying anything stupid to get away. Or maybe anything smart. I'm not really sure which it is, but I do know that there's no shame now.

There's just this intense concoction of fear and anger, and I'm finally going to put it to use.

I look around as we walk, searching for what I need. I pass a couple of bathrooms, but they're too small. Finally, I see one of those huge airport restrooms with two entrances.

Bingo.

I nudge the deputy to get his attention. He glances down at me, but keeps walking. "What?" he asks.

I bite my lip and say, "I have to go to the bathroom."

He sighs. "Hold it."

"I can't."

Annoyance flashes across his expression. "Look, kid, my job is to get you back to your dad safely. I'm not here to change your diaper."

There are a thousand and one things I want to say to him: that I'm not a kid, that he has no reason to be so demeaning, that it's impossible for me to return to my dad and be safe. But instead, I think back to that puppy dog expression Killer always uses on Arrow. Even deputies can't be immune to that level of pathetic, right?

I channel every ounce of inner puppy I have in me, pout my lip a little, and say, "Please? I really, really have to go. I'll come right back, sir."

Maybe it's the puppy look that does it, or maybe it's because I called him "sir." But, for whatever reason, he gives an exasperated sigh and nods toward the bathroom. "Okay, go ahead. But I'll be waiting right by the door, so don't try anything."

I nod and hurry into the bathroom, weaving through the crowd as fast as I can. A couple people shoot me annoyed looks, but to my surprise, not one stops me. With all the Amber Alert stuff, I figured someone would recognize me and try to "save" me. But no one does, and I make it into the bathroom without incident.

I figure I have about one minute before the deputy realizes there's another entrance to the bathroom. Maybe two minutes, considering his level of intelligence. Either way, it's not much time to escape.

I walk toward the opposite entrance, going as fast as I can without drawing attention. I'm twenty feet from the door. Ten. Five. Two . . .

A woman shoves open the door, and I stumble back to avoid smacking into it. I glance up to find the woman gaping at me, her eyes wide with shock. Then she points to me and says, "You're Alison Collins! Sweetie, are you okay? People are looking all over for you!"

Heads turn toward us, and while most people immediately look away, a few start walking toward me. Shit. This is so not good.

I run. It's a stupid thing to do—what better way to attract attention than to go sprinting through an airport? But I don't have any other choice. Nothing I say is going to convince those women to leave me alone, and I'm not going to let go of my escape that easily.

I sprint out the door and dive into the crowd, pushing and shoving people out of my way. My heart pounds so hard that I think my chest might explode. I accidentally knock some guy to the ground, and I hesitate for single second, but then I just keep running.

Ahead, I see the main exit. I still have to get past security, but maybe I can do that. They should be more concerned about people running in than out. So they hopefully will let me by, and then—

Arms wraps around me from behind. I struggle wildly against them, but they're too strong, and I'm trapped. A stream of profanities erupts from my mouth, and I hope I'm yelling them loud enough for the entire airport to hear.

The arms spin me around, and in a gut-wrenching moment, I realize how familiar the hands feel.

Rough. Indifferent. Angry.

Dad.

I have a single second to take in my dad's face. He's glaring down at me, but forcing a smile to appease the people surrounding us. The crowd converges around me. People are pressing in, and my chance at escape is long gone.

My dad keeps his hands on my shoulders as he guides me toward the exit. His grip grows tight, warning me not to try anything else. Tears press against my eyes, but I don't let them fall. I can't cry in front of my dad. Even if he's won, I can't let him see me break down.

His hands dig into my shoulder blades, and I don't think he'll be loosening his grip anytime soon. He talks to the man at the security station, nodding and smiling at all the appropriate times. If I try to look at him objectively, I can see the relieved father happy to have his child back. But I peer closer, and I see the truth all the people around me are missing: he's only relieved because he has me back under his control. And he's not happy to see me, not really. He's just happy he doesn't have to chase after me anymore, and that his reputation as a good man is secure.

I look around, silently hoping someone else will see the truth in this situation. But the airport security is busy ushering passersby away from me, and I'm left alone with my dad. I see two police officers hurrying toward us, and I let out a quiet curse, which just makes my dad dig his fingers into me harder. I shut up and just glare at the officers as they approach. They're no doubt friends of my dad who are here to help escort me away from the airport.

My dad spots the officers, and his brows raise in surprise. Then he lets his smile grow, excuses himself from the airport security guard, and turns toward his colleagues. I watch his lips as he greets them: "What are you boys doing here? You're a little late to the party, you know." He smiles down at me and pats my shoulder a bit too hard. "I've already found my Ali."

The two officers exchange utterly uncomfortable looks. For a moment, I think they're just intimidated by talking to their retired chief. But then a girl steps out from the crowd, and none of the security tries to stop her. My breath catches as I recognize her: it's Avery. Avery's mom strides forward next, followed by her father. They all look deadly serious as they stand next to the officers.

One of the officers steps closer, his throat bobbing as he swallows hard. He looks my dad right in the eye as he says, "Chief Patterson, sir . . . I'm afraid you're under arrest."

I blink a couple times, certain that I'd misread his lips. But then the officer reaches for the pair of handcuffs at his waist, and I realize this is really happening.

My dad smirks, but beneath the cocky expression, I see a tinge of worry. "Come on now. You can't be serious."

I hold my breath as I wait for their response. Avery's parents have tried reporting my dad multiple times, but they're always brushed off, just like me. So why should this time be any different?

The officer nods curtly. "Yes, sir, I'm very serious."

My heart stops beating for a long second, and then starts pounding wildly. Holy shit. This is for real.

My dad's hand tightens on my shoulder until it hurts. "What charges could you possibly be arresting me on?"

A moment of uncertain silence passes, and then the second officer steps forward, finally finding his voice. "Child abuse."

The worry in my dad's eyes pushes closer to the surface. "Those charges have already been looked into and dismissed. They're bogus."

Avery's mouth opens in a disbelieving scoff, and she snaps, "We have six people who say differently."

"Six?"

Everyone turns to me, and I realize I'm the one who blurted out the question. Avery smiles at me and nods. "Yeah, six."

This makes no sense. The only people who have ever dared to confront my dad are Avery and her parents. Everyone else has always turned a blind eye to my abuse, all of them too scared to face my dad's wrath. It's impossible that six people have stepped forward.

"Is this true?" my dad asks the officers.

The first one nods. "Yes, sir."

"Who's claiming I've abused my daughter?"

The second officer squares his shoulders and says, "You know we can't tell you that, Mr. Patterson."

I almost start laughing right then. He'd called my dad Mr. Patterson. Not Chief Patterson, but *Mr.* Patterson. Little bubbles of giddiness inflate my head, and I shake off my dad's grip. He doesn't dare to stop me, and I stride to Avery's side. She reaches out and takes my hand, giving it a comforting squeeze.

I squeeze her hand back, letting her know I'm fine. Hell, I'm more than fine. I'm freaking, flipping, flying *wonderful*.

The next few minutes pass in a blur. I watch the officers step forward and read my dad his Miranda rights as they hand-cuff him. They lead him away, and my dad doesn't resist. He's still trying to reason with the officers and get them to let him go. But the officers won't listen. As they approach the exit, my dad glares over his shoulder at me. He doesn't even try to hide his rage. I just turn away.

The doors close behind my dad, and I turn and tackle Avery into a hug, laughing through a new rush of tears. No one tries to stop our celebration, and Avery's parents even join in on the hug. I'm surrounded by people who care, and for the first time in years, there's no one to get in the way.

I wipe a happy tear out of my eye and sign, *"Who are the six people?"*

Avery quickly signs back, *"My parents, me, two of your teachers, and one of your former doctors."*

I shake my head. *"Why now? People have always been too afraid to say anything."*

"A certain musician convinced them otherwise," she signs as a grin overtakes her expression.

My stomach does a happy little flip. *"Jace?"*

Avery nods. *"He called me last night and explained every-thing. We had to scramble, but we managed to get all six witnesses together. After that, it was just a matter of filing an emergency case with CPS. The police took care of everything else."*

I tackle her into another hug. "Thank you."

She squeezes me back, and then pulls away to sign, *"Don't thank me. Thank Jace. This never would have happened without him."*

I grin, but then the expression falters as the truth slams into me: I'm still seventeen. I'll still need to be in someone's custody for the next couple of months, and that probably means being shoved into the foster system.

Avery takes my hands and says, "What's the matter?"

"Where am I going to go now?" I ask. "I mean, if I'm not with my dad . . ."

She rolls her eyes, like this is officially the dumbest question she's ever heard. *"You'll stay with me, of course. My parents are going to file paperwork to be your legal guardians."*

"And that will work?"

She shrugs. *"Jace already got all this to work. It shouldn't be much trouble to get you in a proper home."* Then her smile grows, and she pulls her phone out of her back pocket. *"Jace told me to show you this text as soon as I could."*

I snatch the phone from her and read the text on the screen: ***Even if I can't love, I will love you. I've never been good at following rules—not even my own. I'm at the Austin airport, and I'll be in LA in a few hours.***

I hug the phone against my chest for a moment, and then hastily type out a message in response. I don't even think about it; the words are just there, and I mean them. ***I love you, too.***

Avery tackles me into another hug, and I squeeze her tightly back, letting out a happy squeal. I flash back to that first night I won the raffle prize, and how Avery and I had acted just like this. Only, this time, it's different. Because this isn't a moment of utter bliss. This is the start of an utterly blissful *life*.

We finally calm down a little, and Avery nods to the phone. There's a new message from Jace on the screen: ***Serva me, servabo te.***

"What does that mean?" Avery signs.

I smile down at the phone as I recognize the familiar motto. *"Hope,"* I sign, remembering what Jace once told me. *"It means hope."*

EPILOGUE
EIGHT MONTHS LATER . . .
JACE

I STRUM THE final chord of the concert as the crowd breaks into wild applause. Over the past few months, Tone Deaf's concerts have grown even larger. Some critics have attributed our success to all the gossip surrounding Ali and me. After the kidnapping charges against me were dropped, and Ali's dad was convicted of child abuse, the media went absolutely nuts. I was proclaimed to be a hero, and Ali's story was broadcasted everywhere.

But I know the truth: the increase in success doesn't come from anything I did. All the credit goes to Ali and the incredible music she continues to write for Tone Deaf.

The crowd slowly quiets, and I hurry through my ending speech. After I say the last thank you and flash a smile, the applause starts up again, and I take it as our cue to leave. I stride off the stage with the rest of the band right behind me. Jon jogs to my side and raises his eyebrows. With a flick of his finger, he turns off his mic, and then says to me, "Excited much?"

"Ali said she'd be waiting backstage," I say as I switch off my own mic.

"That's no excuse to sprint away from your audience. You're going to hurt their feelings, you know."

I know he's teasing, but I still jab him in the shoulder, and he just laughs and jabs me right back. We make it backstage, and the stage crew swarms us. I hear a few people congratulate me on playing a good concert, but I don't really care how well I did. All my attention is on the gorgeous girl pushing her way through the crowd and toward me.

Ali tackles me into a hug, and I wrap my arms firmly around her. I've missed her. Sure, it's only been two weeks since I last saw her, but it's felt like an eternity. She tilts her head up to look at me, and I steal the opportunity for a kiss. Her lips are soft and warm against mine, and when we finally break apart, we're both breathing hard and grinning.

"*I missed you,*" I sign.

She blushes in that adorable way she has. "*I missed you, too.*"

The stage crew dissipates, giving us some room. I reach down and take both of Ali's hands, giving each of them a small kiss. "How's school?"

I didn't think it was possible, but her expression brightens even more. "Amazing, as always."

I laugh a little at her enthusiasm. I've never liked school much, but Ali is completely different. At Gallaudet University, she has an entire school that understands her deafness, and a huge community of students and teachers to support her. According to Ali, she's no longer just deaf. Now she's Deaf— part of a culture that embraces and respects her in a way she's never experienced before.

I have to admit, I miss having her with me all the time. Now that she's living at her campus in Washington, DC, I only get to see her on rare weekends like this one. Since I'm recording a new album, I'm almost always far away in Los Angeles. But it's worth the pain of missing her to see her like this: happy and confident and not at all worried.

"How's the album coming?" she asks, her eyes lighting with excitement. Ali helped me write most of the songs on my latest album, and now that we've entered the recording process, she wants constant updates.

I'm telling her about a song we're struggling to get right when I hear Killer shriek, "Ali!" Of course, Ali doesn't hear him, and she yelps in surprise as Killer leaps forward and tackles her into a hug. As soon as she realizes who it is, she starts chiding Killer at the same time she hugs him. Arrow and Jon step forward, and she hugs them, too.

I take a step back and watch as she easily banters with my bandmates, exchanging updates on all the things that have happened in the past couple of weeks. The topic moves back to the album, and they excitedly talk about it for the next minute. Then Ali turns to me and cocks her head, giving me a curious look.

"What are you so happy about?" she asks.

It's only then that I realize I have a ridiculous grin on my face. I try to shake it away, but it stays right there. I shrug and sign, *"You, I guess. And us."*

Ali steps forward and pulls me into another kiss, and as I savor the touch of her lips, I can feel the curve of her smile against my mouth.

That smile is perfect. Ali is perfect. And, for the first time ever, my life feels perfect, too.

ADDITIONAL RESOURCES

WANT TO LEARN more about the Deaf community Ali joins? You're in luck—there are many resources available to learn about the rich and beautiful Deaf culture. Some of these include:

American Society for Deaf Children: deafchildren.org
Gallaudet University: www.gallaudet.edu
National Association of the Deaf: nad.org
National Technical Institute for the Deaf: www.ntid.rit.edu
World Federation of the Deaf: wfdeaf.org

ACKNOWLEDGEMENTS

FIRST AND FOREMOST, I owe thanks to my mom. Mom, if I listed all the ways you've supported my writing over the years, it would take up every page in this book. Suffice it to say, I never would have made it this far without you.

Thanks also to Ryan, for being an amazing brother and friend, and for encouraging me to write this story from the very beginning.

Thanks to Laurie McLean, who is an extraordinary agent and mentor. Thanks also to everyone over at Fuse Literary, for being the best publishing family I could ask for.

Thanks to Lauren Stewart, for offering valuable critique and invaluable friendship.

Thanks to Verna Dreisbach and Elvira Burlingham, for your dedicated teaching and guidance.

Thanks to Sharon Pajka, for providing information and insight into Deaf culture.

Thanks to Caroline Hanson, Christina McKnight, and Alexandra Mount for offering feedback and support.

Thanks to all my writer friends and critique partners from Stonehenge, Witchy Writers, and Wordforge.

Thanks to all my readers on Wattpad, who encouraged me as I wrote the first draft of this story.

Thanks to the authors of Team Rogue YA, for journeying alongside me on this wild publishing adventure.

And last, but certainly not least, thanks to Adrienne Szpyrka, Kristin Kulsavage, and the entire team over at Sky Pony Press. Thanks for providing my book with insightful edits and a fantastic imprint to call home.